LEAN ON PETE

Described by *Mojo* as 'one of America's most fundamental artists in words and music', Willy Vlautin is the author of two highly acclaimed novels, *The Motel Life* (2006) and *Northline* (2008), and is the frontman of the band Richmond Fontaine, whose latest album is *We Used to Think the Freeway Sounded Like a River* (2009). An avid fan of horseracing, he can often be found writing behind a closed-circuit monitor at Portland Meadows racetrack.

www.willyvlautin.com

D0415082

by the same author

THE MOTEL LIFE
NORTHLINE

Lean on Pete

a novel

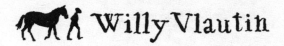 Willy Vlautin

ff

faber and faber

Tremendous thanks to Howard Durand and Twyla Beckner for
sharing their horseracing wisdom. Grateful acknowledgement to
Portland Meadows for being my pal for fifteen years.

Special thanks to the real Lean on Pete and his owner David Duke,
neither of whom bears any resemblance to the characters in this
story. Lean on Pete has had a successful thoroughbred racing career,
and David Duke is a respected Oregon horseman who treats his horses
honorably and with kindness.

First published in 2010
by Faber and Faber Limited
Bloomsbury House,
74–77 Great Russell Street,
London WC1B 3DA
This paperback edition first published in 2011

Typeset by Faber and Faber Limited
Printed in England by CPI Group (UK) Ltd, Croydon, CR0 4YY

All rights reserved
© Willy Vlautin, 2010
Illustrations and Maps © Nate Beaty, 2010

The right of Willy Vlautin to be identified as author of this work
has been asserted in accordance with Section 77 of the Copyright,
Designs and Patents Act 1988

This book is sold subject to the condition that it shall not, by way
of trade or otherwise, be lent, resold, hired out or otherwise circulated
without the publisher's prior consent in any form of binding or
cover other than that in which it is published and without a similar
condition including this condition being imposed on the
subsequent purchaser

A CIP record for this book
is available from the British Library

ISBN 978–0–571–23573–5

2 4 6 8 10 9 7 5 3

For Lee

It is true that we are weak and sick and ugly and quarrelsome but if that is all we ever were, we would millenniums ago have disappeared from the face of the earth.

John Steinbeck

When I woke up that morning it was still pretty early.
Summer had just begun and from where I lay in my sleeping bag I could see out the window. There were hardly any
clouds and the sky was clear and blue. I looked at the
Polaroid I had taped to the wall next to where I slept. It
shows my aunt and me sitting by a river; she has on a swimsuit. She's my dad's sister and she looks like him, with
black hair and blue eyes and she's really thin. In the photo
she's holding a can of soda and smiling as I sit next to her.
She has her arm around me. My hair's wet and I'm smiling.
That was when we all lived in Wyoming. But it had been
four years since I'd seen her, and I didn't even know where
she lived anymore.

My dad and I had just moved to Portland, Oregon, and
we'd been there for a week. We didn't know anybody. Two
days before my school year was done we packed the truck
and moved out from Spokane. We brought our kitchen table
and four chairs, dishes and pots and pans, our clothes and
TV, and my dad's bed. We left all the rest.

Neither of us had been to Portland before. My dad just
knew a guy who told him of a job opening as a forklift driver
for Willig Freight Lines. He applied for it and got it. They
interviewed him on the phone and gave him the job right
then because at the time he was a forklift driver for TNT
Freight Lines in Rock Springs and he'd done that sort of

work for years. We lived in a motel for a few days, then he rented us a house a mile from where he worked. I'm not sure why he wanted to leave Spokane. I told him I didn't want to go, I begged him that I didn't want to go, but he said he'd rather go to prison and get the shit kicked out of him every day than spend any more time in a dump like Spokane.

The house we rented had two bedrooms. There was a kitchen with an electric stove and a fridge, and there was another room that was empty except for a TV we set on a chair. There was a bathroom that had a tub, sink, and toilet, and there was a back room where you could store things and where there was plumbing and electricity so you could put in a washer and dryer if you had them.

Our place was in a neighborhood of small, rundown houses next to a trailer park. The houses were built in the forties. It was called Delta Park. The streets had trees lining them and we had a backyard. Since it was a real house my dad promised we'd get a barbecue and then a dog. I didn't care about the barbecue but I really wanted a dog and hoped this time I would get one.

I lay there for a while longer and tried to go back to sleep but I couldn't so I got up. I put on a pair of shorts and a flannel shirt and my running shoes. It was Saturday and most of the cars in the neighborhood were still parked in front of their houses when I left and started jogging down the street.

Instead of turning left by the mini-mart like I had done every other day I turned right and ran underneath a railroad bridge. I made my way along the road and passed a series of warehouses, a machine shop, a wrecking yard, and an auto parts store. I kept going and went under another bridge and when I came to the other side I saw, in the distance, a horse track. I'd never seen one before and really the only horses I'd ever seen besides on TV were when I once went to a rodeo with my dad and some friends of his. But I always liked horses. Besides dogs, they're my favorite.

It wasn't even 7 a.m., but the backside of the track was already going. The whole area was fenced off in chain link and topped with barbed wire. There were at least a dozen huge buildings that housed the horses. I could see it all from the road. The place went on for acres and people and horses were coming and going out of everywhere.

I ran alongside the fence on a two-lane road. I passed a maintenance shop where two water trucks sat with "Portland Meadows" painted on them. I saw two men welding and a mechanic working on a truck. I passed the main dirt track and saw horses running on it. Then I came to the main grandstand. In front of the building was a huge empty parking lot. The building itself was old and white and green. On the front of it read "Portland Meadows" in huge red neon letters. Next to it was a galloping neon race horse.

I stopped and went up to the building, to the entrance where big glass doors were, but I didn't go in. I just rested for a minute, then did forty push-ups and started running again.

I went for a couple miles before I stopped near a huge river. Off the banks were docks, and the docks held boats and rows of floating homes. I sat there and watched a tug boat push cargo and then I saw a speedboat and a red sailboat and then a few jet skis went racing by, chasing each other around.

I stretched out, then ran easy and slow back to the house. Even so I was dead tired by the time I got there. I went in the front door and to the kitchen to get a glass of water and saw a woman I'd never seen. She was cooking eggs and bacon and she was wearing only a T-shirt and underwear.

"Who are you?" I asked her.

She turned around and smiled. "Who are you?" she said back. She was old, maybe in her forties. There was a cigarette going in a tray on the kitchen table, and she went over to it.

"I'm Charley Thompson."

"You're Ray's kid?" she said, and smoked from the cigarette.

"Yeah," I said. You could see her nipples coming through the shirt she was wearing. Her underwear was black, and it was almost see through. She had red hair and her face had freckles all over it. She wasn't good-looking.

"You look just like him," she said.

"But I'm gonna be taller," I said.

"Is that so?"

"Yeah," I said. "I'm almost as tall as him already."

"I'm cooking breakfast," she said. "Do you want some?"

"Where did you get the food?"

"I made your dad go to the grocery store. All you guys had in the fridge was beer, milk, and Cap'n Crunch. I bet the cereal is yours."

"Yeah," I said.

"You don't have to keep cereal in the fridge, you know."

"There's cockroaches here."

She nodded, then went back to the stove.

"I'm going to get a glass of water, okay?"

4

"It's your house, isn't it?" she said, and looked back again and smiled.

I didn't know what to think but I was hungry. I got a glass of water and sat at the table and waited. After a while my dad came out of the bathroom in his underwear and walked into the kitchen and took a beer from the fridge and sat down. He took a pack of cigarettes off the table and lit one.

"You meet Lynn?" he said, and yawned.

I nodded.

Lynn looked around and smiled at him.

"She's a secretary in the front office where I work." He opened his beer and drank from it. "How far did you go running?"

"Pretty far. Did you know there's a horse track down the street?"

"I've driven past it," he said.

"They were working out when I ran by. I saw maybe fifty horses."

My dad sat back in his chair and didn't say anything. He was looking at the woman and smoking. He was six feet or so and he was skinny and had black hair. His hair was combed back and wet. His chest had this sort of caved-in look to it, and he had a big scar on his leg from burning himself on a motorcycle. But he had a good face, it was kind and he had dark blue eyes and he smiled a lot. Everyone said he was good-looking.

Lynn stood there with her back to us. Her ass was hanging out of her underwear and I looked down at her legs and on her ankle was a tattoo of a flower, and coming out of the flower was some sort of snake.

5

We all ate breakfast sitting around the table. I kept looking at her and thinking about her underwear and her nipples pressing through her shirt and when I did she seemed pretty nice, she seemed alright.

When breakfast was over they went into his room to get dressed. My dad came out a few minutes later and sat across from me at the table and put on his boots.

"Is she your new girlfriend?" I asked him.

"No," he said.

"Is she gonna be?"

"I don't know."

"I like her better than Marlene."

"Marlene was alright."

"She was mean," I said. "She couldn't cook either."

"Lynn and I just work together. Plus she's married."

"She's married?"

"Well, she's separated from her husband. Supposedly he's a Samoan." He leaned over and whispered, "He'll probably chop my head off with a machete."

"What's a Samoan?" I asked.

"You don't know?"

"No."

"Don't they teach you anything in school?"

"They teach me some things," I said.

"Samoans are big fuckers. They play football sometimes. You should know that. There's a few pro ones here and there. They're tough and they love to fight. They come from the island of Samoa in the Pacific. They're the size of mountains."

"Is he that big?"

"She says he is, but I've never seen him. She says he's fucking nuts. This guy at work said the same thing."

"Is he gonna be mad?"

"She said he moved in with a stripper, so who knows."

"Will he come here?"

"You mean to get me?"

"Yeah."

"No. Hell, I'm just talking, Charley. He doesn't know where we live. Don't worry about him. Okay?"

"Okay."

"What did you do last night?"

"Watched TV."

"Was there anything good on?" He finished his beer and lit another cigarette.

"Not really."

He took his wallet out and gave me ten dollars.

"Sorry I can't give you any more."

"I don't need any more."

"You gonna be okay on your own today?"

As I nodded Lynn walked back out into the main room dressed in jeans and a black shirt. She had put her hair back in a pony tail and was wearing dark red lipstick. She went up to my dad and he ran his hand across her ass and then they left.

2

I moved the TV into my room and lay on my sleeping bag and watched it until late afternoon. Then I walked to a main road and stayed on it until I came to a lady and a man walking down the street. I asked them if they knew where a movie theater was and the guy told me to walk two miles down the same road and so I did.

The theater was in a part of town called St. Johns. It was lined with stores and bars, and there were a couple of taquerias and a pharmacy that had an old-fashioned diner in it. There was a bike shop, a dollar store, and a working-man's clothing store. I went into a used bookstore and a Salvation Army thrift store, then I bought a couple tacos and sat down against the wall of a closed-down office and ate.

When the time came for the seven o'clock showing I went inside and sat through two movies. One was about an undercover spy who gets chased all around Europe and the other was about a group of women who get trapped in a cave. The women were good-looking but it was a horror movie and I can never sleep after horror movies.

It was dark out when I left the theater. I walked around for another half-hour or so, then sat back down where I had eaten earlier. I saw a group of girls my age walk by, but they didn't notice me. One of the girls had long blonde hair and she was really good-looking. They were all laughing and having a good time. It wasn't much after that when I saw a fight across the street. Two men came out of a bar called Dad's and started hitting each other. They were near a street light. One man was young, maybe in his twenties, and the other looked old. He had gray hair and a big bald spot on the top of his head. The younger man hit the old man so hard he fell to the ground. Both of them were dressed in work clothes. They had on the same orange-colored T-shirts with the same writing on the back. Then the younger guy kicked the old man in the head and he was about to do it again when people from inside the bar came out and stopped him.

They pushed him against the window of the bar and held him. The old man didn't move from the ground. He just lay there still. An older woman came out of the bar and went to him and kneeled down. You could hear her crying and screaming. I just sat there across the street and watched. A police car pulled up and after that an ambulance. I watched the medics work on the old man and then put him in the ambulance and drive away. The young guy was still there but by then they had handcuffs on him and they were putting him in the back of the police car. I watched until they drove off, then I got up and left. I started off walking, but everything I'd seen that night had made me nervous and before I knew it I was running.

Back at the house I made sure all the windows and doors were locked. I turned on all the lights and got in my sleeping bag and watched TV with the sound down low. Around three or so I got up and ate a couple bowls of Cap'n Crunch before I finally knocked off around dawn.

When I woke up again it was past noon. I looked in my dad's room but he wasn't there, and his truck wasn't in the driveway. I drank a glass of water and did a hundred sit-ups, then I put on my running clothes and left. I turned right like I did the day before and went under the railroad bridge and when I came out the other side I could see Portland Meadows in the distance.

I ran to the grandstand parking lot and did four laps around it before I stopped. I sprinted the last one and by the end I was so tired I could hardly stand. Then I went inside the big glass doors and saw a bar and a food stand and a souvenir shop. There were rows and rows of tables with people sitting at them watching huge TVs with races showing on them. I went outside but there were no horses on the track and I asked an old man why, and he said they only worked out in the mornings and that the real races started in a month or so. I went back inside and stayed there until the food stand closed and the bar closed and the TVs were shut down and I was told to leave.

After that I went to the big shopping center that was next to the track. It had a sporting goods place, a pet shop, and a home improvement store. For a couple hours I walked up and down the aisles of those places, then I went to a mini-mart and bought a can of chili and a can of SpaghettiOs and walked back to the house.

It was night by the time I got there and my dad still wasn't home. I moved the TV into the kitchen and opened the can of SpaghettiOs and heated it on the stove and watched Sunday night TV until I got tired. I moved the TV back to my bedroom and watched from my sleeping bag but the same thing happened that night that happened every night I was alone. I began hearing things, and I got nervous and made myself get up and check the windows and the locks on the door. I turned all the lights off and looked outside. Then I turned them back on and looked in every room. After that I wasn't even tired anymore. I lay back down and watched TV and finally fell asleep around 5 a.m.

The next day I got up and finished unpacking. I had three boxes and a plastic garbage bag full of clothes. I took the clothes out and laid them on my sleeping bag and folded them. I had two pairs of Levi's, a couple long-sleeve shirts, four T-shirts, five pairs of underwear, and a half dozen pairs of socks, a sweater, and two jackets. One was a down parka for when it was really cold and the other was an old canvas work coat my dad had given me.

Two of the boxes had books in them, and in the last one was a clock my dad had gotten me from San Francisco. It was red and sparkly and had a picture of a cable car in the center of it. There were also two football trophies wrapped in T-shirts. One was an award for the best freshman defensive back from my high school in Spokane and the other was older, from Pop Warner football. It was just a normal team trophy that everyone got but I liked it just the same. I cleaned them both off and put them on the window sill.

I broke down the boxes and stuck them in my closet and watched TV for the rest of the day. I left the house in the afternoon and walked towards St. Johns. It was near dusk when I got there and I spent my last four dollars there on a burrito from a taqueria. I sat against the wall of the same closed-down office I had before and ate.

After that I started talking to three men who were sitting in an alley drinking beer. They were older and one guy was missing all his front teeth, and another one had tattoos all over his hands and every time he spoke he stuttered. The other man didn't say anything at all. He just sat there and mumbled and wore glasses with the thickest lenses I'd ever seen. The two guys talked about a friend of theirs who got hit by a car and then they talked about some other guy who stole their backpack. Then the guy with the thick glasses puked. He didn't move, he just sat there and threw up on himself. The other two guys got up and took their things and left and so I did, too.

3

My dad didn't come home that night either and there was no food left and I'd spent all the money he had given me. The next morning I walked down to a Safeway grocery store and stole two cans of soup and a loaf of bread. I put the cans in my coat pocket and carried the bread and left. The second I was outside I started running. I didn't look back or stop until I was nearly a mile away. I was nervous alright but I'd done the same thing quite a bit when I lived in Spokane and I'd never been caught. I walked the rest of the way home and when I got there I ate one of the cans and five pieces of bread. After that I sat in the bathtub and tried to read a spy novel my dad had left in the bathroom.

He came back the next night. I was in bed when I heard his truck pull up. I shut the light off in my room. I could hear him unlock the front door and walk through the living room. After a while he opened the door to my bedroom and looked in. I closed my eyes and kept them shut even when he called my name. He stood there for a time, then turned off the TV and closed the door and I fell asleep right after that.

I woke up early the next morning and got dressed to go running. When I walked out into the main room I could see him in the kitchen sitting in his underwear drinking coffee.

"How have you been?" he asked in a voice that was tired and raw.

"Alright," I said.

"I was on call all weekend but it was slow so Lynn and I drove out to Pendleton to pick up some furniture her uncle gave her. I stopped by once but you weren't here. You get my note?"

"I got it."

"I'll get the phone hooked up next week."

"Maybe we could get cell phones?" I asked him.

"Cell phones?"

"Yeah."

"Then you get people calling all the time and everybody knows where you are. A regular phone is bad enough, with cell phones you end up talking on them while you're on the can, while you're in the movie theater."

"When was the last time you went to a movie?" I said and grinned.

"You know what I mean, smart ass. I'll get a regular phone, but I ain't getting us cell phones. Alright?"

I nodded.

He hadn't shaved and his hair looked like he'd just gotten out of bed. He took a cigarette from a pack on the table and lit it.

"You going running?"

"Yeah," I said.

"How far today?"

"I don't know."

"I've been thinking, we should go to the coast this summer. I hear you can go swimming in the ocean. It's cold, but a hotshot athlete like you could take it."

I sat down at the table and put on my shoes.

"What did you do here?"

"Nothing," I said.

"Did you have enough money?"

"I did alright."

"I was gonna make breakfast but there's nothing here, is there?"

"No."

"We'll go shopping when you get back."

"Alright," I said and he nodded and I got up.

I ran to the mini-mart and turned left and ran past a row of warehouses, then past the Freightliner plant and I came to a small two-lane road and I stayed on it until I began to hurt, then I turned around.

When I got back he was asleep on his bed. It took me a while to get him up but after a while he did and drove us to Jubitz truck stop and we had breakfast in the diner. I ate mine and part of his and then he ordered me a cheeseburger.

Afterwards we walked around the truck stop. It was like a little city. There was a movie theater, a church, a post office, even a medical office, and it was all enclosed like a big mall. We stayed there for a long time and he tried on a pair of boots in a Western store, then we went back out to the truck.

"It's always good to go grocery shopping on a full stomach," he said and started the engine and took us out on to the main road. He lit a cigarette and rolled down the window.

"But you never buy as much when you're not hungry," I said.

"That's the point," he said.

"It's not a very good idea," I said.

"How do you like Portland?" he said after a while.

"I don't know. I haven't seen much of it."

"Meet any girls?"

"I don't think there's anyone my age in any of the houses around us. I haven't met anybody at all."

A man passed us in an old station wagon. His car was smoking. He had his head out of the window and was trying to drive like that.

My dad laughed.

"Do you think the car's gonna blow up?"

"No," he said and paused. "Hell, I don't know. Maybe."

We watched the car. Black smoke streamed from under the hood, then it seemed like it was coming from inside the car too. The man got in the right lane and turned down a side street but he didn't pull over, he kept driving.

My dad turned on the radio and began going through the stations.

"Do you like it here?" I asked him.

"The work's alright," he said, "but I'm a low man and I'll have to work swing and graveyard for a while. It's better than Spokane, though. That's for sure." He took a cigarette from a pack lying on the seat. "There's a Safeway around here, isn't there?"

"I can't go in there," I said.

"Why's that?"

"I stole a couple cans of soup and a loaf of bread from there."

"You did?"

"Yeah."

"When?"

"Yesterday."

"You didn't steal any beer or maybe a bottle of wine?"

"Nothing like that," I told him.

"I should have left you more money."

"I guess."

"I'm sorry."

"It's okay."

"You gonna turn into a bank robber?" he said and looked over to me. He smiled and pushed on my arm.

"No, I was just hungry I guess."

"We'll get you food. Just lay off the armed robbery, alright?"

"Alright."

"So where do we go?"

"There's a Fred Meyer on the way to St. Johns. If you go down to Lombard and take a right."

"How do you know that?"

"There ain't much to do but walk around."

"Then Fred Meyer it is," he said.

We spent over a hundred dollars grocery shopping. We bought hamburger, cans of soup, frozen dinners and vegetables, cereal, bread, hot dogs, pork chops, spaghetti, and donuts. We went to the outdoor section and he bought me an air mattress to go underneath the sleeping bag. It was the kind with the motor and all you had to do was plug it in and it would automatically fill up the pad. He also bought a small hibachi barbecue, briquettes, and lighter fluid. I don't know how he had money then, when he didn't a couple days before, but he did.

Back at the house we put the groceries away and he lit the barbecue. We sat outside on the front lawn. When the coals had burned down enough we put hamburger patties on the grill and he drank beer and watched them cook and I put a can of pork and beans on the stove.

When he left that afternoon he told me he was going to spend the night at Lynn's but that he'd be home in the morning. He gave me ten dollars and got in his truck and left. But the next morning he didn't show up and he didn't show up that night either. I knew he wouldn't but it still made me mad, and I still waited up most of the night for him.

4

I blew the ten he gave me at the movie theater. I watched a comedy about a newscaster, and I bought a hot dog and a Coke and a candy bar. When it was over I snuck into another movie about a ship's captain who sails around getting into fights and a kid gets his arm blown off. When it was over and I had to leave the theater I got pretty down. I knew then, that night, that Portland would be worse than Spokane. At least I had friends in Spokane.

I woke up the next day and decided I'd get a job so I could have my own money. I was only fifteen so I lied on all the job applications and applied to the places I could walk to. There were help wanted signs at Joe's Sporting Goods, Banditos Mexican Restaurant, and Napa Auto Parts. But none of them called me after I filled out the application. I tried for a dishwasher job at Shari's and for a job pumping gas at a 76 station but neither of them called me either. So I just stayed home and watched TV, waiting for the summer to end and for football tryouts to start in August.

I ate through that run of groceries and after that whenever he gave me money I was smarter with it. I'd buy a big package of hamburger, a couple cans of spaghetti sauce, and a box of spaghetti and I'd make a big batch of it. I'd eat on the same thing for days.

* * *

I went running past the track one morning when I saw an old man in a gravel parking lot trying to change a tire on an old horse trailer. He was swearing at it. Each time he tried to get a lug nut off he'd start cussing. He had a low rough voice, and every other word he said was fuck or cocksucker or motherfucker or motherfucking cunt. I stopped and watched from a distance.

He saw me standing there.

"What the hell are you doing?" he said. He had the lug wrench in his hand.

"Me?" I yelled over to him.

"There ain't no one else here," he said.

"I'm just running."

"Are you strong?"

"I'm pretty strong," I told him.

"Come over here," he said.

I walked to him. He was old, maybe seventy, and dressed in cowboy boots and jeans and a flannel shirt. He hadn't shaved in a couple days and even then just meeting him I could tell he was shitfaced drunk. He smelled like beer and his eyes were bloodshot and glassy. He had a big gut and was going bald. The hair he did have was mostly gray on the sides and he had it greased back. His right arm was in a cast and he was chewing tobacco.

"What time is it?"

"Maybe six thirty," I said.

He shook his head.

"I gotta load two horses and get to the Tri-Cities by one, and I got a flat."

I looked down at the tire. There were two cans of Fix-a-

Flat next to it.

"Is that far?" I asked.

"Far enough. Look, my arm ain't worth two shits. I'll give you five dollars if you can get the lugs off."

"I'll try," I told him. I took the wrench and set it on the first nut. I pushed down as hard as I could and it gave. I got four others off but I had to jump on the last one until it broke free. After that he told me he had a jack behind the seat in his truck and asked me to get it. I did and jacked up the axle and pulled off the flat, put on the spare, and tightened down the lug nuts.

When I was done he took three dollars from his wallet.

"I thought I had a five," he said and handed it to me.

"Del," he said and put out his left hand and we shook.

"Charley," I told him. "What happened to your arm?"

"I slipped," he said.

"Why are you going to the Tri-Cities?"

"There's a race."

"A horse race?"

"Yeah."

"Do you need help?"

"Help with what?" he said.

"With anything?"

"You're looking for a job?"

I nodded.

"How old are you?"

"Sixteen," I told him.

"You know much about horses?"

"No."

The old man looked around. With his left hand he took

a can of Copenhagen from his back pocket. He knocked the can of chew into the side of his leg, opened it with one hand, and set it on the hood of his truck. The fingers on his left hand were covered in dirt and grease and his pinky was bent out like it had been broken off and put back on wrong. He put those fingers in the tobacco, took a big dip from the can, and put it between his front lip and gum. He closed the can, put it back in his pocket, and spit on the ground. Some of the spit fell on his chin and he left it there.

"Will your folks let you spend the night away?"

"How far away is it?"

"Four hours, if we're lucky."

"Where will we be staying?"

"I'll be sleeping in the cab. You can sleep wherever you want, or in the back of the truck. I don't care. You got a sleeping bag?"

"Yeah," I said.

"I'll give you twenty-five dollars if you help me up there and back."

"Twenty-five?"

"Yeah," he said.

"We'll be back tomorrow afternoon?"

He nodded.

I had two dollars and change and the three he just gave me.

"Okay," I said.

"What about your parents?"

"They want me to get a job," I said.

"Over there is the backside of the track. There's a café

just off the road," he said and pointed towards it. "You see the beer sign?"

I nodded.

"You'll have to talk to the security guard to get in. Just tell him you work for me, Del Montgomery, and he'll show you where to go. I'll be there for a half-hour, then I'm gonna load up and leave. If you're here by then I'll take you."

He turned and walked away. He dragged his left leg a little and it seemed like it was painful for him to walk. He made his way out of the parking lot, then across the street and through an entrance gate where the security guard stood in a small shack. When I saw where he went I ran back to my house. I left a note for my dad, changed my clothes, rolled up my sleeping bag, and tied it with a piece of rope. I put the five dollars in a plastic bag and folded the bag as small as I could and put it in my shoe and left.

5

Del was sitting by himself at a table in the café drinking a beer and eating eggs and bacon. The restaurant was like a shack almost, but I liked the way it looked. It was rundown and old, and there were pictures of horses on the wall, and a couple of TVs going and two video games in the corner. The floor dipped and raised and the linoleum on it was worn and covered with duct tape in places.

I walked over to him and set my sleeping bag on the ground.

"Have you eaten?" he said through a mouth full of food. There was ketchup on his chin and some had fallen on his shirt.

"No," I told him.

"Can you eat in a hurry?"

I told him I could and he said there was a woman behind the counter named Mora and to order from her and have her put it on his tab. I went to the counter and a lady came from the kitchen. I asked her if she was Mora and she said she was so I ordered a ham and cheese omelet. She wrote it down and told me I owed her six-fifty.

"Del said to put it on his tab."

"Del said that?" the woman said.

"He did," I told her and then I looked out across the room and pointed to him. "He's right over there by the TV."

"I know who he is," the woman said. "He doesn't have a

24

tab. I won't give him a tab."

I didn't say anything.

"He didn't tell you that he doesn't have a tab?"

"No," I said. "He just told me to come up here."

"It's six dollars and fifty cents. Do you still want the breakfast?"

"I only have five dollars. I just started working for him today."

"You only have five dollars?"

"Yeah."

She shook her head and looked over at Del. "Give to it to me, but remember this is the first and last time."

I nodded and bent down and took off my shoe and reached in and got the plastic bag.

"Here," I said and handed her the money.

She took it and put it in the till.

I went back to Del. He was watching a horse race on TV and drinking beer.

"You order something?"

"Yeah," I said.

He nodded, then a race started on TV and he began yelling at it. He seemed pretty upset while it was going and more upset after it was over so I didn't say anything to him about not having a tab or about how the lady made me pay. I should have left right then, but I was flat broke. So I just sat down and waited until my food came up.

Del's truck was a white 1975 Ford pickup and it was parked in the dirt lot across from the backside. There was a blanket duct taped to the bench seat and there were rust holes in the floor. You could see the ground below. The windshield was cracked in three places and it only had an AM radio, but other than that the truck was okay. He started it and moved it in front of a trailer and we got out and hooked it up. The trailer wasn't much either. Just a faded white old rusty stock trailer with two wheels on each side.

He drove up to the front gate and the old-man guard let us in. We went past a couple buildings and then Del parked and we got out and walked down a long shedrow barn where dozens and dozens of horses stood waiting in stalls. The whole building looked like it was leaning to the right. It was dilapidated. The paint was cracked and faded and there was mud everywhere. The stalls themselves were brick on three sides. The brick was painted white, but covered in dust and mud. The gates that held the horses in were metal and most were bent and rusty. A single naked light bulb hung in the center of each stall. There was hardly any natural light shining through at all. It seemed like a prison, a foreign prison in an old movie. There were maybe fifty horses waiting in that single row and Del said there were twenty to twenty-five more rows that had just as many. He said there were almost a thousand horses there.

He came to the end of the row and stopped.

"These two," he said and pointed at two horses that were in stalls next to each other. He opened the gate and went inside and put a halter on the first horse and led him out.

"This is Tumbling Through," he said. "He's a biter. If he goes for you, just hit him on the nose and he'll quit." He handed me the lead rope and told me to walk him down the row and wait for him by the truck.

"And don't let him stop on you. If he wants to stop just give him a quick pull. And watch your feet, don't let him step on you. And if he tries to pull away from you give a hard pull on the rope and he'll stop. And remember, he'll bite the hell out of you. And don't let go. Okay?"

I nodded and took the rope and Del disappeared into another stall. I wrapped the rope around my hand and started going, but the whole thing made me uneasy. Tumbling Through was huge and dark brown in color. I led him out alright and stood there by the horse trailer and I tried my best to keep him from dragging me around. He didn't try to bite me, though. Five minutes later Del came out with another horse.

"Never wrap the rope around your hand unless you want to lose your hand." He spit on the ground.

I nodded and unwrapped the rope.

"This is Lean on Pete."

The horse was black with a small white mark on his face. Del led him to where I was standing and took Tumbling Through from me and told me how to unlock the trailer door and I did. Then I held Tumbling Through while he loaded Lean on Pete. Pete went in easy and calm, but Tumbling Through took a long time to load and you could tell he was nervous. When Del finally got him in and closed the back door we got in the truck and drove to the gate. Del signed out with the old guard, and then we got on the highway. We left the windows down and he spit chew into an old soda cup and left the radio off. We didn't talk. He just sat there hunched over and steered with his good hand and used his cast hand to shift gears. I tried hard not to fall asleep but I always fall asleep in cars and we weren't even ten miles out of Portland when I conked out. I stayed that way until he got off the highway and put us on a small two-lane road somewhere in Washington.

"You ain't much company," he said when he saw that I was awake.

"I have a hard time staying awake in a moving car," I told him.

"No shit," he said.

He had a beer between his legs.

"How much farther?"

"Maybe an hour," he said.

"Hey, Del, how old are these horses?"

"Tumbling Through is two," he said. "He's green but he can run. Lean on Pete's five. He's a piece of shit but he's good enough for this."

"What kind of horses are they?"

"Quarter horses," he said, and then he began coughing and he coughed for a long time so I quit talking and looked out the window. We were out in the middle of nowhere. We passed miles of sagebrush and rocks and hills. Then farms and ranches slowly started to appear. Del turned off on a dirt road and drove down that for almost a mile before we came to a stop. There was nothing around us at all. You couldn't even see the main road.

"We'll get Lean on Pete out first," he said and opened the truck door. He stepped out with his beer, finished it, and threw the can out into the desert. I followed him to the trailer and opened the back door.

He climbed inside, grabbed Lean on Pete by the halter,

and led him around and out. He tied him to the side of the trailer and told me to stay with him. The horse nudged me with his head and I began to pet him. When I did he kept his head still and didn't move. He was like a dog almost. When I'd stop he'd look at me, as if he was startled, and his eyes would look right at mine so I'd go back to petting him and he'd get still again.

Del came back with an old leather travel bag. He set it down on the hood of the truck and took a fifth of vodka from the bag, then a long needle with a huge bottle and plunger. I watched as he filled the bottle with the entire fifth and injected it into Lean on Pete.

"Why do you do that?" I asked him.

"It makes him focus," he said.

Del was sweating and you could tell he was in pain just doing that much work. He threw the vodka bottle into the brush and took a small syringe and a glass medicine bottle. He put the needle into the bottle and filled it with liquid, then injected it into the horse's front hooves.

"These are vitamins," Del said. "And remember, never talk about anything concerning me or my horses or I'll fire you."

"Okay," I said.

"Walk him to that tree and back, and then we'll get back on the road."

I nodded and started walking him. When I was done he loaded Pete in and we drove back to the main road and went another ten minutes until we came to a big ranch house where about twenty trucks were parked.

Del drove past them and up to a big red barn and shut off the engine. We got out and unloaded the horses and I followed him inside the barn and we put them in stalls.

"Do you know how to drive?"

"Sort of," I said.

"You know how to work a clutch?"

"My dad's truck has a clutch. He lets me drive him around sometimes."

"This one's tricky."

"I'll be okay," I said.

"Alright," he said and handed me the keys.

"Take the truck and trailer down the road away from the house, park it, then clean the shit out the trailer. There's a shovel and a broom in the bed of my truck. Then come find me."

I nodded and he walked up towards the house and I got back in the truck and started it. The clutch was going out. I stalled it six or seven times before I finally drove down to where he said and parked it. I shoveled all the shit out of the trailer and threw it into the sagebrush alongside the road. Then I locked the truck, put the keys in my pocket, and walked towards a large group of men who were all wearing cowboy hats and talking Mexican and drinking beer.

Del was standing with them. He had a beer in his hand and was talking to a man who had a patch over his eye. Not long after that another truck and trailer pulled up and three men got out and unloaded four horses.

Del looked around and when he saw me he waved me over.

"That's who we're racing," he said when I got to him.

"Who are they?"

"The old guy is Estrada. He thinks he knows how to train

but he don't. He's just got money. He owns a ranch twenty miles from here. Talking to him is like hammering a nail into your leg. The guy that owns this place has a few that aren't too bad. He's a different story. We'll see."

Del took a can of chew from his shirt pocket, knocked it against his leg, and took a dip from it. "Alright," he said, "let's get Tumbling Through."

We walked to the stalls. He put a bridle on him and tied his tongue down with a strap that went over the horse's tongue and around its lower jaw. Tumbling Through could barely stand still. Del yelled at him, then pulled hard on the bridle to get him to calm down, but even so he wouldn't. We led him out and walked him down the road.

"Who's going to ride him?"

"A semi-friend of mine," Del said.

We stopped in front of the garage and two jockeys stood with helmets on, waiting. They were both dressed in jeans and T-shirts and had protective vests on. Del shook hands with one of them and then that man put a saddle on Tumbling Through. The other jockey did the same to one of the other horses. They both got on and then two men grabbed their lead ropes and led them away.

"Where are they racing?" I asked him.

"A dirt road behind the house. He told me he just graded it and added sand. It used to be a real piece of shit and I told him I wouldn't come out anymore unless he did something about it."

"Will he win?"

"Who, Tumbling?"

"Yeah."

"Shit if I know. Estrada spends some money on his horses. He can't train worth a fuck but money is money."

We walked back to where the men stood. There were big coolers of beer and Del bought a can from an old man who was selling them. We went to the fence, leaned against it, and waited for the start of the race. The track was just a straight dirt road that went for maybe six hundred yards. There was an old metal four-horse starting gate and in the middle, near us, was the finish line and there was some sort of camera on one side of it.

I asked Del what it was and he told me it was a photo-finish camera. He said someone almost got killed there a year ago because of an argument over a race that was too close to call. One of the Mexicans said his horse won the race, the other said his did. They gave it to one of them and the loser got so pissed he rammed his truck into the other guy's truck and totaled it.

"What happened after that?" I asked him.

"The guy who owns this place, the guy with the eye patch, Hector, bought a camera."

"What about the two guys who were arguing?"

"Who knows? I don't give a shit."

In the distance you could see the horses enter the gate and then suddenly the race started. The men around us began yelling. The horses passed me in a flash. Each jockey was hitting his horse with a whip, and one of the jockeys was yelling. It looked pretty close until the end, when the other horse pulled away and beat Tumbling Through.

It took them a while to slow the horses down and they were two hundred yards past us when you could see

Tumbling Through having trouble and then finally, in the distance, he stopped and the jockey jumped off. Del finished his beer in a swallow, dropped the can on the ground, and we went out to where the jockey stood trying to calm the horse. Del kneeled down to look at his front right leg.

"I'm cursed," was all he said and stood up. He took the can of Copenhagen from his pocket. The jockey took the saddle off and said something in Mexican and Del nodded and the jockey left. We walked Tumbling Through back to the barn and put him in the stall next to Pete. He was wet with sweat and was upset and nervous.

Del told me to stay put and left the barn. After a while he came back with two Mexicans I'd never seen.

"He still won't stand on his leg, Del," I said.

Del nodded.

"Will he be alright?"

"I don't know, we'll see." He began talking to the other men. After a while he looked over at me. "You can take a break if you want."

"I don't need to take a break," I told him.

"There's nothing to do right now so go check out the next race, alright?"

"Alright," I said and then I left the barn.

There were two other races before Lean on Pete's and both were really exciting. When the last one ended I went back to the barn to find Tumbling Through gone and Del in the other stall with Lean on Pete. He was holding Pete by his upper lip and twisting it. He put a handful of tablets underneath Pete's tongue and tied the tongue down. Pete started pacing around after that. He couldn't stand still.

I followed them out and the same jockey who rode Tumbling Through put a saddle on Pete. The whole time Pete got worse with the jitters. Del helped the jockey up and the same two men came and led the two horses down towards the start.

Del walked over to where Estrada was and spoke to him, then took money out of his wallet, counted it, and gave it to a bald-headed man who was standing with them. Estrada did the same and they shook hands, then Del went to the fence, leaned against it, and waited.

When the race went off I could see Lean on Pete pulling away. His head pushed forward and his ears pinned back, and the jockey was yelling at him and hitting him over and over with the whip. There was a great sound to it, the hooves on the dirt, the whips hitting the horses, and the group of men leaning against the fence yelling. I couldn't believe the jockeys could stay on when the horses were going as fast as they were. Pete led the other horse by twenty feet and pulled farther and farther ahead. It was like he had wheels, like his feet were barely touching the ground. It was the greatest thing I'd ever seen, and when it was over Pete had won. I looked over and I could see Del smiling as Pete coasted down.

The jockey brought Pete back and Del put a lead rope on him and we led him off the track and to the parking lot. Pete was breathing heavy and he was dark with sweat. The jockey jumped down, took off his saddle, and Del and I walked Pete towards the barn.

"Pete's really fast," I said excitedly.

"If he didn't beat that piece of shit I would have slit his

throat," Del said. "He ain't fast. The other horse is just a pig. We'll hose him down, then we'll get the hell out of here before the spics get drunk and want their money back."

But Del's voice was lighter and easier. You could tell he was happy. We took Lean on Pete to a concrete pad where there was a garden hose. Del turned it on and sprayed Pete down, then he told me to walk him up the road a half-mile or so to cool him off.

"If he tries to get away just give him a snap on the rope. Pete ain't much of a fighter."

I nodded.

"After that, feed him," he said.

"What does he eat?"

"Two flakes."

"Of what?"

"You don't know shit, do you?"

"No," I said.

"There's hay in the barn. You've seen a bale of hay, haven't you?"

"I guess."

"A flake is maybe five inches off one of them. You'll see it. It comes off like a slice of cheese. Ask one of the spics down there if you get confused. And look, don't run off anywhere. The second the last race is done we're loading Pete and getting the fuck out of here."

"What about Tumbling Through?"

"He bowed a tendon on that race," Del said and coughed. "I sold him. I got too many fucked-up horses as it is."

"Is he in a lot of pain?"

"That's not my problem anymore," Del said and walked

off. I just stood there. I didn't know what to think so I just took Pete and began walking him along the dirt road away from the barn.

There were fields of alfalfa on both sides of us, and hills of sagebrush behind them. I talked to Pete and told him how fast he was. He was wet, which made his coat shine, and he was still nervous and jittery. But the farther we got away from the house and the people the more settled he became.

I told him who I was and how I wished I was as fast as he was. I told him about Tumbling Through and to be careful of his legs. We stopped a half-mile from the ranch house and I pet him and told him not to worry and he got calmer and calmer and by the time I brought him back to the barn he seemed easy. I put him in a stall and gave him two flakes of hay and made sure he had water. After that I went looking for Del, and I found him near a crowd of men. He was drinking from a half-pint bottle of whiskey, leaning against the fence, looking out at the hills in the distance.

"I think I got it right," I said when I got to him.

"I won on that last race. Did you see it?"

"I heard it but I didn't see it."

"It was close," he said, still gazing out. I could tell then he was drunk. "You got my keys?"

"Yeah," I said and handed them to him. "Del, I was wondering if I could get a few bucks to buy some tamales? There's an old lady walking around selling them."

He looked at me.

"There's a lady selling tamales?"

"Yeah."

"You'll end up shitting your pants for a week."

"I'll be alright," I said.

"You want your pay, hunh?"

I told him I did.

He went into his billfold and took out five twenty-dollar bills and handed them to me. "There's two more races. By the end of the second I want you down at the stalls. Don't fuck around."

"Okay," I said and stared at him. I didn't know what he was doing giving me all that money. It made no sense but I took the bills from him, thanked him, and ran back to the barn. I took the plastic bag I had in my pocket and set in four of the twenties and put the bag in my shoe. I kept the last one in my pocket and found the lady selling tamales and bought five and two Cokes. Then I walked down to the fence line near the starting gate and ate.

I finished eating just before the last race started. The two horses weren't much past me when something went wrong and the horse closest to me threw the jockey and the jockey went flying into the fence. After the dust settled I could see the jockey laid out on the ground and he wasn't moving. His clothes and face were covered in dirt and you could see his nose begin to bleed. A few men came and spoke Mexican to him and after a while he answered. They let him lie there for a while, then helped him up. I could see tears welling in his eyes and you could tell it was hard for him to breathe. He was hurt pretty bad, and when he tried to walk he stumbled. He leaned on a guy who was standing next to him and was helped away.

6

They took the jockey into the main house and when they did I went to the barn and waited for Del. I was there for a long time with Lean on Pete, just waiting next to him, but Del never showed up. I walked down to the truck to make sure he wasn't waiting for me there, and that's when I saw him in the distance, talking to some men. I went over and stood next to him.

"Where the hell you been?"

"I've been at the barn like you told me."

He shook his head and took a drink off a can of beer, then started talking with the men again. After a while he said goodbye and we started towards the barn. We led Lean on Pete out and loaded him into the trailer and I got in the passenger side of the truck and Del started it up and we left.

"Well," he said and coughed. "We got out of there just in time."

"Why's that?" I asked him.

"I won three grand, that's why. If you stay too long some-one gets drunk and they start blaming you. I'm the only white guy there. It starts with that, then they start accusing you of cheating."

"Of cheating?"

"Yeah."

"How do you cheat?"

"How do you cheat?"

"Yeah."

"Everyone cheats," he said and turned on the radio. We drove for over an hour without saying anything, then we pulled off the highway and drove on a two-lane road. We stayed on that and then turned onto a dirt driveway that led us to a house. It was pretty dark by then, there was only a single light coming off the porch. Del took a flashlight from the glove box and we unloaded Pete and put him in a pasture. There were other horses there and Pete let out a yell when Del let go of him. He went running off into the dark towards them.

"Where are we?" I asked him.

"It's my brother's house," Del said.

"Are we going inside?"

"I'm sleeping in the cab of the truck. You can sleep in the bed or anywhere else you can find."

I looked around. "I'll sleep in the bed," I said. He nodded, then went into his truck and lay down on the bench seat. He didn't even put a blanket over him or take off his boots. He just set his glasses on the dashboard and turned off the inside light. I got into the back of the truck and untied my sleeping bag and rolled it out. I took off my shoes and got in. I lay there for a long time before I fell asleep. For a while I thought of Tumbling Through and where he was and what would happen to him. Then I thought of Lean on Pete and the race he'd won and then I thought about the money Del gave me. It was the most money I'd ever had at one time in my whole life. I lay there and thought if he would remember he gave me that much, and if he'd want it back. Then I thought about what I'd do with it if I got to keep it and that made me relax, and when I relaxed I was suddenly tired and I fell asleep.

The next morning I woke to the sound of Del starting the truck. It turned over five or six times before it finally coughed and rumbled and took. He sat there warming it for ten minutes. It was still dark out. I just lay there unsure of what to do, then Del got out of the truck and walked back to me.

"Are you up yet?"

"Yeah," I said.

"You can stay back here if you want, but I got to get the hell out of here."

"I'll sit up front."

"Then get up and help me catch Pete," he said and walked off into the darkness.

I put on my shoes and rolled up the sleeping bag. I jumped out of the truck and started walking in the direction of Del. The light coming off the house helped but I couldn't see him and started calling out his name.

He turned on the flashlight and pointed it at me.

"I'm over here," he whispered.

I went over to him.

"Keep it down or you'll wake her up."

"Wake up who?"

"My brother's wife. She'd shoot me if she could."

"Why?" I asked him.

"You don't want to know," he said and handed me the halter and a flashlight. "Go get him, but they got four other horses in there so be careful."

"Alright," I told him. I went into the pasture and walked around until I came to the horses gathered near an old bathtub. I saw Pete and I went to him but every time I got near he moved away from me.

I went back to Del.

"He won't let me catch him," I said.

Del shook his head and said something I couldn't make out, then grabbed the halter from me and started walking out towards the horses.

"Do you need the flashlight?"

"Don't talk anymore and get in the truck," he said.

Five minutes later he had the horse in the trailer. He got in the cab of the truck and put it in gear and we got on the road. He drove like he was having a hard time seeing. He held on to the steering wheel tightly with his good hand and only looked off the road to spit into his chew cup.

"That crazy bitch stabbed me," he said finally.

I didn't know what to say so I didn't say anything. I just looked out the window. The sun was beginning to rise. You couldn't see it yet but it was starting to get light out.

"Did you hear me or are you already out?"

"I heard you," I said. "Where did she stab you?"

"In the arm with a pair of scissors."

"Did it hurt?"

"What do you think?"

"Why would she do that?"

"'Cause I came in her," he said and beat on the steering wheel and laughed.

I wasn't sure what he meant. After a while I said, "Was

she your girlfriend?"

"Do you listen? She's my brother's wife and he's as sterile as a castrated dog." He shook his head like I was the dumbest guy he'd ever met.

I didn't know what to say after that so I just leaned against the window glass. We rode silent for a while, then he put on the radio and I fell asleep. The next thing I knew we were driving into Portland.

I yawned and sat up in the seat.

"You're awake."

"Yeah," I said.

"I stopped and had breakfast in The Dalles and filled the truck. You didn't even move the entire time." He was leaned back now. The radio was still going and he had his window half rolled down.

"I'm sorry."

"What do I care?"

"Del," I asked him, "I've been thinking. Can I work for you?"

"What?"

"Do you need help this summer?"

"I'm broke. I don't pay much."

"I just need enough so I can eat."

"What about your folks, they feed you, don't they?"

"I guess," I said. He sat there and spit into his cup a few times.

"There's probably a few things you could do for me."

"Alright," I said.

"I'll pick you up a groom's license if you're serious."

"What's that?"

42

"It's so you can get on the backside and work. You need a license to do that. They only cost twenty bucks. I'll take it out of your pay."

"Thanks," I said, but he didn't say anything back and we fell quiet again. He kept driving and took us to the track, where he parked the trailer and we unloaded Pete and put him in his stall. Then he told me to show up the next morning at six if I wanted to work.

"And look," he said and spit on the ground, "I can't remember, did I pay you?"

"Yeah," I told him.

"What did I give you, forty dollars?"

"Yeah."

"Alright," he said and walked across the backside lot and disappeared into the café. I almost followed him in to tell him the truth, that first he told me he'd pay me twenty-five, and now he thought it was forty, but that yesterday he gave me a hundred. I wanted to tell him all that, tell him that he was wrong, that he'd made a mistake. I wanted to give the extra money back, but really, in the end I just couldn't.

7

My dad wasn't there when I got home. I looked through the fridge and the cupboards but I'd eaten most everything except a can of pork and beans and a can of pears. I put the beans on the stove and ate the pears while I waited. When I was done I walked all the way to Fred Meyer and got a cart and started filling it with things. I bought cereal, bacon, potatoes, spaghetti, canned sauce, bread, milk, a six pack of Coke, TV dinners, cookies, carrots, canned fruit, Hamburger Helper, frozen hamburger, macaroni and cheese, onions, tortillas, cheese, lunch meat, potato chips, canned beans, ice cream, a dozen cans of soup, and a few candy bars.

I went up to the checker and set all the stuff on the belt and the lady rang me up and I figured it out alright. I spent seventy-eight dollars, which left me with sixteen. I kneeled down and took the money out of my shoe and gave it to her. She put everything in bags and put them back in the cart and I rolled it out of the store and pushed it over a mile back to the house.

When I got home I unloaded the bags and made myself a sandwich, then changed into my running clothes. I pushed the cart back to the store and then I ran as hard as I could down to the river and jogged along it until I got tired. I rested for a while on the banks and after that I got up and did my push-ups and sit-ups and headed back to the house.

* * *

That night I made a package of Hamburger Helper and spent the rest of the evening eating off it and watching a movie on TV about a hockey player who gets too many concussions and they make him quit so he ends up as a bartender but even so he still skates and then he meets this girl who's a famous skater and they become skate partners. It was a pretty bad movie but the girl was beautiful and she falls in love with the hockey player and then they win a gold medal.

When I went to sleep that night I couldn't stop thinking about the girl skater. I just lay in my bed and thought about how good-looking she was and how at the end she turned out to be nice and then finally around eleven or so I fell asleep. At five o'clock my alarm went off. I lay there for a while, then I heard noises coming from the main room. I got up and looked out the window and saw my dad's truck and so I got dressed and walked out into the kitchen where he was making bacon and eggs. He was dressed in his work clothes and standing over the stove.

"What the hell are doing up so early?"

"What about you?" I asked him.

"I just got home."

"I got a job," I told him.

"You got a job?"

"I work for a guy named Del at the horse track."

"Is that who you went off with?"

"Yeah," I said. Then I told him about the match race and the jockey falling and Tumbling Through getting hurt and being left out there. I told him about sleeping in the bed of the truck and about Pete and how he won, and how Del gave me a hundred dollars.

"And the guy seems alright?" my dad asked.

"I guess. He paid me."

"Congratulations. You hungry?"

"I'm always hungry."

"Sit down," he said, and then he went to the fridge and took a can of frozen orange juice and put it in a pitcher and filled it with hot water and stirred it until it thawed. He set the pitcher on the table and went back to the stove and put in two more eggs.

"You didn't steal all these groceries, did you?"

"No," I said. "I went to the store and paid for them."

"Jesus, you're something," he said. He went to the fridge and took a beer from it and opened it. He flipped the eggs over and let them sit for a minute, then put them on a plate with some bacon and sat down across from me.

"I'm not so sure about Portland," he said. "How about you?"

"I don't know," I said. "I ain't done anything yet. I hear the football team at Jefferson High is pretty good. I'm just waiting for that and hoping I make the team."

"You'll make the team. Spokane ain't that much smaller than Portland."

"Maybe."

"When do practices start?"

"August 12th."

"I'll make sure we stick it out for the whole season, alright?"

"We could always go back to Spokane."

"We ain't going back there."

"We could go back to Green River, then."

"There ain't any work there and I hate it there. We'll stay here for a while. Sooner or later I'll get dayshift. I'm just too old for graveyard, that's all. I'm just complaining. Alright?"

"Alright."

"You want to hear something?" he said.

I nodded and began eating.

"There's this new kid at work. He's on parole, he was in prison in Pendleton. He'd gotten three DUIs, then got busted driving without a license and he was drunk with an eight-ball of cocaine on him so they sent him off. He's only been out a couple months, but his uncle is the head dock supervisor so that's how he got the job. Anyway, he and I get paired off together. It's only his fourth or fifth day and he's drunk, and not just sorta drunk but fucked-up drunk. This operation is so big that you never really talk that much or have to be in a closed room with anyone so no one noticed. Plus he's always got about five pieces of gum in his mouth and with all the forklift exhaust nobody smells anything on him. But me, hell, I'm in a trailer with him and he can't stop talking and his eyes are glossed over and I know he's drunk; I can smell it. He starts talking about prison and about how he doesn't drink anymore and how moving freight was worse than being in the can. In prison he said all he had to do was drop acid and do heroin and play cards and watch TV.

"So we keep loading boxes, and pretty soon we get to these chairs. These wood chairs that aren't in boxes but wrapped in cardboard and plastic. He starts throwing them into the back of the trailer and breaking them. I ask him what the hell he's doing and he just starts laughing. So we finish the load and then we move into another trailer and this time he's on the forklift. I'm just marking off the freight bill and he loads in a pallet of spices and sets it down, then backs up and raises his forks and starts ramming holes into the boxes. Spices cost a lot and he's ramming the hell out of them with the forks. No one notices 'cause the place is a madhouse. Then he loads in another pallet and does the same thing."

My dad started laughing.

"Did you stop him?" I asked.

"What?"

"Did you get him to stop?"

"His uncle's a boss. Anyway, I'm too low on the pole to do much but try and get paired up with someone else."

"Will he get you in trouble?"

"No. I made him sign the freight bill. They'll know he loaded it. My name's nowhere on there. He'll be done in a week or two. You worry too much. I know how to work these situations out in my sleep. I just thought it was pretty damn funny, a guy killing freight like that. I got to say this is a real different layout than Spokane."

"Then maybe we can go back to Spokane," I said and looked at him. "We could probably get our old place again and I could go back to the same school."

"Shit, I can't go back there. I'm lucky I got the hell out of there when I did."

"We could try."

"It's not going to happen. How's breakfast?"

"I didn't know you knew how to cook."

48

"I was a cook for three years when I got out of high school."

"Really?"

"You didn't know that?"

"No."

"I was," he said. "But it's no way to live. Getting up at four in the morning and getting hit with grease all day. People complaining to you, orders backing up. It ain't much of a life."

"But you get free food, right?"

"You get free food but you end up hating food, let me tell you. But there's waitresses. You like waitresses, don't you?"

"I guess," I said.

"All the best women have been waitresses at one point."

"Really?"

"Of course," he said and finished his beer. He went to the fridge and got another and opened it.

"So what have you learned?"

"Don't be a cook, and go out with waitresses," I said and smiled.

"See, besides being a star athlete you're smart too."

8

I left the house at five forty-five and walked down the street to the track and stood outside the gate until the guard came out of his office. I told him I had just started working for Del Montgomery and he let me through. I went over to the café but Del wasn't there so I went looking for him, but I couldn't remember where his horses were. All the shedrows looked the same, and there were so many of them it was confusing. I asked a man walking by if they knew him and he pointed me to a distant corner of a shedrow and I found Del bent down on his knees trying to put leg wraps on a horse.

"What are you doing here?" he said when he saw me.

"You said I could work for you."

"You got to be here earlier than this."

"You told me six."

"Make it five."

"Alright," I said.

"You know how to clean a stall?"

"No," I said.

He didn't say anything, he just picked up the lead rope of the horse he was working on and led it outside to a hot-walker and hooked him to it. He showed me eight empty stalls and told me what to do, and I started working. I had a pitchfork and a wheelbarrow and I picked out all the manure and the piss-soaked straw. I'd never been around horseshit but it really didn't smell, although the urine did, like ammonia. When the wheelbarrow was full I unloaded it inside a big building that sat in the center of the shedrows. The place had nothing but straw and horseshit in it, and it was so big you could probably park an airplane there. When I was done I put fresh straw down in each of the stalls and made sure the horses' automatic drinking fountains were working. There was a girl who fed Del's horses and I met her but she didn't really talk much. Her name was Maxine and she wasn't much older than me and her face was scarred and Del said she'd been kicked in the face by a horse when she was a kid.

After I was done, I followed Del around and listened to him talk. He would stand and have long conversations with people. One conversation would end and then he'd walk to the next row and start up with someone else. I followed him to the café and he got a cup of coffee and talked to people there. The cook had made maple bars and set them out on the counter, and I ate two and drank a carton of milk while Del stood there rambling on to some old guy whose right ear was half missing.

I followed him around for another hour, then we went back to the café and he ordered lunch.

"Do you want anything?"

"I can't spend the money," I told him.

"Are you hungry?"

"I'm always hungry," I said, and then, just like that, he bought me lunch. We sat at a small table near the window and waited for our food. Del had chew spit stuck to his chin but I didn't say anything about it. His hair was messed up and his shirt had old dried sweat stains on it but I couldn't really smell him. He just sat there and sighed heavy, like he was having a hard time breathing. Then he took off his glasses and spit into them and cleaned them with the bottom of his shirt. He didn't talk to me once, he just sat there reading a newspaper that was sitting on the table and twenty minutes later a guy with a big gray beard set down our food.

When I was done I looked up and Del was staring at me.

"You don't have any manners, do you?"

"What'd I do wrong?" I asked.

"You're not supposed to lower your head to the plate and shovel it in. And you got to let yourself chew. I don't know how you eat so fast without choking. What does your mom say about it?"

"I don't know. I don't know her," I said.

"Is she dead?"

"I don't think so."

"Does your dad have any manners?"

"I've never noticed," I said.

"Your mom has never shown up?"

"No."

"You don't hear about that often. A mom leaving her kid."

"I guess."

"It's rare. She must have been a real piece."

"I don't know."

"You don't have a step-mom?"

"No."

Del opened his shirt pocket and took a toothpick out of it and began picking his teeth. "The way you eat makes me lose my appetite. If we're gonna eat together you have to get manners. But don't ask me. I don't have time to teach you everything. Alright?"

"Alright."

"That's it for today. I'm going home."

"Can I work tomorrow?"

"Be here at six."

"You said you wanted me here by five."

"You can get here at five if you want."

"Do I get paid every day?"

"You don't get paid until you know what you're doing. I don't pay anybody for teaching them something. Plus you owe me for the groom's license. I'll take that out first and then I'll let you know."

"Do I have to take any tests for the groom's license?"

"No," he said. "You just have to be fifteen."

"So when do you think I'll get paid?"

"When you've learned something."

"Alright," I said and got up. "I'll be here at five tomorrow."

"Suit yourself," he said and went back to the paper.

When I got home I took a shower and fell asleep in front of the TV. I woke up around six and put on my running clothes and headed towards the river. When I got there I did my push-ups and sit-ups and ran sprints down the street. I'd run as fast as I could for a block, then I'd jog the next block, then I'd sprint again. Every time I wanted to quit I thought about them not letting me on the team, about them making fun of me 'cause I wasn't tough enough, and I kept going until I couldn't go anymore.

* * *

For the next two weeks I worked for Del, doing whatever he told me to do. I got there in the morning at five and stayed until eleven or so. He was the moodiest guy I'd ever met. Sometimes it was like I was his grandson. He'd walk around and tell everyone he'd finally found a kid that would work, that could put his nose to the grindstone. Then maybe an hour later he'd tell me I was the dumbest kid he'd ever had work for him, that I wasn't worth a rock on the side of the road.

At the end of the first week he paid me fifty bucks and I was more than relieved. But at the end of the second week he only gave me thirty when I'd worked more hours and learned more. I knew the names of his horses and which ones needed what. I knew how to clean stalls and which order he did things in. I put on leg wraps and helped him do anything he couldn't do with one hand. It didn't make sense that he'd pay me less. I wanted to say something about it but he didn't look like he cared if I did. When he gave me the money it was like he knew I didn't deserve it, like he might hand me the money and say, "I don't need you anymore." So I just kept my mouth shut.

That first time I got paid I went to the grocery store and spent most of the money there. When I got home I put the groceries away and made a batch of spaghetti. I cut up onions and garlic and put in canned tomatoes and ground beef. My dad had a bottle of Italian spices that he'd gotten from work and I put some of that in the sauce as well.

After I was done eating I moved the TV into my bedroom and watched a movie about a guy who becomes a mountain man and lives by himself for a long time in the middle of nowhere. He meets a mute boy whose family got killed by Indians and he adopts him. Then he gets married to an Indian girl and then both the girl and the kid get killed and the mountain man spends the rest of the movie trying to murder every Indian that did it. It was a horribly sad movie because the girl and the kid were really nice and they all tried to start a family together. When it was over I shut off the TV but I thought about it for a long time before I went to sleep.

Around one or so my dad came in. I woke up when I heard him open the front door. He went into the kitchen and turned on the radio and it sounded like he was making something to eat. I dozed off again and the next time I woke it was because someone was beating on our front door and I could hear a guy yelling. The second my eyes opened I knew something wasn't right. I could just feel it. I was asleep one moment and then nervous and scared the next. I sprung up from the bed and went out to the main room in my underwear. My dad was still in his work clothes and he was pushing against the door, trying to keep it shut. I stood in the back near the kitchen. The man outside kept banging on it and you could see it shake. I wanted to say something to my dad but I couldn't get any words out.

"Fuck you," the man screamed through the door. "Fuck you, fuck you, fuck you."

"Look," my dad said. His voice shaky and nervous. "She told me she was single. It ain't my fault. It's her fault. She told me you guys were over."

"I heard about what you two did tonight," the man said.

"Look, it's not my fault she ain't sure what to do. It ain't my fault she calls me."

And then the man broke down the door. He kicked it in. You could see the wood around the bolt lock give way and all of a sudden a man who weighed over three hundred pounds was in our house. It was the Samoan. He had his curly black hair in a ponytail and he was dressed in a T-shirt and sweats with flip-flops on his feet. I don't know how he kicked in a door with flip-flops on but he did. My dad moved back in the room, but he didn't run, he just stood there. The Samoan hit him in the face as hard as he could. My dad fell back into the wall and then the man picked him up and threw him through the big window that overlooked our front yard. He picked up my dad like you would a little kid and hurled him into the glass and my dad went all the way through and fell outside on the ground.

I couldn't move. Then the Samoan saw me and I froze in panic. But he didn't do anything to me. He just stared at me then turned around. He walked outside, got into his car, and drove off.

When I saw his tail lights disappear I went out to my dad. He was lying on the ground and he wasn't moving. There was glass everywhere and his face was bloody, but I could see he was still breathing. I went inside and called 911 and got dressed while I talked to them. Then I took two towels from the bathroom and a flashlight I kept by my bed and went to him. I shined the flashlight on him and it was then I could see a big piece of glass coming out of his stomach. There was a dark pool of blood around it. There were cuts on his arms and on his neck and on his chin. His nose was bleeding.

I didn't know if I should put the towel around his stomach or if that would move the glass and make it hurt worse, make it bleed more. I didn't know the right thing. So I just stood there with the flashlight on him and the towels in my hand. I tried to tell him he'd be alright but every time I spoke I started crying.

I got so scared I couldn't move.

The ambulance and police came and I watched them work on him. They left him on his back, put a neck brace on him, and then put a pack around the piece of glass in his stomach and put him in the back of the ambulance and drove off. They didn't even tell me where they were going.

There were two cops and they asked me who I was and my relation and I told them.

"Where did they take him?" I asked.

"They took him to the hospital," one officer said.

"Which hospital?"

"Good Samaritan," he said.

"Oh," I said, but I didn't know where that was. And then I thought about how big Portland was and how I didn't know anybody and I started crying.

When I calmed down they asked me my name and I told them.

"What happened tonight?" the other officer asked.

"I was asleep and this guy started beating on the door and yelling at my dad, and then he broke the bolt lock and came in the house. I was up by then and standing in the kitchen. I saw this big huge guy hit my dad and throw him out the window."

"What did the man look like?"

"He was huge. I think he was Samoan."

"Samoan?"

"My dad's going out with a lady whose husband is Samoan. I think it was him."

"Do you know his name?"

"No."

"What's her name?"

"Lynn, but I don't know her last name. They work together at Willig Freight Lines."

"What did the man do after he threw your dad through the window?"

"He got into his car and drove away."

"What kind of car?"

"I'm not sure. I know it wasn't a truck."

"Do you have anyone coming to stay with you tonight?"

"What?"

"How old are you?"

"Fifteen."

"Do you have someone to look after you tonight?"

I paused for a while.

"My uncle's coming," I said.

I looked around. There were neighbors out on their lawns. Everyone's lights were on and they were all looking at us, watching us.

Another police car came up and the officers told me to wait. They walked over to the car and when they turned around I went back in the house, grabbed my coat, and walked out the back door. I hopped over the fence and went through our neighbor's gate and began walking down the street.

9

I walked for a mile or so, then hid in some bushes alongside the road. It was hours before I went back to the house, and when I did the police cars were gone. All the neighbors were back in their houses and their lights were off. I went inside and made myself look in each room but there was no one there and everything looked the same as it had. I sat in the kitchen and tried to figure out what to do, then I went into my dad's room and got his toolbox. I took a hammer and broke out the rest of the glass from the big window. When I did a neighbor across the street came out in his bathrobe, but he didn't say anything. He just stood in his yard and stared. I waved to him but he didn't wave back. I put the hammer down and went to the closet where we kept an extra sleeping bag and I unzipped it and nailed it to the wall over where the window had been. When I was finished I called a cab to take me to the hospital.

It was almost 4 a.m. when I got there and just going inside made me sick to my stomach. I'd never really been in a hospital. Not a big one, anyway. I asked the front-desk lady at the emergency room about my dad and she said he'd been admitted and that he was in surgery. She was nice and asked me if I was his son and I told her I was and she told me I could sit in the waiting room if I wanted. She told me she'd come get me when I could see him.

It was past morning when I saw him. He was in intensive

59

care and asleep with tubes going in and out of him. The nurse said the glass cut up his bowel, spilling infection into his gut causing a bad case of peritonitis. I asked if that was serious and she said it was like he'd been poisoned, so yes, it was really serious.

He had stitches on his face and on his arms. He looked terrible. He barely looked like my dad, more like an old man. I sat down on a chair next to the bed and stayed there until a nurse came in and told me it would be alright if I took a break. She said he'd be asleep for most of the day.

I went back out to the waiting room and watched TV until I fell asleep in the chair. When I woke it was hours later and I stood up and got a drink from a water fountain, then went to the bathroom and washed my face. I went back to his room and looked in on him, but he was still asleep so I went to the cafeteria and ate. Then finally, in the afternoon, a nurse came out to where I was watching TV and told me he was awake and led me in to him.

"Are you okay?" he said softly when he saw me. "Did he hurt you?" His lips were chapped and his face was swollen and pale. He had sweat on his brow. He looked bad off.

"I'm okay," I said. "Nothing happened. Are you okay?"

"I don't know."

"Does it hurt?"

"Not yet, they got me pretty doped up."

"But you'll be alright?"

"I hope so."

"Do you think the guy will be back?"

"Which guy?"

"The guy that threw you through the window?"

"No, I'll tell the police about him. He's a big fucker, isn't he?"

"Yeah," I said, and then, just like that, I started bawling.

"Don't worry about him, okay?"

"What am I going to say to the police? They'll take me away if they know no one else is in the house."

"If you see cops just go the other way until I can get my head together, alright?"

I nodded. "I'm sorry that guy threw you through the window."

"Me too," he said. "You don't have to stay here with me. You can go back to the house if you want."

"The house scares me."

He nodded.

"I nailed a sleeping bag over the window."

"That's good thinking. It'll be alright, Charley. It'll take a bit but I'll be alright. My clothes should be here somewhere. Get my wallet if it's still here. Take the money out of it. I might be stuck here for a while. I'm having a hard time staying awake, alright?"

"Okay," I said and then he closed his eyes.

I got up and went through the drawers and found his wallet and his car keys. He had seven dollars and I put that in my pants pocket and shut the drawer. I sat there for most of the day and into the night and then they made me leave. It was late by then and I walked miles before I found my way back to the house. I put the TV in my bedroom and locked myself in. I hammered nails into the floor by the door to keep it shut and I slept in my clothes.

When I woke up it was four-thirty in the morning. I didn't

know what I was going to do. I wanted to go back to the hospital and see if my dad was alright, but I had less than twenty dollars and I knew I'd have to try and keep the job with Del. So instead of going to the hospital I went to the track.

10

It was still dark out when I got there and Del's horses were in their stalls and hardly anyone was around. I looked in on Pete and pet him and whenever I'd stop he'd move towards me and stomp and shake his head. I turned on the light in his stall and went in. It was the same as all the others. The floor was covered in straw and there were no windows, just three walls of painted brick that was worn and covered in dust, and a gate keeping him in. There was a bulb hanging from the roof rafters, and an automatic drinking fountain for him to get water. I scratched his neck and when I did his lips quivered. There were scars on his face and long scars on his rear. I'd asked Del what they were from and he said most were from when Pete was laid off and put back in a herd. Horses are always arguing, Del said. But the scars around his leg were from when he'd reared back in a starting gate and threw the jockey and got himself cut up. Del said Pete used to be full of it, that he used to be a handful, but now he was tired out and had thrown in the towel.

I stayed in there with him and kept petting him, then I turned off the stall light and sat down on the ground. I told him about the Samoan and my dad in the hospital and about what had happened. I told him how there was blood and glass everywhere and how in the hospital there were tubes running in and out of my dad and how I didn't know what I was going to do if he wasn't alright. How I wished he and I could just disappear. We could live in a place where there was no one else around and it would be warm with miles of grass for him to eat and no one would ever make him run. There would be a barn and a house and the house would be lined with food from floor to ceiling and there would be a TV and a huge swimming pool.

It was almost six o'clock when Del showed up. I saw him walking down the shedrow. "What are you doing here?" he said.

"Getting ready to work."

"You weren't here yesterday."

"I couldn't work yesterday," I said.

"You can't choose the days you work for me. I tell you when to work, you don't tell me."

"I'm sorry," I said.

"I got enough problems."

"I couldn't work yesterday. I wanted to."

"Just go home," he said.

"My dad's in the hospital."

"No shit?" He smiled and gave me a look.

"And I don't have your phone number or I would have called you. I've asked you for it. Remember that day in the truck? You told me I didn't need it."

"Your dad isn't in the hospital. That's a load of shit."

"You can call down there if you want."

He took his fingers and pulled the chew from his mouth and threw it on the ground.

"What hospital?"

"Good Samaritan."

"I'm gonna call down there," he said and paused. "Here's the deal. You can work for me but I ain't paying you for this week. I'll pay you next week same as usual but you got to learn a lesson. Take it or leave it."

"I want to keep working," I said, but I was really mad at him. I began to hate him. "I need your phone number though. My dad really is in the hospital so I'll call you the night before in case I can't come in."

"I guess that's fair enough," Del said and shook his head. He reached for a pen in his shirt pocket and took an old receipt from his wallet and wrote his number on it.

"I'm going to put three on the hotwalker so you'll have three stalls to clean right off." He took a can of Copenhagen from his pants and put in a fresh chew and began getting the horses out and we hardly talked the rest of the day.

When I got off work I went back to the house but even in the daylight it made me nervous. I went up the drive where my dad's truck sat parked, and unlocked the door.

"Is there anyone in here?" I asked and stuck my head in. "Hello?"

I stood there for a minute but I didn't hear anything so I went inside. I walked through each room and checked the windows to make sure they were still locked and I checked that the sleeping bag still covered the broken window alright. Then I locked myself in the bathroom and took a shower. After that I left. I took the bus downtown and went to the library and found a Wyoming phone book. I looked in the white pages under the city of Rock Springs for my aunt's name, Margy Thompson. There were a couple M. Thompsons but there were no Margys. I wrote down all the numbers that were near it and then I wrote down all the Thompsons in the whole state, dividing it up by the city.

I remembered one of the jobs she had at an auto parts store in Rock Springs. It was a place called Scottish Sam's and I got the number for that as well. I put the list in my pocket and decided I'd try to find somebody's phone that had long distance and if I couldn't I'd wait until I got paid and use a payphone. After that I used one of the library computers and put in her name and the state of Wyoming but nothing came of it.

Five years before that we were living in Green River and she was living in Rock Springs, and we used to visit her and she would visit us. But after a while my dad and her didn't like each other. Then when we moved to Spokane he told me she had moved as well but he wasn't sure where. Before that she'd always sent me cards and things like that but it stopped. I knew she didn't know where we were 'cause when we moved to Spokane we didn't leave a forwarding address, we just snuck out. We didn't even have a phone for the first year.

When I left the library I walked to the hospital but my dad was asleep and he wouldn't wake up. I stayed with him for a couple hours, then the nurse came and she told me he wasn't doing very well. She said a doctor would be by to talk to me, but I never saw one. I just sat there and got more and more worried. It was midnight when I was told to leave and I walked all the way back to the house.

Everything was the same when I got there but just being inside made me so nervous that I changed into my work clothes, rolled up my sleeping bag, and took it and my alarm clock and headed towards the track.

The backside was shut down and dark except for a few overhead lights shining off the buildings. The main guard was there sitting in his shack so I walked along the chain link until I couldn't see him and found a place to crawl under. When I got to the other side I went as fast as I could to the shedrows and in near darkness went past the horses in their stalls until I came to the end and Del's horses.

His tack room sat next to Pete's stall and was shut with a padlock that I had the combination to. I opened it and went inside in the dark, closed the doors behind me, and turned on the light. I plugged in my alarm and set it for 5 a.m. and laid my sleeping bag down on the floor and turned off the light. It was completely black in the room and every once in a while I could hear a horse move or kick or make a noise but it all eased my mind more than worried it and before I knew it I had conked out and the alarm was going off.

When I got up I hid my things behind a metal filing cabinet. The morning wasn't cold and I walked out into the shedrow. I locked the tack room and visited Pete and said good morning to him. I pet him for a long time and he just stood there calm and still and I told him that I was living next door to him now and that I'd visit him every night. When I'd woken up enough I walked over to the café. I went inside to the bathroom and washed my face and combed my hair with my hand. I went to the counter and ordered breakfast.

It was just past five thirty when I went back to Del's horses. I put a halter on Pete and led him out to the hotwalker and cleaned his stall. I did the same for all the horses and by the time Del showed up at six forty-five I was almost done.

"What the hell are you doing?" he said in a huff when he saw me. He was wearing jeans and there was a wet spot around his crotch like he'd pissed in his pants.

"I'm cleaning out the stalls," I told him.

"Don't ever start before me getting here."

"Okay," I said.

"What are you doing tonight and tomorrow morning?"

"I don't know," I said.

"I'm heading to a place near Richland, Washington. I'm leaving in a couple hours. They don't start the race until five. I can't drive long distances at night or I'd come back. We'll get up in the morning and be back here by ten. You want to go?"

"Do I get paid if I go?"

"I'll pay you."

I didn't want to go with him, I really didn't. I wanted to go back to the hospital but I didn't know what else to do because I needed the money to get by on.

"Okay," I told him.

"Finish cleaning out the stalls and then be ready to go. We're taking Lean on Pete and Broken Blue. We'll load them in an hour or so." I nodded and Del turned around and walked away. I finished working, then I called the hospital from the café phone, but my dad wasn't awake and they didn't say anything different about how he was so I just left a message with his nurse telling him I would be gone for a day if he woke up and wondered where I was.

We loaded the horses and drove to a trailer park. We pulled to the side of the road and Del shut off the engine. He turned on the radio and found a station and we sat there for a while until a guy came up to the passenger side door and knocked on the glass.

"Let him in," Del said, and so I opened the door.

"Where the fuck have you been?"

"I was down the street," the man said and threw a duffel bag in the bed of the truck. I moved to the center of the seat, next to Del, and the man got in and set a paper sack on the floor.

"This is Charley," Del said and looked at me.

"Hey, Charley," the man said, and he put out his hand and we shook. "My name is Harry Durand."

"He's too fat to be a real jockey anymore," Del said and laughed.

"That's the only reason I'd work with you," Harry said back. He was short and thin and dressed like a cowboy with boots and jeans and a Western shirt. He wore a baseball cap and I'd guess he was probably in his thirties. He had a long scar on his chin and a missing side tooth.

"Are you related to Del?"

"No," I said. The truck and trailer lurched forward.

"I can smell you already," Del said. "If you get too drunk to ride I'll leave you out there."

"I ain't drunk. I spilled a beer on myself. I was eating a bag of chips and reading the paper and I reached for my can without looking and it went all over my lap."

"What the hell are you eating chips for?"

"A guy's got to eat."

"Where were you?"

"The Chinese Village."

"What time did you go there?"

"I was already done working, if that's what you're asking. You're like an old lady."

We got on the highway and stayed in the right lane and Del turned up the radio. Harry looked out the window and everyone was quiet. Then after a while Del took a can of Copenhagen off the dash and opened it.

"I've never seen a guy chew as much as you."

"Well," Del said, shook his head, and paused. "Look, I ain't gonna have this conversation with you. I'm tired of it."

Harry laughed. "Then I'm gonna have a beer. You want a chew and I want a beer. You want a can of beer, Del?"

"Might as well," he said.

"What about the kid?"

"He's under age," Del said.

Harry handed a beer to Del, then knocked me on the side. "How about it?"

"No thanks," I said.

They both drank their beer and then they had another and I fell asleep. It wasn't until we were in Umatilla that I woke up. We were parked at a gas station. Both Del and Harry were gone. I got out of the truck and could hear banging coming from the horse trailer. I walked behind it but I couldn't see anything really. It rang out and the trailer rocked and everyone around the station noticed.

Del and Harry came out at the same time. Del had a cup of coffee and Harry was carrying a paper sack.

"You're up?" Del said.

"They're beating on the trailer."

"It's alright," he said. "Don't worry about it."

"Is it okay if I go into Wendy's and get something to eat?"

"I ain't gonna wait long."

"Okay," I said and ran inside. When I got back they were waiting on the side of the road. Harry was leaned against the passenger side door and he looked asleep. I knocked on the glass and he looked over. He opened the door and got out so I could get back in.

"I bought you guys some fries," I said and handed Harry the bag. He took it and Del put the truck in first. He turned on the radio and Harry started eating.

"You want any, Del?" Harry asked.

"No," Del said. "And you shouldn't either."

I opened up my sack. I had two cheeseburgers, a jumbo fry, and a large Coke.

"Why do you eat so goddamn much?" Del said when I was done.

"I'm trying to gain weight," I told him.

"Why the fuck would you do that?" Harry asked.

"I play football."

"Where?"

"I played in Spokane. I was on the freshman team there. We won eight games in a row."

"What position?" Harry asked.

"Safety," I told him. "But I can play cornerback or wide receiver. I'm too little to play anything else and I'm waiting to lift weights until I'm done growing but I haven't grown in six months and I'm almost as tall as my dad so I'll start lifting when I start my new school."

"You're probably too young, but Spokane had a great track called Playfair," Harry said.

"I hated Playfair," Del said.

"You hate every track I ever mention," Harry said.

"That ain't true. I liked Longacres."

"I've never mentioned that one and you know why."

Del shook his head and took the chew off the dash, looked over at Harry, and put in a dip.

"So why'd you move down to Portland?" Harry said, ignoring him.

"My dad wanted to work here."

"What kind of work does he do?"

"He works for a trucking company, Willig Freight Lines."

"I always wanted to play football," Harry said, "but I was too small. I was barely five-four when I graduated from high school. I weighed about a hundred and three pounds. Hell, I couldn't grow a moustache until I was thirty."

"It didn't stop you from betting," Del said and let out a laugh.

"I can do that, sure," Harry said.

"Not too well, either."

"I ain't seen you quit and you're worse than me."

"Maybe," Del said.

"I used to be a runner, though. In high school before I started riding I ran the mile. I did alright too."

"I go running every day," I told him.

"I never really liked it," Harry admitted.

"You've never liked anything but drinking and watching TV."

"Del, I ain't talking to you," Harry said. "I'm talking to

the kid. I was tired of talking to you twenty minutes after I met you ten years ago."

"That's a good one," Del said.

"I just tell it the way I see it."

"Well I'm trying to concentrate on driving, so keep it down," Del said, and then he turned up the radio and hunched over the wheel. Harry knocked me on the ribs and I looked at him and he smiled and shook his head, then he leaned back against the door and the window glass and fell asleep.

When we parked the truck and trailer we were at a ranch near Pasco, Washington. There was a house and a huge white barn and a couple other outbuildings. Del got out and went up to the house and knocked on the door and went inside. Harry and I opened the trailer, got the two horses out, and led them into the barn and to a couple empty stalls. There was a black and white dog walking around. He came up to me wagging his tail, and I pet him for a while.

Harry went out to the truck and got his duffel, then came back in and changed his clothes across from me and the dog. He was in his underwear when I looked up at him. Even though he was thin and bony he had a small gut. There was a scar on his left leg that ran from six inches above his knee to a few inches below it. There were two scars on his shoulders, and when he turned around I could see a long scar running down his back.

"Do any of the scars hurt?" I asked him.

"They all do a bit, but my knee's the worst and I didn't even hurt that one riding. I did it when I wrecked my car."

73

"You wrecked your car?"

"I fell asleep and went off the side of the road and ran into a tree."

"And you didn't get hurt except your knee?"

He nodded. "The worst part was that they took my license away. I like having a car."

The dog pulled on my pant leg with his teeth.

"You've got a friend," Harry said.

"I've never had a dog," I told him. "But I'd like one."

"They're a pain in the ass, but I like them too," he said as he put on a T-shirt and a padded vest. He put on jockey pants and boots too, then a long-sleeve Western shirt. He went over to a sack and took a beer from it and sat down across from me.

"So what do you like about football?"

"I like that you can hit people," I told him.

"I always thought I'd like that part of it."

"Plus you're a part of a team. Everyone helps everyone else. And if you do, if you do act like a team, then you win, and if you don't, you lose."

"What the hell are you doing hanging out with Del?"

"I'm only fifteen," I said. "I tried applying for a real job but no one would hire me."

"Don't let him bully you and watch out. He's tight, he'll rip you off."

I nodded.

"And don't listen to half of what he says."

"Alright," I said.

"Does he still lecture on and on about the *Daily Racing Form*?"

"He tests me on it sometimes."

"I've never met a guy who hates the Beyer number as much as he does," Harry said. "You can learn from Del, but watch out, alright?"

"Can I ask you a question?"

"Sure," he said.

"I heard somebody at the track say Del runs his horses into the ground. Will he do that to Lean on Pete?"

"Is Pete the black one Del brought?"

I nodded.

"If Del's broke he has the tendency to run his every week or every other week, but Pete's probably alright 'cause the season hasn't even started yet and I don't think Del did the fair circuit this year. Plus he's a quarter horse so he's got that going for him, and he's probably been laid off all winter. Once it gets going, who knows. Del runs them sore, that's for sure. A lot of guys do. But listen, don't get attached to a horse. They ain't like that dog over there. If they can't run they ain't worth a shit to anyone."

We sat there for a while longer and then the dog went over to Harry and sat on his lap and tried to lick him in the face. Harry laughed and pet him for a while, then asked me to call the dog back and I did.

Del came into the barn and told me to clean out the trailer and handed me the keys. I moved the truck behind the barn, in a clearing, and cleaned it and from where I was I could see a saddled horse tied to the side of a red horse trailer and six Mexican men standing near a round pen. There were three horses in it. They were talking in Mexican so I couldn't understand anything they said.

A car pulled up and a kid got out. He didn't look much older than me and he was small and skinny and wearing jockey boots and carrying a helmet and a whip. He went over to a guy who looked like the main boss and started talking to him. Then another guy went into the round pen, took out a horse, put a bridle on him, then a racing saddle, and they led him out onto the dirt road.

It wasn't much after that I saw Del and Harry coming out leading Broken Blue. Del and one of the Mexicans began talking and Harry held on to Blue until two men came on horseback. Del gave Harry a leg up, and I saw another guy help up the Mexican kid. Del handed the lead rope to one of the men on horseback and they headed down a long dirt road away from the house.

Del and I leaned against a fence near the finish line to watch the race. The starting gate was nothing but two-by-fours, and it was old. There was no finish-line camera, and Del said that his horses had to lead by a full head to win. If they didn't, it was the same thing as a loss.

He let out a long sigh when the horses left the gate. It seemed close for a time but as they neared the finish you could see Broken Blue was trailing by half a length. Harry was whipping the horse and yelling at him but it was no use.

"He's always been a fucking pig," Del said and spit on the ground.

He looked over at me, and you could tell he was upset.

"What are you doing?"

"Watching the race," I told him.

"I told you not to leave Lean on Pete alone."

"You didn't tell me that."

"You don't know how to listen," he said, looking at me.

"I know you didn't tell me that."

"Just get back there. Who knows what these motherfuckers will do."

I turned around and went back to the barn and stood by Pete.

He looked at me and moved closer against the gate. I just stood there scratching him and talking to him. His dark eyes stared off and every once in a while he'd yawn or shake his head up and down. I told him that he was the fastest horse there today and the fastest horse in the whole state. I told him to be careful and not to get hurt, and that he should win 'cause then everyone would be nice to him and Del wouldn't be such an asshole on the ride back. Then Harry came in trailed by Del and Broken Blue. Blue was put in an empty stall and the saddle and bridle were taken off.

Del looked at me. "Hose him down, but that's it. Stay close. When this race is over we're getting the hell out of here, okay?"

"Okay," I said.

They pulled Lean on Pete out of his stall, put the bridle on, and saddled him. Del put a handful of tablets underneath Pete's tongue, then tied it down. He cinched up the saddle one more time.

"You're a crazy fucker," Harry said quietly to Del.

"We'll be alright if you're not too drunk."

"I ain't drunk," Harry said.

Del shook his head and they led Pete to where the two horsemen were. Del gave the lead rope to one of them and helped Harry up. The same Mexican kid hopped on another horse and they were both led down the dirt road track. Del walked over to the men. He spoke to a man in a gray cowboy hat, then took his wallet out and handed a wad of money to an old man who was standing next to him. The man in the gray cowboy hat did the same and the old man counted the money.

I walked down the fence line near the midway point of the straight track when I saw them break out of the gate. It was neck and neck for the first bit, then suddenly Lean on Pete took off. He exploded with speed and by the time he passed me he was nearly a full length ahead and when the race finished I knew he had won by even more than that. I stood there for a bit, then went back to the barn.

Ten minutes later Harry came in.

"It's time for us to get going," he said. He was out of breath and looked worried.

"Give me the truck keys, then get Blue and meet me at the trailer." I gave him the keys to the truck and he grabbed his gear and left.

I brought the horse out and took him to the truck. Lean on Pete was tied to the side of the trailer and was wound up and more nervous than I'd ever seen him. He pulled at the lead rope and it made the trailer rattle. He couldn't stand still. Del was down the way arguing with one of the Mexicans. They were pointing to the dirt track where two men wearing cowboy hats were walking around looking at the ground.

Harry untied Pete and pulled hard on his lead rope, trying to get his attention. Then he walked Pete back and forth in the driveway and when Pete had settled down enough he came to me and handed me the lead rope.

"Don't lose him, alright?" I took the rope and held it as tight as I could while Harry opened the trailer door, but when the door slammed against the side of the trailer Pete got uneasy again and began circling me in panic. I didn't know what to do, and Harry had to come and help. He took the rope from me and settled Pete down and we loaded Pete and did the same with Blue, then shut the door behind them and got in the truck and waited for Del.

"What's going on?" I asked him.

Harry sat back on the truck's bench seat and rubbed his face with his hands and let out a long sigh.

"They think we've cheated."

"How could you cheat?"

"There's a lot of ways to cheat."

"Did you?"

Harry let out another sigh.

"What are those two guys looking for out there?"

"A buzzer," Harry said and looked out the window.

The trailer began to rock and shake.

"Don't worry. It's probably just Pete. He's scared shitless right now. It ain't right to load him just after a race like that but Del's got a point. We probably need to get the fuck out of here."

I looked outside the cab to see Del still talking to the man in the gray cowboy hat. They both were staring off into the distance at the men doing the search. Del kicked at the ground with his boot. I counted the other men. There were seven.

"Are they gonna find it?"

"The buzzer?"

"Yeah."

"Not where they're looking," Harry said and laughed. He reached down to the floor and took a beer from the sack and opened it. He pulled his baseball cap down low and acted like he was asleep and would only move when he took a drink of beer. I kept looking at Del but he kept talking to the guy and, even at that distance, you could tell they weren't getting along. The trailer would fall silent, then all of the sudden there would be loud bangs.

It must have been a half-hour before Del got in the truck and started it and we drove out of there. He was sweating pretty heavy and he had both hands on the wheel. The cast on his arm looked worse. It was thick with dirt and it was cracking around his hand. He used that arm to shift the truck and after he'd got us up to fifty and on the main road he hit the steering wheel with his other hand.

"Goddamn," he said. "That Rodriguez is one untrusting son of a bitch."

"I wonder why," Harry said.

Del laughed and turned on the radio. He set it to a country station and started humming along. Harry took the last beer from the sack and we drove for nearly an hour until we were on the outskirts of Walla Walla. Del took an exit and drove us to a ranch and parked. He got out of the truck and talked to a man there, then they both walked to the back of the trailer and unloaded the horses. After that Del backed the trailer off to the side of the barn and we unhooked it and left.

We got a room in Walla Walla at the A & H Motel. Harry

walked down the street and came back with a twelve pack of beer and pint of whiskey. He set it on the table between the two beds, then took off his boots and his racing pants and put on his regular clothes. He sat on the bed closest to the door and started drinking. Del was lying on the other bed watching TV. I stood there for a while, then saw there was a pretty decent place for me to lie down in the corner by the window. I put my sleeping bag out and sat down on it.

Del took a long drink off the whiskey and opened a beer.

"That was a close one," he said.

"It seemed alright until they started looking for it."

"I thought it was pretty chickenshit that they'd accuse me."

"I haven't seen a horse take off like that in a long time," Harry said. "They had to know."

Del nodded, then sat up and took a can of chew from the bedside stand and took a dip from it.

"Just watching you do that makes me want to puke."

"If you weren't such a drunk we wouldn't have to get a room," Del said.

"You're just complaining 'cause you're so goddamn cheap the thought of spending money on a room makes you break out in a rash."

Del spit into a wastebasket between the beds.

"I can't help it if I can't see good at night. At least I still have a license. And I don't mind getting a room. I paid for it. I didn't hear you speak up when that fat old Indian wanted fifty bucks."

"I risked my life for you today."

"I paid you for it," Del said and sat back. "And look, if

you'd lay off the beer you wouldn't have to be here in the first place. If you weren't so fucked up you'd get on at a track or two."

"How many times are you gonna bring that up?"

"As many as it takes."

"You're the guy that needs to lose fifty pounds."

"I ain't a jockey, am I? The last time I checked, you were."

They went back and forth and back and forth like that, then all of a sudden Harry threw a can of beer against the wall, put on his boots, and left.

I just sat there. I didn't say anything and Del didn't say anything either. He just watched TV and channel jumped for the next hour before he settled on news.

I got up and put my coat on.

"Del, I'm gonna go and get something to eat."

His eyes were half shut. He sat up and rubbed his face.

"I gave him rides when he was at 124 pounds. I gave him rides when everyone else gave up on him."

I nodded.

"I guess you want your pay?"

I nodded.

"How much did I tell you?" he said and sat up and took his wallet out.

"You never did," I said.

"Here's sixty," he said and handed me the bills. "Just leave the door unlocked."

I put the money in my pants pocket and left. I went to a grocery store and got a roll of quarters and found a payphone and called the hospital and asked for my dad. They put me on hold for a long time and then they told me he was asleep so I hung up. After that I called Scottish Sam's Auto Parts in Rock Springs. A girl answered but she said she'd never heard of Margy Thompson and that she'd worked there for three years. I asked her if anyone else would know, but she said the only one who'd worked there longer than her was the owner and he'd just gotten out of the hospital and wasn't coming back to work for a while.

I walked down a main street and saw an Elmer's Restaurant and went in and sat at a table and my waitress was old and nice and filled my soda three times. She and I started talking and she said I looked like her brother when he was a kid. She said it made her head hurt how close we looked to each other. I ordered the ham and scalloped potato dinner with soup, and afterwards she gave me a free piece of pie.

I called the hospital again after dinner but they said he was still sleeping. I looked at stores windows, then went to a park and watched a group of kids skateboarding. They each took turns going off this jump, and then they all left together and were talking and laughing. As I watched them I knew I'd probably never be like that. I laid back on the grass and looked up at the sky for a while, then finally went back to the room.

When I opened the door I could see Del sitting on the bed laughing and drinking a beer. There was an overweight woman in there and she was wearing a blouse and a denim skirt and was holding the skirt up with her hand. She wasn't wearing any underwear and you could see her naked down there. She had dyed blonde hair that was growing black on the top and she wore bright red lipstick. She had two Band-Aids on her leg and was wearing sandals. One of the straps was held together with black tape.

I went inside and shut the door behind me.

Del put his face up to her ass and let out a long breath.

"Even her ass smells good."

Harry was sitting on the other bed. He wasn't laughing or smiling. He just had this blank sort of expression on his face, and had his hands around one of the woman's breasts. Her shirt was open and they were just hanging out. The TV was on and the woman held a beer in her hand and was humming along to a commercial.

I didn't want to be there but I wasn't sure where else I'd go. Harry and Del hardly noticed I came in and I don't think the woman saw at all. I sat down in a chair near the bathroom sink and tried to watch TV.

"You wouldn't think Walla Walla would have this sorta ass," Del said. He set down his can of beer and pulled her ass apart. He took his finger and put it in there.

"What in the Christ are you doing back there?" the woman said.

"I'm exploring," Del said and laughed.

"It's gonna cost you."

"I got the money," Del said, then he spit and you could see that he put most of it in the wastebasket but that some went on the side of the lady's ass. Harry was on the other side of the woman and he started kissing her breasts.

I got up and grabbed my sleeping bag, took my backpack, and left the room. I stood there in the parking lot for a long time, then I got into the bed of the truck. I moved things around so I had enough room to lay my sleeping bag down. I took off my shoes but left the rest of my clothes on and got in.

The night was clear and I could see stars. The motel was quiet. Once in a while you could hear laughing coming from the room, but it was faint and hardly noticeable. I just lay there and I was warm, I wasn't really scared at all. I just thought about my dad and then I thought about my aunt. I thought about the times we'd go to the movies or the time when her car broke down and we left it on the side of the road and walked to a restaurant. I remember her not even worrying about it, her just sitting there smoking cigarettes and talking and laughing and eating.

It was just past dawn when I heard a tractor trailer rig start. It rumbled and smoked and then it calmed and just sat there and idled. When I looked up into the sky there weren't any clouds and it wasn't cold. I lay there until the truck left, then I went into my backpack and took out my running clothes and changed into them.

I got up and put on my shoes and grabbed my roll of quarters and jumped out of the truck and started running. I was almost out of the parking lot when I got worried that they'd wake up and leave me so I turned around and went back to the truck. I opened the hood, found the distributor, unhooked it and took out the rotor. I set the rotor under my sleeping bag and started running again.

I had learned that from a kid in Spokane. He tried out for football but he was small and never got to play. I used to spend weekends at his house eating and watching TV. We were both trying to gain weight.

His brother had a 1983 Cadillac. My friend would take out the rotor to make him late for work. He said his brother would wake up late and grumpy and then he'd get in the car and try to start it. He'd sit there and turn the key over and over but the engine would never take. He'd start beating on the steering wheel and start swearing, then he'd get out and take off down the street trying to get a bus.

The kid hated his brother and wanted the car. Once his brother was gone he'd put the rotor back so when his brother tried it after work it would start right up. His brother thought the car was cursed and quit driving it and finally sold it to his little brother for two hundred dollars.

I ran to a payphone and called the hospital, but they said he was sleeping. I hung up and started running again. I ran downtown and through the university campus. I ran up and down a big courtyard and around all these college buildings, then I went back to the motel. The truck was still there. I grabbed my backpack and went into the room. Del was asleep on one bed with no covers over him. He was completely naked. Harry was on the other, conked out with a sheet over his head. The woman was gone. There were beer cans on the carpet and the dresser and the bedside table. The TV was still on. There was an ashtray full of cigarette butts and there were two empty whiskey pints sitting next to the telephone. The bedside clock said 7 a.m.

I went into the bathroom and took a shower and got dressed. They were still both conked out when I went back into the room so I walked downtown and found a restaurant and ate breakfast. When I got back they still hadn't moved and Del was snoring. I put the rotor back in the distributor, then lay down in the bed of the truck on my sleeping bag and fell asleep. The next thing I heard was the truck starting. I don't know how much time had passed. I looked inside the cab, they both were there, and I lay back down as Del got us out on the road.

We stopped at the ranch where we'd left the horses. Harry got out of the truck and headed over to them. I jumped down and followed behind him. He took our two halters that were resting on the fence and opened the gate.

Harry got Broken Blue and told me to get Pete and so I walked down a bit further and found him. He moved his head right next to me when he saw who I was. I pet his face and neck, then put the halter on him and headed back up. When we got there Del was leaning back in his seat and his eyes were closed. Harry loaded up Broken Blue. He took Pete and got ready to load him, but Pete was walking slow with short steps and Harry noticed. He leaned down and put his hands around Pete's front legs and moved them slowly up and down.

"You should probably go get Del."

I went to the truck and knocked on the driver's side window and Del slowly sat up.

"What?" he said and rolled down the window.

"Harry said to come back."

Del shook his head and opened the door. He got out and stood there for a moment. He looked sick. He coughed and coughed, then he walked back to the trailer.

"What is it?"

"Is he the guy you think is navicular?"

"It ain't that bad yet."

"He looked like he was walking on nails when the kid was coming up the road with him."

Del just stood there staring at the horse, then he bent down and ran his hands all down Pete's leg. "I don't know," he said, and you could see his mood getting worse as the seconds passed.

Then he stood up again. "If I had a gun I'd shoot him right here."

"If I had a gun I'd shoot myself," Harry said, and he looked like he might puke.

Del took off his glasses and rubbed his face and put his glasses back on.

"Load him and let's get something to eat."

"I thought you said you weren't hungry."

"Well, I'm hungry now," Del said and walked back to the truck.

11

No one said anything on the ride back. Del didn't even play the radio. He just chewed and every time he put in a new dip Harry would take out a can of beer from the sack by his feet and open it. It was late in the afternoon when we finally got back to Portland. We left Harry at a mini-mart near his trailer. He went inside the store and came out with a twelve pack of beer and a can of Coke for Del, then he said good-bye and walked across the street. Del just sat there lifeless, his face pale and his eyes raw and bloodshot.

He opened the Coke, then started the truck and drove us to the track and we unloaded the horses.

"Look," he said, "things are gonna be changing soon. The race meet here starts up next week and I'll have horses running every week. We're gonna have a lot of work to do. We can't fuck around."

"Okay," I said.

"Clean the stalls before three. The night feed's at four, alright?"

"Alright," I said.

Then he got back in his truck, moved the trailer to the lot, unhooked it, and left.

After I cleaned the stalls I stood there with Pete. I looked at his legs but I couldn't see anything. He wasn't swollen and he wasn't lame. He didn't seem upset either. I didn't know Del well enough to know if he'd really shoot Pete, but

I couldn't stop thinking about it.

When I was done I walked to the hospital, but when I got to my dad's room he wasn't there. Only one bed was occupied and there was an old man in it. Next to him in a chair sat an old lady. I asked her if she knew where my dad was but she said she didn't know. I looked in all the rooms on the floor but he wasn't in any of them.

I found a nurse behind a desk and I asked her. She wore glasses and had long brown hair. She wore rings on her fingers. I remember all that about her, I can still see her. She stood there and told me he'd died. She'd met him. She was one of his nurses and said that when they sewed up his bowel there was a leak. When they X-rayed it they didn't see it, but it was there, and he became septic and his organs shut down. She went on about it, but I didn't really understand. She said he was sleeping when his heart stopped.

Tears fell down my face and I felt like I was going to hyperventilate, but I didn't make a sound. I just stood there. My eyes stared at the nurse. She tried to hug me but I don't like to be hugged. I backed away. Tears began falling down her face and I turned around and left. She called out to me but I didn't stop. I got out of the building and walked around but I didn't know where I was going. Everything blurred. My thoughts swirled and then I started crying. I was in deep trouble, I knew that. My dad was lying somewhere dead, and I was all alone.

It was dusk when I walked back to the track and locked myself in Del's tack room. I sat there and got more scared. I had no idea what I was going to do and no plan I had made sense so I just lay down on my sleeping bag and waited out the night.

When I got up again it was 5 a.m and I hadn't slept at all. I put my sleeping bag away and went out and looked in on Pete. His legs still seemed alright and I pet him and talked to him and told him what had happened. I started crying again and I felt worse about things than I had the day before.

Del didn't come in until seven o'clock and hardly said a word all day. He worked three of his horses on the track and the others he put on the hotwalker for an hour, then sent them back to the stalls. Towards the end of the day he went to his truck and came back with a black bag. He told me to halter Pete and I did. We took him to a stall that had no bedding on the ground, it was just flat concrete. I tied Pete to a post and Del pulled Pete's shoes and told me to fill a bucket with water and grab a couple towels out of the tack room.

When I came back he soaked the towels in the bucket, then took one out and wrapped it around Pete's front right leg. He had me hold his foot like we were going to pick it and grabbed a small paint brush and a glass jar of liquid. He opened the jar and put the brush in it and brushed the liquid on the bottom of Pete's hoof.

"What is that?"

"Jet fuel," he said. He let it sit for a bit and then he took a lighter from his shirt pocket and lit the bottom of the hoof. It flashed in flames for a second, then died out.

Del told me to put his foot down. I did and looked at Pete but he just stood there like it wasn't bothering him.

"What's it for?" I asked him.

"To kill the nerves in his feet. They're causing him a lot of pain and he won't run worth a shit if I don't try something."

"Does it hurt him?"

"Does it look like it hurts him?"

"No," I said.

"We gotta do his three other feet, so hurry up."

I nodded and we did the same for his three other feet and then Del had me put him back in his stall and left.

I finished my work, then walked back to the house, and everything was the same when I got there. I went into my room and put some clothes in my duffel, then took the picture of my aunt and me and my two trophies and packed them as well. I left everything else.

My dad's room had a double bed and a dresser with a lamp sitting on it. He had a black and white TV sitting on a chair and in the closet he had hangers holding his clothes. I took a few things. I found his leather belt that had his name on it, Ray, in silver letters. I took off my belt and put on his. There wasn't a notch small enough for me so I went to his toolbox and found a hammer and a nail and made one so the belt would work.

I went through his drawers and found ten dollars and a handful of change. There were two snapshots underneath his clothes in the dresser. Both had me in them. One was when I was just a kid and I was sitting in a shopping cart. The other was of him and me at a pizza parlor. We were both smiling and he had his arm around me. I took that one and left the other.

In the kitchen I took two knives and forks and spoons and wrapped them in a paper towel and put them in the duffel. Then I turned on the TV and heated a can of soup and ate. After that I took a shower. When I was done I grabbed the towel and the soap and shampoo and put that stuff in the duffel as well and left.

It wasn't late at all, not even five o'clock, when I walked back to the track. I looked in the parking lot for Del's truck but I couldn't find it so I went through the backside gates and walked down the shedrow. Inside the tack room I looked around for a place to hide both my clothes bag and my sleeping bag but there wasn't enough room. I could hide the sleeping bag or the clothes but not both. I didn't know what to do and finally just stuck my duffel on top of a filing cabinet and wrote a sign on it. "Charley's Football Gear."

As it neared evening I left the backside and went to a Chinese restaurant and ate dinner. After that I just went back to the tack room. I tried to go to sleep but I couldn't and there was nothing to do in there. I turned the light back on and went through Del's things. There were a few boxes and a file cabinet, but besides papers there was nothing but horse gear in there. I turned the light off again and lay down but I was restless. My mind got darker and darker thinking about my dad and the uncertainty of things and the only thing I could think of to do was to go back to the house and get the TV. So I got up and turned on the lights and put on my shoes. I'd explain to Del that he might like a TV in the tack room. That if he didn't mind, I'd hang out there and watch TV on breaks. It seemed like an alright idea and so I headed back to the house.

It was dark when I got there. I'd left all the lights off. The door was still locked and I found my key and opened it and turned on the lights in the living room. I called out but no one answered. I looked through the place and everything seemed okay so I went to the fridge and made myself a triple-decker peanut butter and jelly sandwich and wrapped it in a paper towel and put it in my coat pocket. The TV was in my bedroom. I unplugged it, picked it up, and left.

It was a 16-inch TV and it was hard to walk with. I made it down the street, but it was slow going. I passed the mini-mart and started down the main road. I was almost a half a mile on it when a police car pulled up behind me. I didn't notice it and then all of a sudden there were flashing lights and I stopped and turned around.

The officer got out of his car. There was a gun hanging from his belt. He was big and had a moustache and he wore his police hat back on his head almost like a cowboy hat.

"Where are you going with the TV?"

"To my house," I told him.

"Where's your house?"

"What?" I said.

"You heard me. Where's your house?"

"It's the pink one near the horse track," I said. It was the only house I could think of. It sat alone by itself near a Motel 6 and the track parking lot.

"Whose TV is that?"

"It's mine. My dad bought it for me."

"Why are you carrying it down the street?"

"What?"

"That's the second time you heard what I said and didn't answer. Why are you carrying it down the street?"

"I just got it fixed."

"You had it fixed on a Saturday night?" he said.

"My friend fixed it."

"What's your name?"

"My name?"

"What's your name?"

"Ray."

"What's your last name?"

"Thompson," I said.

"Do you have an ID?"

My hands started shaking.

He asked me again and I dropped the TV and started running. He yelled at me to stop, but I didn't. I ran underneath the overpass and came out the other side. I looked back and I could see he'd gotten in his police car and was going to follow me. I started running again but there was nowhere to go. On one side there were warehouses and on the other was the barbed-wire fence that lined the track. I kept running and then I jumped up on the chain link and climbed over the barbed wire. One of the barbs went into my hand but I barely felt it. I got to the top and another one caught on my coat and ripped it and another cut into my leg. I fell to the other side. The cop stopped and his spotlight looked around until it found me. I got up again and started running. By then I was on the track itself and I didn't look back until I made it to the backside and by then I couldn't see him at all. I ran down the shedrows until I came to Del's tack room. I unlocked it and

95

went inside and shut off the light.

I sat down on the floor and waited. With every sound my nerves got worse and I was sure the policeman would find me. I could feel blood leaking out of my hand and I could feel the cut on my leg and when I felt around it, it was wet. I sat in darkness for a long time. It seemed like hours even though I know it wasn't. Then my leg started to hurt so much that I turned on the light.

My hand was covered in blood. I went to my duffel and found a sock and wrapped it around my palm. My pant leg was torn and it was dark with blood. I pulled it up and saw that my calf had a long cut in it. Blood was coming out pretty fast. I took a T-shirt and wrapped it around my leg and tried to stop the bleeding.

I didn't know what to do. If I went to the hospital they'd want to know where my folks were. I had no insurance. I only had thirty dollars. I put pressure on my leg and held the sock tight around my hand. I looked around the room. There wasn't a first-aid kit, but I found a cardboard box full of leg wraps. I took one and looked through Del's desk until I saw a pair of scissors. I grabbed another T-shirt from my things and cut it in a continuous strip the best I could. I took the other shirt off my leg. The cut was still pushing out blood and the shirt was soaked with it. I rolled the cut-up shirt around my calf, then put the leg wrap over that. There was a roll of duct tape hanging from a hook on the wall and I put strips on it to hold it in place. Then I took the sock off my hand. It was still bleeding so I took another clean sock and re-wrapped it, then duct taped it as tight as I could. My pants were all covered in blood so I took them off and put on my other pair.

I set out my sleeping bag and lay down, but my hand wouldn't stop leaking blood and I got nervous about it and decided I'd have to get real bandages. There was a Walgreens pharmacy a half-mile away so I put on a red windbreaker that was hanging off Del's chair and left.

I walked on the side of the road and kept a look out for the cop. Every once in a while I stopped and pulled up my pant leg to see if there was any blood leaking out, but there never was.

At Walgreens I bought a box of gauze, a package of white bandages, a bag of cotton balls, a bottle of hydrogen peroxide, two ace bandages, a roll of white tape, a bottle of aspirin, and a tube of Neosporin. When I went up to the counter I kept my hurt hand in the windbreaker pocket, and I got my money out with my good hand and paid for it. Afterwards I walked out of the store into the parking lot and looked again for the police but they weren't there.

It was late when I got back to the tack room. My leg hurt bad, but when I took off my jeans there was only a little blood leaking through the bandage. The cut itself was red and filled with blood but it wasn't gushing out like it had before. I poured hydrogen peroxide on it, and it spit up and foamed but it didn't hurt. After that I covered the cut with Neosporin, wrapped it with the new bandages I'd bought, and covered it with the ace. I did the same with my hand, then I tried to clean up the place the best I could. There was blood soaked into the plywood floor, and I couldn't think of anything to do about it except cover it in dirt and straw. I took four aspirin, got in bed, and shut the light off.

As I lay there I kept imagining the cop walking down the shedrow looking for me. I tried not to move at all or make any sound and time passed. I tried to sleep but every time I got tired I began thinking about the cop and then I started thinking about the Samoan and my dad in the hospital and I hardly slept at all.

When I got up at six-thirty my hand hurt right off but my leg felt alright until I started moving around; then it hurt pretty bad. I put on my pants and hid the sleeping bag and put the duffel away and went out and cleaned the stalls.

Del didn't show up until eight and he was in a foul mood and yelled at me a couple times, then he yelled at the girl, Maxine, who fed the horses and she started crying.

Del didn't work Pete at all so he was just stuck in his stall. He wasn't favoring any of his legs, and he didn't look like he was hurting, he just looked bored. When I was done working I pet him and talked to him and told him about my cuts and the cop and the broken TV. Then Del found me and I helped him wash down a horse named Simmer Slew.

"What happened to your hand?" he said when he saw the bandage.

"I was helping my neighbor tear down a fence and I wasn't wearing gloves."

"Is it gonna get in the way of you working?"

"No," I told him.

"You feel like making some extra money?"

"Sure."

"You know how to stack wood?"

"I've never done it," I said.

"It's not hard," he said.

"And you'll pay me?"

"I'll give you ten bucks."

I only had seven dollars and change left so I agreed. I followed him to his truck and we drove a couple miles to a neighborhood in Northeast Portland, where we stopped in front of his house. In the driveway was a huge load of split firewood.

He unlocked the door and I followed him. I could smell something bad in there right off but I couldn't tell what from. The entry was full of boxes and you could hardly walk by. There were stacks of *Daily Racing Form*s and newspapers and magazines and there were a couple bales of hay stacked against a wall. He led me to the living room where on a couch was an old dog. It wagged its tail but didn't get up. The smell was coming from him.

The wood stove was in that room and Del wanted me to stack the wood behind it, along the wall. He brought in a chair and said I could use it to stand on so I could get the wood all the way to the ceiling. Then he went into another room, turned on a TV, and shut the door.

I stood there for a while and just looked around. There was nothing on the walls, no pictures or photos, and nothing really in the room except the couch with the dog on it and the stacks of boxes. On the floor was a worn-out tan carpet that was covered in dirt and pieces of bark and scraps of wood. I made sure the bandage on my hand was alright, then I walked back out to the front and started bringing in the wood, but it took forever. For a start I could only really use one hand, and there was so much stuff in the hallway I couldn't bring very much at one time anyway. The old dog just lay there and Del stayed in his room with the TV going.

I stopped an hour later to take a leak and check my leg. The bathroom was right off the kitchen and it wasn't much to see either. The toilet hadn't been cleaned and the tub was full of mold. The shower curtain was black with it and there were only a few hooks still holding it up. Scattered everywhere were empty toilet-paper rolls and old newspapers and racing forms. I pulled up my pant leg and the bandage was holding alright and I couldn't see any blood.

His kitchen wasn't like a real kitchen. There was a fridge but I don't think the sink worked as there was a box in it. The kitchen table was covered with stacks of racing forms and the counter didn't have any room left on it either. The floor was white and green linoleum but it was coming up in areas and worn down in others. The only normal thing on it was a big dish of dog food and a bucket of water.

I went outside and got a drink from a hose, took three aspirin, and kept stacking. It took me two hours to get the rest of the wood in. I put three full rows behind the wood stove. Then Del came out and showed me a large walk-in closet that was empty except for carpet on the floor and a few scraps of wood and told me to stack the rest in there. So I filled it to the ceiling all the way to the door.

By the end my hand was bleeding again. I could see it beginning to soak through the bandage, but it didn't hurt that bad. When I finished I knocked on Del's door, but he didn't answer so I yelled out his name. When he came out I could tell he'd been sleeping. He didn't say anything, he just looked in the closet and then outside to see if I'd left any wood out there and when he saw I hadn't, he paid me and told me I could go.

As I walked down the street I realized that even with the ten he'd given me I only had seventeen dollars to my name. I'd have to quit eating out so much. I stayed on the sidewalk for a mile or so until I came to a Safeway. I went inside and bought three cans of chili, three cans of soup, a loaf of bread, and a can opener.

12

By the time I got back to the track it was dark. I snuck underneath the fence and walked down the shedrow and opened Del's tack room and locked myself inside. I laid out my sleeping bag and took off my pants and looked at my leg. The bandage was still clean, and when I took it off I could see that a lot of the cut was healing over, that only the lower part was still bleeding. I washed it with hydrogen peroxide and re-bandaged it. My hand looked worse off and it was still bleeding. I poured the hydrogen peroxide over it, then coated it with Neosporin and put a new bandage on it as well.

I opened a can of chili and ate it cold with three pieces of bread. Then I tried to sleep but I just lay there restless and then I turned on the light and looked through Del's things again but I didn't find anything interesting that time either.

I got dressed and went outside and visited Pete. I told him about Del's house and his sick dog.

"You should have seen the poor old dog," I told Pete. "He was going bald in places and he stunk so bad it almost made me puke. Maybe his teeth are rotten, I don't know. And Del's place is the worst house I've ever been in. He's never cleaned the toilet and he's a pack rat and he doesn't even have any pictures on the walls. I'd at least put up the win pictures, wouldn't you? If it was our place, Pete, I'd paint the whole house inside and out and I'd pull out the carpet and give the dog a bath and buy a new shower curtain."

Pete just stood there. There was no one around, and the old man who guarded the track couldn't see me from where he was, so I put a halter on Pete and led him out and walked him along the gravel road towards the edge of the backside where there's a patch of grass. We stood out there and the night was clear and there were stars. He seemed to walk without any problem and I let him graze for a long time. When I took him back I still wasn't tired so I walked up and down the shedrows. I did that until I passed an open tack room and saw a person inside watching TV.

I looked in and the person saw me.

"Who are you?" It was a woman. She was older, probably in her thirties. She had short brown hair and a man's haircut. Her clothes were men's clothes, too, but you could tell by her face and from her voice she was a woman.

"Charley," I told her.

"I'm Bonnie Sparks," she said and stood up. "Who do you work for?"

"Del Montgomery."

"Del?"

"Yeah."

"You related to him?"

"No."

"How do you like him?"

"He's alright, I guess."

"You friends with him?"

"No," I said.

"I shouldn't tell you, but he's a pervert."

"A pervert?" I said.

She nodded. "You've been staying in his tack room, haven't you?"

"No," I said.

"I'm staying in this one right now," she said.

"You're spending the night here?"

She nodded.

"Is it against the law?"

"Sort of, but people do it. I'm not living here. I'm just spending the night."

I nodded.

"Are you staying in Del's?"

"Not really," I said.

"It's alright if you are."

"You won't tell Del?"

"No," she said, and then she asked me if I wanted to watch TV with her.

I told her I did and I walked in and she unfolded a chair for me. There was a black and white TV sitting on a desk and there was a movie playing. It was an old one set in a prison in Africa and two guys were trying to escape but they got caught and tortured.

When a commercial came on she told me to shut the door so I got up and shut it.

"Do you smoke weed?"

"No," I told her.

She lit a joint and smoked from it. She held the smoke in for a long time, then looked at me and blew the smoke in my face.

"They say Del likes to watch women go to the toilet."

"Really?"

She nodded. "What happened to your hand?"

"I cut it mowing my dad's lawn," I told her.

"How?"

"How?"

"You're full of shit," she said, and smiled.

"I'm not lying."

"You're not much of a liar," she said. She went into another drawer and took out a package of cookies and set them next to the TV.

"You can have some if you want."

I took two of the cookies and ate them.

"Let me see the cut," she said.

"It's not bad."

"I've seen enough cuts to know." She looked at me again so I took the tape off, then the bandage, and she looked at it.

"You should go to a doctor."

"I can't," I said.

"You can't?"

"No," I said.

"Why can't you?"

"I just can't," I said.

"Let me clean it out, at least," she said. "Come here to the sink."

Her tack room had a sink with hot and cold water. She washed out the cut and put iodine on it and it really hurt. After that she wrapped it in a bandage and taped it. When she was done I told her about my leg. I pulled up my pant leg and showed her the bandage and she told me to take off my pants and so I did. She had me stand on a chair and put my hurt leg in the sink while she washed it out. It hurt pretty bad but I didn't say anything. She put iodine on it and I let out a cry and she laughed, then re-bandaged and taped it. She told me it looked worse than my hand. She thought it looked pretty bad.

Afterwards we sat back down and she kept smoking weed and we ate the whole package of cookies and watched the movie. In the end one of the convicts escapes by swimming away on a bag of coconuts and the other gives up and lives on an island and grows his own food. When it was over we left and walked about a mile to a Burger King.

We ate inside and under the bright fluorescent lights you could see her eyes were bloodshot and you could see that she looked old. Her face was weather-beaten, wrinkled and leathery, and her hands and fingers were rough and they looked twice as old as the rest of her did. I knew I shouldn't have spent the money, but I got two cheeseburgers and an order of fries.

On the way back she told me she used to be a jockey. In high school she'd worked out horses at a track in Fresno. Then after she graduated she moved to Portland and worked out horses at Portland Meadows for a couple trainers in hopes that they'd put her in a race or two, but they hardly ever gave her rides. It was hard for a woman, she said. They all told her if she would keep galloping their horses she'd get her chance but when they assigned mounts each week her name was never called. She didn't have an agent so she just had to wait until the worst of the horses came up. No real jockey would touch any of them, but she had to prove herself so she'd take anything. She'd broken her foot, her jaw, and her wrist on a couple of those horses. She ended up being a jockey on the Oregon fair circuit and rode a lot out there. She went to places all over the state.

"I once raced in Union, which is way out in eastern Oregon, and I was in the gate and the horse reared up and flipped over backwards. I couldn't get out and he landed on me. He got stuck, he was in a real panic. He was just a baby, a two-year-old. I didn't know the trainer. I wouldn't have ridden him if I knew what I know now but I was just an apprentice. I needed all the rides I could get. I broke my pelvis and punctured a lung. I healed up alright but it took a long time and the guy I was living with at the time wanted me to quit so I got a job as a cook. I worked at Red Lobster for almost seven years and then I started coming back. I couldn't help it. I worked out horses for a while, then I started riding for a guy who makes Del seem like a good guy. He began putting me on horses and I did alright. Then there was another horse who spooked and threw me into the rail and I broke my back. The horse broke both its forelegs, which is something I've only seen a couple times. After that I quit trying to be a jock."

She kept talking about it and about all these horses that had tried to kill her or had broken down while she was working them. Then her voice changed and got sad and quiet and she told me how she got in a car wreck. How she was driving and her friend was sitting next to her and she lost control and the car flipped over and ended up in a bunch of blackberry bushes. When she woke her friend was gone. She had her seat belt on and got out alright but she couldn't find her friend. She had to go to the road and flag someone down and then the police and fire trucks came but none of them could find her, and then finally they started cutting back the blackberries and found her dead.

We walked past the backside until we came to the trailer park where her trailer sat. We stood there in the darkness and she looked at it but there wasn't anyone in there and there wasn't a car parked in front of it. I'm not sure why she wasn't living there, she didn't say anything about it. She just pointed to it and told me it was half hers, but most likely she wouldn't see a dime out of it. After that we walked to the track and said goodbye and she went back to her tack room and I went back to Del's.

13

That night I lay awake for hours. It was almost four in the morning when I finally fell asleep. I woke to Del standing over me, kicking me. I looked at my alarm clock and the radio on it was playing, it was just after six.

"What are you doing?" he said.

I tried to wake up but it was hard. I got out of my sleeping bag but I was hazy and I couldn't find my pants.

"What happened to your leg?" he said.

"Nothing," I told him. I found my pants and put them on.

"Are you living here now?"

"No."

"Then what is it?"

"My dad's still in the hospital and I heard some noises at the house last night. I thought someone was breaking in and I got scared and came down here."

"With a bag of clothes."

"I didn't want to have to go back there. Our next-door neighbor, she got broken into last week."

"When's your dad getting out of the hospital?"

"Pretty soon, I think."

"Look, I don't want you living here, and from now on you got to be ready at five thirty. The meet is starting this weekend. It's Portland Meadows until Christmas. Get your shit together. I'll be at the café."

He turned around and left and I rolled my sleeping bag and set it and the rest of my things in the corner.

After that day I found a different place to put my clothes and sleeping bag. There was a crawl space over an empty stall and I left my things there. Also I began to spend most of my time away from the track when I wasn't working in case Del came around. Sometimes I'd sit by the river and try to sleep and other times I'd go to the library to look at magazines, or walk downtown and go in and out of shops all day. I never bought anything except once at a thrift store. I got a shirt, a pair of pants, a hotplate, and a pan. I showered in the shower room at the track and Bonnie let me wash my clothes in the washer and dryer in her tack room.

I quit eating out altogether because I got paid less after that day Del caught me sleeping in his tack room. And then, to make things worse, one morning Del told me to put his horse Forestville on the hotwalker. He told me this while he was walking around with a fat old man he was trying to get as a client. I guess the fat man had a lot of money and wanted to buy race horses and Del was trying to convince him that he was the right guy to find and train the man's horses. They went to the café to talk and I finished cleaning, then I went to get Forestville. He was in his stall pacing around, and when I went in he tried to bite me. I bopped him on the nose and got the halter on but it took a while. Del said Forestville turned into one of the meanest horses he'd ever had. He said some horses just got meaner and meaner the longer they ran and the sorer they got. Forestville was like that.

I had a hard time controlling him when I brought him out, but I thought I'd get him to the hotwalker alright. Across the way on the next shedrow two men were on the roof. They had pulled off the metal roofing and were replacing the rotten wood underneath, and as I brought the horse out I could see them trying to get a plywood sheet up there. One of the men was on the ground and the other was on the roof, but the man on the roof wasn't strong enough to bring the sheet all the way up and he let go. The sheet fell on the ground and then the man lost his balance and dropped from the roof as well. It all made a loud crash and Forestville reared back. I held on to him the best I could but he spooked and tried to get away and I fell and let go of the rope and he sprinted off.

When I got up I saw him running down the main gravel road and I chased after him. He nearly went into a man who was a pushing a wheelbarrow, then he turned the corner and I lost sight of him.

Forestville stayed loose for more than five minutes. He ran onto the main track and a man who was galloping a horse finally caught him. I got Del out of the café but by the time we got Forestville back he had a long cut on his leg and blood ran down it, pouring onto the dirt.

Del brought him back to the stall and I followed him. Forestville was in a panic, he was lathered with sweat and breathing heavy. Del went to the tack room and came out with a syringe. He went into the stall and it took him a while but he injected Forestville with something, then came out and threw the syringe in the garbage and took his can of chew and banged it into his leg and opened it.

"That'll calm him down and then we can take a look at the cut."

He put the chew in his mouth.

"I'm really sorry, Del."

He didn't say anything at first. He just spit on the ground.

"A guy over there fell off the roof with a big piece of plywood and Forestville spooked."

Del spit again.

"I'm sorry," I told him.

Then he looked at me. "You know how much this is going to cost? I'm gonna have to call the vet. It's going to cost me more than the piece of shit is worth."

"I'm sorry."

"I'm sorry," Del said in a high whiny voice. "That old guy was going to sign up with me. Now he's probably talking to Freeman or said fuck it and is driving up to Emerald Downs as we speak."

Del started breathing heavier. You could tell he was getting more upset.

"I thought you were alright." He spit on the ground again. "I took a chance on you and you paid me back by ruining one of my best quarter horses. I'll probably have to put him down."

I began thinking about them killing Forestville and tears welled in my eyes. I'd caused the whole thing, I'd ruined Forestville's life.

Del looked over at me.

"And now you're gonna cry?"

"No," I said but I couldn't help it and I started.

"Stop crying," he said.

"I'm trying," I said.

We stood there silent for a long time watching as Forestville calmed down.

"It's alright," Del said finally. "This shit happens. Why don't you get out of here."

"Are you firing me?"

"No," he said. "I just don't feel like being around you anymore today. You're an alright kid. You just fucked up. I'll see you tomorrow."

"Okay," I said, and then I left him alone.

But at the end of that week Del only gave me twenty bucks, and when the meet started none of his horses won or were even in the money. The first race was Lean on Pete in a 350-yard claiming race. In a claiming race all the horses are for sale. They're the horses that the owners don't care about losing. Del said it was "like lining up a bunch fat guys to run a sprint race. It's only fair because they're all fat and worthless."

Del and I walked him from the backside to the track paddock. The paddock is inside the main grandstand building so people watching can see the horses before the race. They can see the horses come in, get saddled, and the jockey mount them. The only thing between the people and the horses is a chain-link fence. There are open stalls for each horse in the race, and a circle path so the horses can be paraded.

Del told me to walk Pete around and I did and we fell in line with all the other horses. Then he called me back and we put a saddle on Pete and a bell rang and the jockeys came out of a room and Del talked to an old-man jockey and helped him up on Pete and guided him out of the paddock to the pony horses. After that we went inside and Del got a beer from the bar.

Portland Meadows was a big old place. At one time it probably held twenty thousand people, but right then there were less than a thousand showing up. Del said a lot of tracks were falling apart, that no one was going anymore. Portland, Turf Paradise in Phoenix, Arapahoe Park in Denver . . . Del had worked at all those and they were all struggling. He said Portland was the worst, though. The purses were too low, and it was hard to make any money betting when all they could come up with is five-and six-horse fields. Del said Portland was like a single-A baseball team on a never-ending slump. They were pro, but not by much.

We went outside and stood by the rail and waited on Pete's race. When I looked back at the building I could see the entire grandstands were closed off and Del told me they hadn't been used in ten years.

The track was beautiful though, and I felt good that Pete was racing on a real track and not a dirt road. I hoped his feet would feel alright and that he wouldn't get hurt. I wished more than anything that he would win so Del would treat him right.

The horses went into the gate and then the race began. An announcer over a loudspeaker began calling out the leading horses and his voice got more excited as the race went on. It was an amazing thing to see, all the horses running as fast as they could, and the jockeys all in different colors, whipping the horses. The only people outside watching were three drunk men yelling for their horses and a guy who was kissing his girlfriend and an old lady sitting on a bench. Pete started out alright, he was in the lead pack and the announcer said his name twice, but by halfway through he began to fade and as he passed us he was in fifth place and he stayed there.

When the race was over Del shook his head, let out a sigh, and finished his beer. They brought the horses back to the finish line and the jockey jumped down and Del helped take the saddle off and I led Pete back to the shedrows. He seemed alright though. He wasn't limping, he wasn't jittery either, he just seemed tired.

After the races I decided to go back to the house to see if I could get my dad's toolbox. I was hoping I could sell some of the stuff in it, but when I got there his truck was gone and there was a "For Rent" sign on the lawn. The broken window had been replaced. There were no cars in the drive or lights on so I walked up and looked inside and it was empty. The sheets we had over the windows were gone. I tried my key in the lock but it didn't work. I walked around back but there were no boxes or anything of ours still there.

That night I couldn't sleep at all. I thought about my dad's things and what would happen to them. If they would be thrown away or given to a thrift store. I thought about him lying there dead in a freezer like on a TV show. I didn't know what they'd do with his body, if they'd bury him or cremate him, and the more I thought about it the worse I felt. I tried to make myself lie still and I tried to think of things to relax me but none of it worked and the second the sun came up I got dressed and started working.

When the next week's races came, Del put Lean on Pete in a maiden 350-yard claiming race and he got second. It was a great race and even Del seemed happy about it. But later on another of his horses, Little Tramp, broke its right front leg on the stretch of a six-furlong race. He was in the back of the pack and then suddenly he stumbled and the jockey fell. The other horses kept racing but Little Tramp stopped and even from where I was I could see the bottom of his leg swinging back and forth. He stumbled around on three legs and the jockey lay on the track and he wasn't moving.

I was standing next to Del when it happened and he swore more than I'd ever heard him. We ran out to where the horse was. They got the jockey up and they loaded him into an ambulance and then a tractor pulling a large green box on wheels came out and they loaded the horse into it. Del said they had to put him down right after that.

For the rest of that day Del was in a horrible mood. Every other word he said was fuck or cunt and then later on when his three-year-old Dash's Dart came in fifth Del took him back and hosed him off and said horrible things to him. He sprayed water in his face and told him he wanted to slit his throat and then finally he threw down the hose and yelled at me and I came over and finished and he walked off.

An hour later I found Del in the café. I knew it was the wrong time to talk to him but I was broke. I only had a dollar-fifty left. I asked him for my pay.

"I lost a horse today," he said. He was sitting with two

other guys I didn't know and they were playing cards and drinking beer.

"If you even have ten bucks I'll take it," I said.

"Look, you're sleeping in the tack room. I could charge you for that but I don't." He shook his head, then spit in a cup and started talking to one of the guys.

That night I put fresh bandages on my hand and leg and walked to an Albertsons grocery store. It was a pretty big place in a strip mall. I got a basket and walked up and down the aisles and put in canned spaghetti, canned soup, and canned chili. I had eight in all when I went out the door. I started running through the parking lot carrying the basket. I looked back to see if anyone was following me and when I did a car pulled out of a space and hit me. It didn't hurt that bad but all the cans went flying everywhere and rolled away on the asphalt.

I got up and started running. I left the cans on the ground and ran out of the parking lot and kept going until I was in a neighborhood and saw that nobody was following me. My leg felt alright though. I checked it for bleeding but I couldn't see any and it didn't hurt. I walked for a while longer, then went to a mini-mart and asked the cashier where another grocery store was and he told me and I walked a long time to get to it. It was a Safeway and I went in there and got a couple plastic grocery bags and put one inside the other to make it stronger, then I went to the canned food aisle and set in six cans. I didn't do anything after that. I didn't look around or stall, I just went straight for the exit. As soon as I was out of there I ran as hard as I could. I turned around a couple times but no one came after me.

That night I hid the cans in the rafters, then I lay there for a long time in the tack room but I wasn't tired at all. I got up and went out to see Pete. I stood there and pet him in the faint light and then I went into the stall and sat down and leaned back against the wall and talked to him.

I told him about a time when my aunt Margy and I went grocery shopping and how she let me get anything I wanted. We stacked the cart up to the top and then as we drove back to her apartment we passed a movie theater and she told me we should see a movie. She stopped the car in front of the theater and checked the time listing, then we raced home as fast as we could and put all the frozen and refrigerated groceries away and drove back to the theater and made the start of the movie.

I told him of another time when she and I went camping. We drove way out to a place my dad and her went to as kids. We were onto a dirt road for fifteen miles or so and then we turned on another road and parked near a creek.

"You could see a fire pit and a clearing where people had camped before us," I told him. "There was a grass meadow. If you were there you could have eaten for a month on it. It was really nice. We set up a tent and then together we got firewood. That night she cooked us dinner on a camp stove and we sat by the fire and ate. It was really good food, too. It was macaroni and cheese with broccoli and ham. And for dessert we had s'mores. If you don't know what that is I'm sorry. They're good. You toast a marshmallow on the fire, then put it on a piece of chocolate and then you put that on a graham cracker. You make a sandwich out of it. The graham crackers are like the bread. Anyway, we ate, then we just sat there looking at the fire. There was no one around for miles. Just the trees and the sky and the mountains. But then we both started hearing things. Sounds of things moving and rustling around. We heard coyotes howl in the distance. We let the fire die out and we went to bed, but as we lay there we got more and more scared, and finally my aunt sat up in her sleeping bag and said, 'Would it be alright if we left? It's spooky out here and I'm starting to get scared.'

" 'I am too,' I told her.

"She turned on a flashlight and we got dressed and threw everything in the back of her car and drove away and when we hit pavement she let out a long sigh.

" 'I thought we were done for,' she said and grinned. We drove back to town and ate at a diner. She let me get whatever I wanted and when we got back to her house we set up the sleeping bags in the living room and watched TV and spent the weekend camping there."

Pete looked at me half asleep. Once in a while he'd move his head around but that was about it. I pet him a bit longer, then put the halter on him and we walked down near the fences and I let him eat grass. After I put him back I walked up and down the shedrows. I passed the tack room where Bonnie Sparks was staying. The door was closed but I could hear a TV going and there was a light on so I knocked.

You could hear the TV shut off and then maybe a minute passed and she answered.

"What are you doing?" she said. Her eyes were bloodshot. She had dried mustard on the corner of her mouth, and she was dressed different. She had a red shirt on with white buttons and was wearing black jeans. She was dressed up.

"Nothing," I said.

"Do you want to watch TV?"

I nodded and she let me in. She turned on the black and white and we watched a show, then she told me of a party she was going to and invited me to come along with her and I told her I would.

We walked out to the parking lot and got into an old Volkswagen Bug and she drove us pretty far out in Northeast Portland and parked us in front of a house. We went inside and everyone there was older than me, and I didn't recognize any of them from the track. Bonnie left to use the toilet and I just stood by myself for a long time. There was music playing on a stereo, and there was a dining-room table that had a bowl of chips and some dip set out. There was also a plate of lunch meat and next to it a loaf of bread.

I waited for her to come back but she didn't. I stood there for maybe an hour, then I went over to the food. There was a cooler on the floor underneath the table and there were Cokes and I drank one and made a sandwich. Then I just sat down on a couch and listened to the music and watched everyone talk. Once in a while they'd look at me and I'd say hello but mostly I just sat there.

A couple hours passed and I didn't know what to do because I still hadn't seen Bonnie. A few times I went outside to make sure her car was still there and it always was. Finally, I went from room to room and knocked on the doors. No one answered any of them so I began opening them and looking inside. I found her. She looked asleep, sitting on the bed with her back resting against the wall. She didn't have her shirt on. There was a naked man next to her who had a needle going into his arm. He looked up at me so I shut the door. I went back out to the party and left.

I didn't know where I was. I walked down one street and then another and then I was running. The thoughts in my head were swirling. I'd seen a lot of things. I'd seen my dad do things. I'd seen him having sex with women. I'd seen him bending women over our couch and ramming into them and I'd seen them in the kitchen sitting on top of him saying things to him. I'd seen him puking his guts out in the sink and snorting cocaine and smoking weed. I saw a woman passed out in the back of our car in nothing but a bra. I saw her pee on the seat. I saw a guy get a broken beer bottle pushed in his face while we were at a daytime barbecue. I'd seen my dad hit my aunt in the face and call her names when all she did was tell him to come back when he wasn't so drunk and mean. I'd seen him wreck her car and then abandon it. I'd seen him talk to the police. I saw a kid get hit so hard that he began to foam at the mouth and go into seizures and I'd seen a kid shoot a dog in the head with a .22. I'd seen another kid tear the pajamas off his sister just so he could see her down there. She was screaming and crying. And I'd seen Del punch a horse as hard as he could and I'd seen a horse break his leg and wobble around on three while the broke one was held on by only skin.

I kept running and running until I was so tired I couldn't think about anything like that. It took a long time. It always takes a long time, but it always works.

14

A couple days later I met a guy named Johnny Billson who had been a jockey at Bay Meadows and Golden Gate Fields. After that he started riding at Portland Meadows before he quit altogether. He told me he hated horses more than anything, he told me that if never saw another horse in his whole life he'd be happy. Even so he said he was still drawn to being a jockey, that he still couldn't completely shake it.

He was a swing-shift cook at the Shari's Restaurant down the street from Portland Meadows. He knew Del and I guess Del told him about me and Johnny hired me one morning to help him move from one apartment to another. His old place was on the second floor and his new place was across town on the third floor. So we carried all his things down to a pickup truck, drove to the new place, then carried them back up three flights of stairs. He had a lot of stuff and we had to move his record collection, which was really heavy.

When we were done I had to ask him for the twenty dollars he said he'd pay me. He looked through his wallet, but I could see he didn't have any money in it. He just stood there and lit a cigarette. He told me he thought he had the dough but he guessed he didn't. He said he'd give Del the money later that week.

"I got to buy food today," I told him.

"I can't get the cash today," he said.

"Please," I said.

He looked at me, then finally said he'd feed me if I went to the back door of Shari's during the dinner shift from Sunday to Thursday. All I had to do was ask for him. He said he'd give me three free dinners instead of the twenty. I told him okay and made him shake hands on it.

I went to the restaurant that evening and knocked on the back door and a man answered and led me in. Johnny Billson was standing over the grill and he smiled when he saw me. He got me a Coke and made me a cheeseburger and fries. He told me to sit in the corner next to the employees' lockers and eat. When I was done he let me have a bowl of soup and made me a sandwich to go. All in all I must have eaten there ten times and he never seemed sore about it.

It was late July by then and football practice was to start in less than a month. I stopped by the high school and it was three times the size of my last school. It was called Jefferson High, the Democrats were their mascot. I wanted to go to school, but I knew they wouldn't let me live on my own, I knew they'd put me in some sort of home. I decided if I couldn't figure anything out by the start of football practice I'd ask Del if I could move in with him.

I used my spare money to call the M. Thompsons from the list I'd written down. There was a payphone in the main grandstands at the track and I called all the numbers I had for that name in Wyoming but I never had any luck. I tried the place my aunt had worked again, Scottish Sam's Auto Parts, but the same girl answered and told me the same thing she had before. I got on the library computer again to try and find her that way but I couldn't. For a few nights I just lay in my sleeping bag and bawled about it. People say crying makes you feel better but it didn't, it didn't change anything, it just made me tired and embarrassed.

I began buying my food at a mini-mart that was maybe a mile away. There was an Asian girl my age who worked behind the counter. She would always smile at me, and a couple times we talked and she said she was going to Jefferson High, the same school I was supposed to go. She was really good-looking and she always had her nails painted fluorescent green and when she talked she always said my name. One time she said it five times and we only talked for a couple of minutes.

That week Del had four horses racing. Mr. High Pockets, Go Buster Go, Easter Sonny Boy, and Lean on Pete. He was in a horrible mood when he began talking about the upcoming races. It was early in the morning, the sun had barely come up and he was eating a candy bar and drinking a can of Coke. He stood there wearing jeans that were falling down and an old red flannel shirt that was stained with dried white paint.

"All I know is with all the bullshit happening you can't even call this a track anymore. Back in the seventies this place was at least a real track. People don't give a shit anymore. They'd rather sit in front of a goddamn box with lights and sound effects and shove their money into it. No one wants to go to the track. They'd rather go to the fucking mall. That's all casinos are. Longacres, that was a track. The seventies were a hell of a lot better than this. Shit, even the eighties were alright. I had some real horses back then and I had jockeys I could trust. You can't trust anyone now. You can't even trust the *Daily Racing Form*. And you can't tell me that the Beyer number is worth a shit at this dump. I've spent hours trying to teach you the form and it's like I'm pouring water onto a rock. It just bounces off and never takes. Every goddamn kid nowadays is like that. The world's a mess, a real mess if guys like you end up running things. Did I tell you I saw that kid Luis looking through my truck the other day? And a couple weeks ago I caught Hopper siphoning gas out of it with a garden hose. I ask him what the fuck he thinks he's doing and all he says is, 'Del, is this your truck?' Well he knows its my fucking truck. I let him have it. I'm an inch away from murdering his ass. Then all he says is, 'Jesus, I swear I didn't know this was your truck, honest.' But he doesn't apologize, he just walks away with five gallons of my gas and let me tell you gas ain't cheap anymore. Nothing's cheap. The goddamn farrier goes up, feed goes up, medicine goes up, and the purses go down. You tell me what to do."

"Me?" I asked him.

He shook his head. "All you ever do is ask for money and eat and I've never seen anyone make eating seem so goddamn unappealing. What can you tell me? I'll tell you what you can tell me, nothing. I got an ulcer and I can't feel my toes and I haven't taken a decent shit in a year and all my horses are pigs."

I just stood there and he stared right at me and went on. He talked about how the vet was charging him too much and that the café used expired food, and how since computers started you couldn't win anything on horses and how his ex-wife owes him two thousand dollars and how the hot-water heater in his house was broken and how he paid a guy to fix it and how the guy took the hot-water heater back to his shop and went on vacation without fixing it. He didn't have hot water for two weeks. He put in a chew and told me how he had to buy a brand-new one, and how they don't make anything that lasts anymore. Then he started talking about a woman he lived with who used to get so drunk she'd throw up in bed in her sleep. Then he told me about a brake job he got where they said they'd changed the pads but hadn't. They said they turned the rotors but they hadn't done that either.

"They didn't do a goddamn thing but I caught those lousy fuckers and what do I get? Nothing, that's what."

Del kept going on like this until an old man came up to him and they started talking so I went back to cleaning stalls.

Pete came in sixth that day, beating only one horse. Mr. High Pockets was last, Go Buster Go got fourth, and Del's best horse, Easter Sonny Boy, came in second but got claimed.

That night I gave Pete two apples and he ate those and kept nudging me, looking for more. He wasn't lame but he hardly moved at all in his stall. He just stood there almost lifeless. Del had raced him three weeks in a row, plus the match races before that, and his times were getting slower each week.

The next morning I went to Bonnie's tack room to ask her about him. I knocked on the door and waited until she came out.

"What time is it?" she yawned.

"Almost six."

Her hair was messed up and you could see her legs. She wasn't wearing anything but a black T-shirt. She told me to hold on and closed the door, and I could hear her in there getting dressed, then she came out in a different shirt wearing jeans and boots. We walked over to the café and she ordered breakfast, and I sat there and watched her eat part of it, then push it away. She let the plate sit there and drank coffee and watched the TV they had going.

"Are you done eating?"

"Yeah," she said.

I looked at her.

"What?" she said.

"Would it be alright if I ate the rest of your breakfast?"

She smiled and nodded so I took the plate and her fork and finished it. We sat there for a while longer while she drank coffee and then on the way out I bought two maple bars with my last dollar and gave one to her. We walked over to Del's stalls and she went in and looked at Pete. She bent down and ran her hands up and down his legs.

"There's a lot of heat."

"Is that bad?"

"It's not good."

She told me to put a halter on him.

"What time does Del get here?"

"He'll be here in an hour or so," I told her.

"Then let's put him on the hotwalker right now," she said and led him out. She stood back and watched him.

"He's sore alright. Just look at the way he walks. How old is he?"

"Five, I think."

"How often has Del been racing him?"

"Five weeks in a row. I'm not sure before that."

She just stood there.

"Will he be alright?"

"I don't know. If Del keeps racing him all the time he won't be."

"Del says he thinks he might be navicular."

"That's bad if that's the case," she said.

"What's gonna happen to him?"

"It depends," she said. "Quarter horses are pretty tough. They can take a lot more than thoroughbreds, but look, Charley, don't worry too much about one horse, okay? You can't think of these guys as pets. They aren't. They're here for racing, not for anything else. If they lose too much they get fired. When I had horses as a kid we had winter pastures and summer pastures. We wouldn't even begin breaking them until they were four. These guys get broke and rode hard at two and are stuck in a stall for twenty-three hours a day for months at a time. You can make a nice horse fucked-up as hell in no time at all. So be careful, alright."

"It seems like Pete's in prison."

"I guess that's what I'd call being stuck in a cell for twenty-three hours a day, then taken out and run and put right back. The thing that gets me is that there's over a thousand horses here and not one of them is good enough to race at a real track like Santa Anita."

"What happens if he keeps losing?"

"Del will sell him to whoever will buy him. Maybe he'll get claimed, but don't think about that," she said and smiled. It was the first time I'd really seen her smile. Her teeth were brown and they were crooked but she had a nice smile.

"What if no one wants him?"

"You mean if he really is navicular?"

I nodded.

"Nothing good, Charley. There used to be a slaughter-house outside of Salem. Most of the horses went there, but they've outlawed slaughtering horses in the U.S. now so they ship them down in stock trailers to Mexico and kill them there."

"They ship them to Mexico and kill them?"

"Don't think about it," Bonnie said and put her hand on my shoulder.

The next Sunday, Del's horse Go Buster Go was in third place coming around the stretch when the other two horses in front began to fade. He moved past them on the outside and suddenly he was in first.

"Don't let him lug out," Del screamed. We were watching the race from a TV near the main floor bar. "Goddamn it, don't let him lug out." The jockey was whipping the horse and trying to hold him in. The number three horse came up next to Buster, but Buster pinned his ears back and held him off and won the race and Del's share of a $3,500 purse. Del smiled in relief and finished his beer and we both went outside and got in the win picture. We stood with two people I didn't know and Maxine, the girl who helped feed his horses. Del put his arm around her while the picture was taken and told me he'd get me a copy of the photo.

I helped him walk Go Buster Go to the backside and we brought him to the test barn to be drug tested. They had a hotwalker there and we put Buster on it and waited for him to piss and Del smiled and talked to anyone who would talk to him.

Later that afternoon his horse Dash's Dart ran a six-furlong stakes race and came in second and won over $2,000. The odds on her were 23-1 and Del whispered to me that he had her second in a hundred-dollar exacta and won that as well.

"Miracles sometimes happen," he said and I'd never

seen him so happy. When we went out to the track to get Dash's Dart Del wasn't walking slow like an old man, he was nearly skipping.

That evening I found Del in the back room of the café playing cards. He hadn't paid me yet and I'd already asked him twice. He was drunk. I stood there for a long time just watching him and waiting.

"Well, what do you want?" he said when he finally noticed me.

"I was hoping–" I started to say.

"You want your money, right?"

I nodded. He pushed his chair back and took out his wallet and he gave me forty dollars.

"Yesterday you said you'd give me eighty."

"That's all the cash I have on me tonight," he said. But when he took the forty out of his wallet I could see a big wad of bills in there. "I'll get you the rest tomorrow, but I'm busy now, alright?"

"Alright," I told him and then I left, but I couldn't go back to the tack room while he was still there so I took the money and walked all the way to St. Johns to a taqueria that was in the back of a Mexican grocery store. While I was there a couple came in and started arguing with each other. The woman got up and left him there. He stayed but he didn't eat anything. He just lit a cigarette and then after a while a Mexican guy came from behind the counter and told him that smoking wasn't allowed. The man looked like he might start a fight but he didn't, he just left. There was no one else in the place except me and the counterman. After a minute or so he went into the back and, when he did, I got up and went to the table where the man and woman had sat. The woman's meal was half done but the man's was untouched and I took it and set it on top of my empty plate. I went to the counter and rang the bell and the guy came out from the back and I got a to-go container and put the man's meal in it and left.

It was still pretty early so I walked around for a while, then I went to the movies and saw one about a good-looking girl who has a crazy father who thinks there is treasure buried underneath a Costco. They end up jack-hammering through the concrete floor and finding a hidden river and a bunch of gold. After that I walked back to the track and by then the café was closed and Del's truck was gone so I went inside the tack room, laid out my sleeping bag, and ate the rest of the Mexican food.

Del showed up at nine the next morning carrying a paper sack. He was hungover and dressed in the same clothes he wore the day before. He went into the tack room, sat at his desk and turned on the radio. In the sack was a six pack of beer and a package of hot dogs. He began eating the hot dogs cold and washing them down with beer. It was a pretty sick thing to see. Him just taking them out of the package and putting one after another in his mouth. I stood outside watching. Then he swallowed a handful of aspirin, lay down on the tack-room floor, and fell asleep.

A couple hours later he coughed and sat up.

"What time is it?" He felt around his shirt pocket and took out a can of chew and put in a dip.

"It's eleven-thirty," I told him.

"Okay," he said and stood up. He took a can of beer off the desk and opened it. "Pete's up first. Let's hope to God he gets claimed." Del moved his hands through his hair and put on his cowboy hat and coughed and it was a heavy, sick sort of cough. "I got to hit the can. Be ready to bring him over in twenty minutes."

The race was a $4,000, 350-yard maiden claimer. Del didn't say anything at all when we brought Pete over. There were lines of sweat leaking down from under his cowboy hat and he hadn't shaved. I stood with him in the paddock and held Pete while he put on the saddle and he didn't say anything then either.

When the bell rang and the jockeys came out, a woman jockey got on Pete. Del didn't tell her anything, he just gave her a leg up, then led them out of the paddock and handed Pete's lead to a pony girl who took him out.

While the horses paraded Del went to the bar and ordered a beer so I walked down next to the track and waited. When the race went off the announcer didn't even mention Lean on Pete. From where I was I could tell he was near last and by the time the winner passed the finish line I could see Pete struggling three lengths behind.

Del walked out on the track as the jockey brought Pete back. She jumped down and they took the saddle off and she said a few things to Del but I couldn't hear. As we walked Pete back to the stalls Del remained quiet. We hosed him down and set him on the hotwalker and then put him in his stall. Del went to him and felt both his front legs.

"Is he gonna be okay?" I asked.

"It don't look good. I guess he probably really is navicu-

lar. I ain't certain he's got it, but I ain't paying for X-rays."
He picked up Pete's right hoof and when he did it you could
tell it hurt and Pete jerked and Del fell back and hit his
head on the stall wall.

When he got up you could tell he was mad. He stood
there for a moment or so, then just walked over to Pete and
hit him as hard as he could in the neck. Pete moved away
from Del and bumped into the back of the stall.

"You're a pig," he said as he opened the gate and left.

I followed him down the shedrow until he walked to a
sani-hut. He went inside and was in there for a long time.

When he got out I asked him, "What are you gonna do
with him?"

"With who?"

"Pete."

"Can't a man shit in peace?" he said. He put in a chew
and looked at me. "No one wants a five-year-old that can't
run and could be navicular. We have to get rid of him."

"I still don't understand what navicular is," I said to him.

"It's a fucked-up bone in his foot. How many times do I
got to tell you? It's a degenerative disease. There's nothing
to be done about it for a horse like him. I ain't paying to cut
his nerves and he's barely worth Therapain. Now I gotta run
a few errands so leave me alone, alright?"

I nodded and he left the backside, got into his truck, and
drove off.

I went to Pete's stall. He seemed okay but I wasn't sure.
When the races were done that day I went to Fred Meyer
and bought him apples and a bag of carrots, then I pulled

up a chair next to his stall and tried to read a novel that Del had lying around. I spent the afternoon that way. That night Del showed up again to play cards in the café so I left and decided to walk to the trailer park where Harry Durand lived, hoping he would know what to do about Pete. I knocked on a few trailer homes before this old lady told me which one he lived in. I went to it but he wasn't there. I waited for a while but he never showed up so I walked back to the track.

I went into the café to see if they were still playing cards and they were. Del saw me and waved me over.

"You still know how to drive my truck?" he said. He was drunk.

"Sure," I told him.

"Hook the trailer to it. You know which one, right?"

I nodded.

"Bring the truck and trailer over here and park it in front of the café, okay? We're gonna load Pete tonight. I'll be out in an hour or so."

"Where's he going?"

"I'm going to sell him."

"You're gonna sell him tonight?" I asked.

Del nodded.

"To who?"

One of the other trainers playing cards started laughing.

"Why should you care?" Del said.

"I was just asking."

"It's not any of your business."

"I could buy him off you," I said.

Del laughed. "You don't have any money and you can't

keep him in one of my stalls. Just go get the truck."

I stood there staring at him, but he didn't say anything more, he just handed me the keys. I went out to the lot and found his truck. It started easy enough but I stalled it twice trying to get it in gear. I drove it around to where his trailer was and backed it up the best I could and hooked the old stock trailer to it. The whole thing took a long time, but I did it. I drove to the front gate and the security guard came out, opened it, and I drove in.

I took the truck down the main backside road until I came to Del's stalls and I cut the engine. I went to Pete, put a halter on him, and loaded him. Then I went to the tack room, took my bag of clothes and sleeping bag, and put them in the cab of the truck. After that I went into the rafters and got my last couple cans of food, then took two bales of Del's hay and set them in the bed of the truck.

I got back in and circled around and drove to the main gate. The old-man security guard came out and I rolled down the window.

"What are you doing?" he asked.

"Del's selling Lean on Pete," I said. "He told me to load him and park across the street. He's in the café finishing up playing a card game."

The security guard turned on his flashlight and looked in the back of the trailer and then shined the light on him.

"Alright," he said. "Just sign here." I signed where he told me to, then he opened the gate, and I drove out.

I had the truck in first. It was hard to get it in second but I did and drove down the road towards the freeway. I didn't mean for all of it to happen like that, I really didn't. But I could tell by the looks of the other men at the card game that Del was going to sell Lean on Pete to what the people at the track called the killers. I knew sooner or later he would be in a stock trailer full of other horses he didn't know heading for Mexico.

16

When I came to the stoplight I headed south on the freeway. I could have gone either way, but there was more traffic heading north. I got the truck out of second and into third alright but I kept grinding gears and I couldn't figure out how not to. It took me three tries to get it into fourth. I was scared to go over fifty but I knew I had to. The old truck seemed to rattle and shake more than it did when Del drove it and I wasn't sure why. Every ten seconds or so I checked the rearview to make sure the horse trailer was still there and it always was so I just kept driving down the road.

I passed through downtown Portland and up some hills and then the road leveled and the traffic thinned and we left the city. I began to relax. I looked at the dashboard and I saw that I still had a quarter tank of gas. I drove until it was near empty, then I got off the highway and pulled into a gas station.

A fat lady came out, I gave her all the money I had, and she put thirty-four dollars' worth of gas in the tank and I went back to Pete. He looked pretty small in the big old stock trailer, but he didn't seem upset or worried. I went inside and found a map of the western United States and when the counterman wasn't looking I walked back out with it. The truck started easy and I drove back towards the highway and pulled over. I looked at the map for a long time and decided I'd go to Wyoming and try to find my aunt for real. I had to drive through Oregon and Idaho to get there; I had to drive more than a thousand miles.

It was almost ten o'clock when I began heading east on Highway 20. It was a two-lane road and the further we were from the interstate the windier it got. Then the mountains started and I began grinding the gears so much that I just left it in second. Cars passed me because I was going so slow, a few of them even honked and I was worried that if a cop saw he would pull me over. Eventually I made it through the mountains but when I did I realized I'd missed the turn-off I was supposed to take and ended up in a town called Prineville.

I was dead tired by then and I parked in the lot of a closed Safeway grocery store. I tried to sleep but I just lay there in the cab and worried. I had less than a third of a tank of gas and no money. I looked through the glove box but there wasn't anything in there except a bunch of receipts, a flashlight, some fuses, a lighter, and a pocket knife. I took the lighter and pocket knife and put them in my coat pocket.

I got out and looked in the bed of the truck and there was an empty five gallon gas can. I took it out and set it on the ground then went back to Pete. He stood there motionless in the darkness and really I had no idea how he was doing. I went to the bed of the truck and got him a flake of hay, then I opened a can of soup and we ate together.

It was still dark out when I left the truck and walked to the first house I saw and stole a garden hose. I went back to the truck and cut off a six-foot section. There were a handful of cars in the lot and I moved the truck next to one so the gas tanks were right next to each other. The other car had a lock on the gas-cap cover, but I broke it off and stuck the hose down the tank. I began sucking as hard as I could and after a while gas poured into my mouth and started spilling out. I put the end of the hose in the gas can and it began to fill.

I filled Del's front and back tanks like that. It took me three different cars to do it, but I didn't get caught and I was too worried to feel bad about it. When I was done I got back on the road and drove out of Prineville as the sun began to rise. Not long after that I got so tired I could hardly keep my eyes open. I passed a sign that said I was entering a national forest, and in the distance I could see mountains and trees starting. I pulled off on a forest service road that ran alongside a creek and I stayed on it until there was a good turnout and I cut the engine.

I went back to the trailer, unloaded Pete, and took him down to the creek. He looked around for a long time, then he drank a little. I could see the muscles on his neck move as the water went down his throat, and he seemed pretty fine.

"I hope it's alright I took you," I said to him. "Del was gonna take you to Mexico, I know he was."

Pete leaned down and looked at the water but he didn't drink again.

"Del said a lot of mean things to me. He told me that I'd never amount to anything, that I'd be lucky if I ended up working a fryer at a fast-food place. He used to say I was useful as a bag of concrete that had been pissed on. He said stuff like that all the time. The only reason I'm telling you all this is that I know he said some things to you too. But remember, when he was talking about you he was just being grumpy. Everyone knows you're a good horse."

Pete looked up, then stepped into the creek. The cold water ran over his feet. His coat was black as asphalt and his eyes were half shut. It was like he was asleep right then.

"One time my dad left me at this guy's house for a week while he went to Las Vegas with a woman he was dating. I can't remember her name but she won a free trip to a casino. This was when I lived in Green River, like I told you earlier, but the guy who I was staying with lived all the way over in Cheyenne and my dad and his girlfriend dropped me off there on the way to Denver. That's where they were gonna get the plane to Las Vegas. I'd met the guy before but I didn't know him. He was my dad's friend from high school. This guy's voice was so loud you never could tell if he was just talking or if he really was mad and yelling. He worked swing shift and I had to sleep in the living room, but the problem was he never went to bed so I just sat there with him and watched TV. I never once saw him sleep in his bedroom. He just watched shows until he fell asleep on the couch. I slept on the floor, which I don't mind, but it was a small room. It made me nervous. It was summer, so I didn't have to go to school, but my dad signed me up for a week of day camp so I'd have something to do. The problem was that the guy lived ten miles away from town. He told my dad he'd drive me in. He owed my dad a bunch of money and they'd agreed to call it even if the guy took me to the camp and let me stay at his apartment. But he was hard to get up when morning came. The first day I had to stand over him and shake him. He was so mad and startled when he woke I thought he was going to hit me, but he got up and drove me in. It was the same way the second day but he was even grumpier about it then. On the third day he wouldn't get up so I missed the camp. I ended up just sitting around outside his building. He took me the next morning but the day after that he didn't even come home. And there was hardly any food at his place. All he had were Banquet frozen dinners and they're the worst. The Salisbury steak's alright, but he'd only bought one of those.

"When the last day came I got up at six o'clock and waited outside in the parking lot for my dad. He showed up with his girlfriend around noon and I got in the car and we went home."

Pete lifted his head.

"I won't make you sleep at that guy's house. I guess that's what I'm trying to say. I'll make sure you're alright and we'll find someone to fix your feet. Okay?"

Pete just stood there with his eyes half shut. I walked him back and tied him to the side of the trailer and cleaned it out with a broom. I led him in, gave him a flake of hay, then lay down in the front seat and conked out until it was late afternoon.

When I woke up I walked Pete up the road to let him stretch out, and he went along slow like he didn't feel good, and when we went to the creek he didn't drink at all.

I put him back in the trailer and threw in another flake of hay. I went in my bag and took out my last can of soup and ate it. I looked at the map and figured out which way to go and got back on the road.

I kept the truck at fifty and drove for hours. By the time night came I turned onto Highway 395 and headed south, but the longer I drove the harder it became to shift gears. One time when I was going up a hill the engine suddenly started revving, but I wasn't going any faster. It was like I had the clutch in but I didn't.

I can't remember what time it was when I got to Burns, Oregon, but it was late and I had less than a quarter-tank of gas. Burns is a small desert town and everything was closed except for a gas station and an all-night restaurant. I drove around until I saw a few trucks parked on a side street across from a motel. I pulled up alongside a white pickup and killed the engine. There was no lock on the gas cap and I grabbed my hose, stuck it in the truck's tank and began sucking. But when the gas came I wasn't ready and I swallowed some. It was horrible. I couldn't stop coughing and gas poured out of the hose and on to the street. I must have let a gallon run out before I got the hose in the gas can and it began to fill. The whole time I just stood there spitting and coughing and then finally I puked out onto the street.

I filled Del's front tank to the top, then pulled the hose out, threw it in the back and started the truck. This time it barely went into first. It was grinding worse and it took me a couple minutes to get moving. The whole time my heart raced and I was certain some big ape-looking cowboy would come running from a motel room. I began heading out of town but my stomach was still sick and felt worse and I knew I had to eat. I turned around and drove towards the restaurant, and parked a block away next to an auto body shop.

When I walked into The Apple Peddler there was hardly anyone there. I sat at the counter and a waitress came and set down a menu and a glass of water. She was middle-aged and sort of heavy, and she and the cook looked like the only people who were working. There was an old-man truck driver in a corner booth reading the paper and there was an obese guy sitting at a table near the door doing paperwork.

I ordered the full chicken fried steak dinner with baked potato, soup, and a large Coke. I also got two cheeseburgers to go. When the waitress finished taking my order I went to the can and washed my face and hands and rinsed out my mouth, trying to get rid of the smell and taste of gas. When my food came out I ate as fast as I could. The lady filled my Coke once and when I finished eating she set down the sack with the two cheeseburgers and the bill.

I watched her for a while, then she disappeared into the back. I took the sack and headed for the door. I passed the register where I was supposed to pay and saw the old-man truck driver still sitting in his booth. I couldn't see the other man even though the table was still full of papers, but as I passed it and was halfway out the door something grabbed my shirt from behind.

It was the obese man.

His face was pale and bloated and it looked like he was trying to grow a moustache. He must have weighed over three hundred pounds. On his shirt there was an Apple Peddler name tag. It said his name was Mitch and that he was a manager.

I hadn't noticed the tag before.

"I knew you were going to dine and dash," he said. It

didn't seem like he was angry or anything, but he wouldn't let go of my shirt.

I tried to say something back but nothing came out.

"Do you want to pay now?"

I looked at him and then after a while I said, "I don't have any money."

"You ordered twenty-five dollars' worth of food and you don't have any money?"

I shook my head.

"You're serious?"

I nodded.

"Let's go," he said. He kept hold of my shirt and took me past the restrooms and down the hall to an office. We went inside and he shut the door behind us and told me to sit in a chair that was in the back of the small room. If I tried to run I'd have to go past him.

"I didn't want to steal the food," I told him.

"You didn't want to?"

"No."

"Then why did you do it?"

"I was starving."

"Do you live in Burns?"

"No," I said.

"How old are you?"

"Fifteen," I told him.

"Where are your parents?"

"I don't know."

"Are you a runaway?"

"No," I said.

He picked up the phone and dialed the police. He talked

to them for a long time, and told them what I'd done. He said he thought I might be a runaway, and by the end it sounded like the police were going to come and get me.

"But my friend's sick in the car," I said when he hung up. "I can't leave him. If the police come and take him he'll die."

"What's wrong with your friend?" he asked.

"I don't know," I said.

"What's your name?"

"They'll kill him," I said, and suddenly tears were leaking down my face. If Del got Pete back I knew he'd put him down, but if I didn't say anything Pete would be stuck in the trailer and when day came he'd die in the heat.

I stood up and started for the door but the manager moved in front of it, blocking me.

"Sit down," he yelled, and this time you could tell he was really mad. He was beginning to sweat. It was coming off his forehead and his shirt was growing dark under his arms. I just stood there. He told me again so I sat back down. Then the waitress came into the office.

"The bus just showed up."

"How many got off?"

"At least twenty," she said.

"Great," the man said and shook his head.

"The driver wants to talk to you."

"Why?"

"I don't know," she said.

"The sheriff hasn't shown up, has he?"

"No," she said.

"This kid," he said and pointed to me, "tried to dine and

dash. I'll go check with the driver. Watch him and don't let him leave, okay?"

The woman nodded and he left the room. She sat on the edge of the desk and looked at me.

"I should have known," she said. "You don't look like you got a dime."

"I'm sorry."

"You at least have to tip," she said.

I nodded.

"Waitresses are the ones who get screwed when you don't pay. Some places make us pay. Stealing from a waitress is pretty low."

"I really am sorry," I said.

She took a pack of gum out of her uniform pocket, opened it, and put a piece in her mouth.

"I bet you're a runaway."

I nodded.

"So you don't live around here?"

"No," I said.

"Where are you headed?"

"Wyoming," I said.

"Wyoming?"

I nodded.

"Why?"

"My aunt used to live there. I'm trying to find her."

"Where are your parents?" she asked.

"I don't know," I said.

"I'd be madder, but I could tell you were hungry, and you look like you've been sleeping underneath a car. Maybe the sheriff can help get you to your aunt."

"I can't go with the sheriff."

"Why?"

I just can't."

The manager came back in.

"There's twenty-eight total and they all want food." He looked at his watch. "I've waited an hour for the sheriff. I don't know what to do. I'm not going to leave him alone in the office and we have forty-five minutes before they get back on the bus and head to Winnemucca."

"I shouldn't say this, but just let him go," the waitress said.

"You saw how much food he ordered."

The waitress nodded.

"I just don't know why it's taking them an hour to get here," he said, and you could tell he was tired.

She stood up. "I got to go back out there or the whole bus will stiff me."

The man shook his head, then sighed heavily and told me to leave. The waitress looked at me and moved her eyes, telling me to go, so I grabbed the sack with the cheeseburgers and went out the door and into the main dining room where a bus load of black people sat.

I went out the main door and ran through the parking lot and made it to the truck and got in. I ground the transmission into first and the truck lurched forward. I kept to the back roads until we were out of town, and soon it was pitch-black dark. I kept the truck going the best I could and for a while it was easy as there were no hills. Behind us there was nothing but darkness.

17

I drove for a long time without seeing anyone. I was out in the middle of a desert. I checked the rearview every once in a while but there were never any police cars or headlights behind me. Then the road began to incline and the engine lugged. I tried to shift down but it wouldn't. It was stuck in third gear. I pushed the clutch in over and over and used all the strength I had to try and get the gear shift out of third but it wouldn't go. The hill kept getting steeper. The engine lugged more and the truck slowed until the engine finally quit.

I made it to the side of the road and stopped. I tried again and again to take the truck out of third but it wouldn't go. I sat there for nearly a half-hour trying. I found a flashlight in the glove box and opened the hood but I didn't know what to look for. I waited until the truck cooled down and I then tried again but it still wouldn't leave third. I started the engine and revved it and tried to go forward but it just lugged and stalled. I looked around but there was nothing but darkness. No house lights or headlights or moon. I gave up. I turned on the cab light and gathered everything I could. I kept the flashlight and took the road map and there was a pack of gum on the dash. Under the seat I found an old *National Geographic*, a pair of gloves, and an old yellow rope. I took all those things and got out of the truck.

I left the headlights on and went to the truck bed and

took my duffel bag and emptied it out. The only things I kept were my two trophies and the picture of my aunt. I put the photo in my back pocket and wrapped the trophies in shirts and put them back in the bag. I put on my coat and stuck the two cheeseburgers and the flashlight and the map and magazine in the pockets. Then I filled the bag with hay. I took the rope I'd found and cut a piece and tied it around my sleeping bag in two places so I could put it over my shoulder. There was an empty gallon water jug and I took it and tied it to the sleeping bag, then I went back to the trailer.

I turned on the flashlight and opened the door. Pete's eyes looked worried but I don't know if he was. I took the lead rope and led him out. I carried the sleeping bag and the duffel of hay and we started walking up the hill. There were no cars but it was spooky out there alone. I couldn't hear anything 'cause Pete's shoes were banging and clanking against the asphalt. We walked for an hour before we saw a truck pass. It slowed down for a bit but it didn't stop. Soon it started to get light so we moved off the highway and started walking through the desert sagebrush. I kept the road in sight to have something to follow, but I tried to get far enough away so no one could really see us. The walking was pretty easy and Pete went alright. His steps were short and it seemed like he hurt, but he never once stopped.

The hills around us were covered in sage and rock. Once in a while there'd be a tree but not very often. In the far distance were a couple of ranches and I saw cars and trucks pass on the highway but there was nothing much else out there. We walked for hours. It was hot out by then. We came to the top of a hill and started down the other side and I saw what looked like a creek in a small gully. When we came to it, it was wet with water and mud. The water was moving slowly. Pete went to it and stood in the middle of it but he didn't drink. I filled the jug and the water was muddy but it tasted alright.

There were little patches of grass by the water and Pete ate off those and I moved alongside the bank with him. We walked maybe a quarter mile that way until we came to a pine tree and an old campsite. There were rusted-out cans everywhere and a fire pit and broken glass. I tied one end of the yellow rope around the tree and the other to the lead rope. Pete seemed uneasy about it at first and leaned back against it but my knot held and then after a time he calmed down and started looking for grass. I sat down in the shade, ate one of the cheeseburgers, unrolled my sleeping bag, and conked out.

When I woke it was afternoon and it was hotter than it was before. Pete stood half asleep. I was hungry again and ate the other cheeseburger, then I sat for a long time and did nothing. I lay back down. When I got up again it was late in the day. I took some hay out of the duffel and set it in front of him. There was a jet flying overhead and it was leaving a contrail that seemed to go on for miles and miles. I watched Pete eat and then I went to the creek and washed my face and tried to dunk my head in the shallow water.

I filled up the gallon jug, then rolled the sleeping bag and untied Pete and brought him to the creek and this time he drank and he drank for a long time. Then we started walking again. We went over a hill and came down another gully and saw a dead deer that was rotted out. Its lower jaw was ripped off and its guts were gone, as was most of its body. Pete didn't seem to notice and we kept going. Every once in a while I thought I heard a rattlesnake, but I never saw one. We came across a bunch of beer cans and every so often we'd see old used-up shotgun shells or the skeleton of some animal. The sun was still hot but the worst of the day was over and I kept watching the highway and only a few times did I lose sight of it.

I passed the time by talking to Pete. I told him about football and how my freshman coach sent me up to varsity to practice after our season was over and how they let me go to the varsity banquet as well as the freshman one. I told him about each of my four interceptions and how I made friends with a linebacker named Collin and how he used to invite me over to his house to spend the night.

I told Pete about Collin's house and how nice it was and how he had three sisters. I told him about the first time I spent the night and how the next morning we all sat around the kitchen table and ate breakfast. There were two older sisters and one younger. They were in their pajamas and they were beautiful and they sat and talked and laughed. The mother was there and she made pancakes and bacon and a pitcher of orange juice. She was in a bathrobe and she was also good-looking. She stood by the stove cooking and her hair was back in a ponytail and every once in a while she'd come by with another batch of pancakes. It was the nicest place I'd ever been. I told Pete how I almost called them one night a few weeks back, but that I didn't want to beg them for anything or have his sisters know that I was living like I was. If they ever thought of me I'd rather have them think of me as alright. I'd rather never see them again than let them see me the way I was.

We kept going until it was dusk. We came to a huge bluff that was impossible to pass over. It was a wall of rock that went sixty feet straight up. I had to make a decision. I could go back to the highway or I could follow the bluff along in the opposite direction, hoping there would be a place I could pass through or a trail that would take us over. I stood there for a long time trying to think. In the far distance I could see the highway and every so often a truck or car passed. I was scared to lose sight of the road, but the thought of a car stopping or a truck dashing past and spooking Pete worried me enough that I chose to go away from the highway.

We walked until it was almost too dark to see. We stopped at the bottom of a shallow gully. There was nothing there except a dried-out creek and sagebrush. I set down my sleeping bag and opened the duffel and poured out half of the hay. Pete ate and I drank as much water as I could, then I cut the plastic jug in half so Pete could drink the rest.

It was almost pitch-black dark by then. I turned on the flashlight but I couldn't find anything to tie Pete to. There were no big rocks or trees or anything. I held on to him but I began to fall asleep, so I tied the yellow rope around my foot and tied the other end to the lead rope, but every time Pete would hear something and startle he'd move around and stomp and drag me with him. Finally, I just sat up and held the rope and waited for night to end.

Just before sunrise we started walking again. Pete seemed okay but he went along slow and every once in a while he'd just stop and I'd have to pull him forward. We went for a long time before we found a place to cross over the bluff. When we got to the other side I couldn't see the highway or any houses. In front of us was nothing but desert.

It was midday when we finally came to a washed-out dirt road. I was hungry and thirsty and it was hot out. There were no clouds and no shade. We took the road and walked on it for miles. I could tell Pete was hot and tired, but he never stopped or acted up.

After a while the road split in two and I took the nicer-looking one. We went over a hill and then down the other side. I could see nothing. No main road or trees or anything. It was late afternoon. We walked for a long time, then climbed another hill and from the top of it I saw a trailer parked off in the distance. And further behind it I saw what looked like the highway.

We headed toward the trailer. As I got closer I could see a red car parked in front and there were trees and outbuildings. People were living there.

The sun was still beating down when we walked up the drive. I could see it was an old trailer. It was white and the outbuildings were nothing but a carport and a rundown barn and paddock.

The car in front of the trailer home was an older Toyota that looked as though it ran. It wasn't dusty and the windows were down. I went to the barn and tied Pete to a fence post and set down the duffel and the sleeping bag and walked up to the trailer door and knocked. I waited, but no one answered. So I banged on it again, then I heard talking and the door opened.

A white man stood behind the screen door. He had short, almost shaved hair and he didn't have a shirt on. His chest had tattoos all over and he was missing two fingers.

"My truck broke down on the highway," I told him.

"How did you get all the way out here?"

"I walked. I got lost. I broke down maybe twenty miles back."

He shook his head.

"I have a horse," I said.

"You have a horse?"

"I need to get him some water. Would it be alright if I got him some?"

The man looked at me, puzzled, then called out to someone and not long after that another man came. He was Indian and was heavy with the same sort of haircut. His shirt was off too and he had tattoos like the other man had.

"What's going on?"

"This kid says his truck broke down and that he's got a horse."

"Where's your horse?"

"I tied him to the fence down there."

"You walk him here?"

"Yeah."

"From the highway?"

"I was on the highway for a while but I was worried he'd get spooked so I took him off it and now I'm lost."

"No shit?" the Indian said and opened the screen door. "Let's go take a look."

He walked out and the other man followed. They were both dressed in shorts that came down to their knees, and flip-flops.

"I grew up around horses," the Indian said.

"Everyone calls him Pinto," the other man said.

"Pinto's just a piece-of-shit car."

"You ain't named after the car," the other man said.

"I know," the Indian said and laughed.

We walked down the drive to the fence where Pete stood tied. The Indian walked up to him and pet him.

"What's his name?"

"Pete," I said.

"That ain't much of a name for a horse," the other man said.

"Do you think it would be alright to get him some water?"

"We'll get him some chow, too," the Indian said, and untied Pete and led him towards a gate. He opened it and pulled Pete through and unhooked the halter. Pete just stood there. Then the Indian ran his hand down Pete's back and hit him as hard as he could on the ass.

Pete ran off. He kicked and ran and bucked.

The Indian and the other man started laughing.

"He's got bad feet," I said.

"He looks alright to me," the Indian said.

"He's not," I pleaded.

"Okay," Pinto said.

Pete kept running around for a while, then calmed and

stayed at the other end of the pen.

"Would it be okay to get him water?" I asked again.

The Indian nodded and went over to an old metal tub, turned it over, and shook it out. There were boards in it and an old window screen and a rim off a car. He walked to the barn, turned on the hose, and dragged it to the tub. He rinsed it out and flipped it back over and filled it.

But Pete wouldn't come near us.

"He don't seem thirsty," the other man said.

"He's just scared," I said.

"He'll drink sooner or later," the Indian said and looked at me. "Do you need to use the phone?"

I nodded.

"What did you say was wrong with the truck?"

"I'm not sure," I said. He asked me what it was doing and I told him and he told me that the clutch had gone out and that it would cost some money to fix it.

I followed them into the trailer. It was clean inside and there was a swamp cooler going so it wasn't too hot. There were wood-paneled walls with paintings of mountains and rivers hanging on them and there was a kitchen with a table and chairs and a stove and fridge. They sat down on a couch and began playing video games. The Indian pointed to the phone and I walked over to it and picked it up. I dialed my old number in Spokane and waited for a while, then hung up.

"The line's busy," I said.

They both were smoking cigarettes. The Indian got up and took two beers from the refrigerator and sat back down.

"You're out in bumfuck here," the man said.

"Why ain't you traveling with a phone?" The Indian said.

"I don't have the money for one."

"How old are you?"

"Sixteen," I told them.

"Where you taking the horse?"

"To Wyoming," I said.

"Why up there?"

"I don't know. I'm just supposed to drop off the horse."

"You're in a world of shit, then, aren't you?"

"I guess."

"Well, you can use my phone until you find someone," the Indian said. "And my name ain't Pinto, it's Mike, and that over there is Dallas."

I told them my name.

"Maybe we should go get his truck and bring it back here," Dallas said and looked at me. "What's wrong with it again?"

"It's the clutch. We'll go after this game," Mike said. He took a beer off the table, drank it, then threw the can towards a big trash basket in the kitchen.

"How many is that?"

"Seven," Mike said.

They kept playing the game. I asked them if it was alright if I got a glass of water and Mike said it would be and I went into the kitchen. All the glasses were dirty so I washed one out and drank as much water as I could. They weren't able to see me from there, and on the counter near me was a loaf of bread and it was open. While they were playing I began shoving bread into my mouth. I ate three pieces that way, then washed it down with more water. I went back to the living room where they were.

"You can try the phone again if you want," Mike said.

I picked up the phone and dialed the same number and acted like someone answered. I explained about the truck and I asked Mike where we were and the phone number and then I talked a bit longer and hung up.

"Is someone coming to get you?"

"Yeah," I said. "They'll be here tonight or tomorrow morning early."

"You can stay here if you want," Mike said. "Dallas's best cooking is worse than an MRE, but you can stay the night."

Dallas busted out laughing. The video game was one where they were both soldiers working together to kill aliens. The characters had guns and walked through dark corridors and shafts and hallways and aliens would pop out and try to kill them. They played game after game and drank beer and smoked cigarettes. After a while I went outside and checked on Pete. He was in the shade under a shelter that came off the barn. I looked at the metal tub and could tell he'd drunk quite a bit. I sat down on an old milk crate next to him.

It was hot out. There wasn't a cloud in the sky and the sun was still strong. Mike had said it was past ninety degrees and I could tell Pete was tired. I leaned against the barn and fell asleep.

When I woke Mike and Dallas were standing next to the horse. Mike had on black army boots. They were still both in shorts and wore no shirts, and I stood up and went over to them. Mike took the lead rope and threw it around Pete's neck and tied it to the other side.

"This is how you make a hackamore," Mike said. He had a cigarette in his mouth. Dallas was standing behind him holding two beers. "It's how you turn a lead rope into reins."

"How you know all this shit, Pinto?" Dallas said.

They were both pretty drunk.

"My folks had ten horses and two hundred head of cattle," Mike said. "My grandfather, the one who gave me this place, had five. I used to spend a lot of time fucking around with horses."

He walked Pete out into the sun and grabbed a bunch of his mane and tried to get on bareback. Pete was uneasy and scooted out from under him. Mike took one rein and pulled it hard to the left and jumped up. When he got on you could tell Pete was spooked. Mike moved him around in circles until Pete finally stopped and was still.

Mike walked him around a bit, then kicked him hard with his feet and Pete took off. He ran him, then stopped him and got Pete to go in circles again.

He did this for a while, then came up to us.

"He's hardly broke," Mike said.

"He's only ever been a race horse," I said.

"No shit. So he's got speed?"

"Some," I said. "But his feet have a disease. He's sick."

"I looked at his legs and his hooves. I didn't see anything. Somebody probably sold you a bunch of shit."

Dallas laughed.

Pete started moving around nervously. Mike yelled at

him and his face got serious. He pulled as hard as he could on the right rein until Pete was going in small circles and finally stopped moving.

"If I ran him up that hill a couple times he'd calm his ass right down," Mike said, then rode him around the pen some more. A couple times Pete acted worried, and when that happened Mike would be rough with him until he'd calm down.

I didn't have the guts to stop him. I just stood there and watched.

Then Mike got off. He handed me the reins and took a beer from Dallas and drank from it.

"Why don't you get on?"

"I've never ridden a horse," I told them.

"You've never ridden a horse?"

"No," I said.

"Get on," Mike said. "I'll show you what to do."

He brought over the milk crate and told me to stand on it. He brought Pete around. He handed me the reins and I grabbed them and a handful of mane and got on the way Mike told me to and then I rode him around the pen for a while. Mike and Dallas were talking and laughing. I kept going in circles and tried to say things to Pete to ease his mind and he seemed alright but he held his neck stiff and walked slowly, with short steps.

Mike came over to us and moved right beside me and hit Pete hard on the ass. Pete took off like a shot. I held on to the mane the best I could but I fell off and hit the ground so hard it knocked the wind out of me.

I lay there and tried to catch my breath. Dallas and Mike

came over and once they saw I was alright they couldn't stop laughing.

"I was just joking around," Mike said. "That horse of yours is a spooky fucker. I didn't think he'd take off that hard. Just remember, if a horse bolts on you, you have to get him to stop or you have to jump off. But you got to do something, alright?"

I was still lying on the ground. I couldn't breathe, then finally my air came back and I nodded. My nose started to bleed and my ribs hurt. Mike gave me his hand. I took it and he pulled me up.

18

My right leg hurt when I stood on it but when I walked around it got better and it got easier to breathe. Pete moved back underneath the shelter in the shade. Mike and Dallas went back into the trailer. I got the milk crate and set it by Pete, sat on it, and apologized to him and tried not to cry, but after a while I did.

My thoughts got to me again. I was a horrible person, and I had gotten us in a huge mess. I felt as lost and lonely as I ever had and I couldn't stop worrying about Pete. I sat out there and I didn't know what to do. Then Mike and Dallas came from the trailer and walked over to me. They were both wearing shirts now and had sunglasses on and Dallas carried a twelve pack of beer.

"We're going to get you a bale of hay," Mike said. "You can come along if you want."

I stood up and followed them to their car. I got in the backseat and Mike lit a cigarette and started the engine. Dallas gave him a beer. He opened it, took a drink from the can, then drove us out to the main road. Dallas turned the stereo on and he played it so loud you couldn't hear anything. The windows were rolled down and there was a breeze and the day was almost over.

We drove for a while on a paved road, then we came to a yellow house set back on a dirt drive and we drove down it and parked in front of a barn. Next to us was a rusted-out pickup truck and a horse trailer and a tractor and farm gear. The barn was twice the size of the house. It was yellow too but the paint was coming off and the whole place seemed like it was leaning.

Mike finished his beer and cut the engine. He lit another cigarette, then we all got out, walked up to the house, and he knocked on the door.

An old man answered.

"Hey, Mr. Kendall."

"Is that you, Mike?"

"It is," Mike said and he introduced Dallas and me. Then the old man opened the door and led us through the house and out the back door to where there was a deck. He had the radio going and was drinking a can of soda and we all sat out there on folding chairs. His eyes were gray and he wore glasses and his hands were so bent with arthritis that he had a hard time holding the soda can.

"Can I offer you a beer, Mr. Kendall?" Mike asked.

"It's too early for me but I don't care what anyone else does."

Dallas grabbed the twelve pack at his feet and took out two.

"So you're back?"

"We have two more weeks until we have to report again."

"You boys are doing us a good service."

Mike lit another cigarette.

"We're doing something over there alright."

Dallas laughed at that. Then Mike told us about a friend of theirs who lost both his legs and got a concussion so bad he can't talk. He listed a few guys he knew who were killed over there. Then he told us about having to shoot a guy in the head. How the man's head just blew off but his body stood there for a time. And then he talked about a morning they saw a truck in front of them blow up and then about a guy he knew that blew a girl in half. She was really cut in two parts. He split her at her belly.

"It's a real fucking mess over there," Mike said finally, and no one said anything for a while after that. The sun was going down over the hills. The radio played the news and then the farm reports.

"When you come back, are you going to take over your granddad's place?" the old man asked.

"I don't know," he said. "We just had a few weeks off and I wanted to show Dallas. After I get back I don't know what I'm gonna do."

The old man took out a short cigar from his pocket and lit it.

"I came across a mom coyote and her cubs last week. They were eating on something. There must have been seven of them. They were down in the gully. I had my rifle. I hit the first few while they were eating and a few others as they tried to run up the gully hill and escape."

"Did you get them all?" Dallas asked.

"I think so," the old man said.

Dallas laughed at that, but Mike didn't even smile. He just looked at the hills and seemed tired.

The old man got up.

"Can you stay for dinner?"

"Sure," Mike said. "If you don't mind."

"It's sloppy joe night. Let me just make sure Laurie has enough."

The old man went inside and Mike leaned over to Dallas and said something I couldn't make out and they both busted out laughing.

When dinner was ready we sat in the kitchen. A huge woman stood there cooking. She was so big she used a walker to get around, but she looked young and he introduced us to her as his granddaughter. She was the largest woman I'd ever seen. You could tell it was hard for her to just walk, you could hear it in her struggle to breathe. It was like someone had blown up her body with air.

Her red hair came down to her shoulders and her face was alright. She wasn't pretty but she wasn't the other way either. We all sat around the table while she worked, and no one said anything to her and she hardly spoke at all. Dallas and Mike kept drinking beer and then the old man started drinking them too.

Dinner was sloppy joes with green beans, and there were two bags of potato chips on the table. She set down a plate in front of me and asked me if I wanted a soda. I nodded and she came back with two.

"Just in case you're really thirsty," she said and then she sat down at the end of the table. Everyone was eating and the food was good. She opened a can of soda for herself and when she did her grandfather stopped eating and wiped his mouth with a paper towel.

"Mike, she won't even drink diet soda. She won't even do that to help herself."

Mike looked at the old man and nodded.

"I don't understand it. I don't understand how a person

166

can get like she is."

The woman just sat there and ate. She had the same amount as us, she didn't have any more.

"If I were as big as a semi I'd try something. I've caught her in her room eating a whole bag of Snickers bars."

"I was not," she said. "You know that's not true." She had a nice voice. It was soft and warm. "You shouldn't drink beer. You get ugly when you drink beer."

The old man looked at her and we kept eating. When she got up to get us seconds the old man started talking about her even though she was just a few feet away.

"When she came to live here she was getting big and now she's so big she can't go up the stairs. I had to put in a shower downstairs because she can't take a bath 'cause she can't fit in the tub. It cost me three hundred dollars to do that. Look at her. She won't eat much around me, but God knows when I'm asleep she puts on the feed bag."

Mike and Dallas and I just sat there and listened. Then Mike set down his fork and said, "You're lucky you got someone looking after you, Mr. Kendall."

The old man just looked at Mike, but Mike looked right back, then smiled and drank from his beer. Laurie set down a plate with extra sloppy joes on it.

"Do you boys need any more beer?" the old man asked.

Both Dallas and Mike nodded and the woman went over to the fridge and brought back two. We all kept eating until the food was gone, then I helped clear the table and Laurie did the dishes. Mr. Kendall brought out a bottle of whiskey and they all went back out to the porch.

"Do you want me to dry?" I asked her.

"If you want," she said and handed me a towel that was hanging from a hook on the wall. "What are you doing with Mike?"

"My truck broke down. I'm waiting for my ride. I just met Mike today."

"He's alright, I guess," she said. "Do you like ice cream?"

"Sure," I said, and when we'd finished cleaning up she made us two bowls of vanilla ice cream with chocolate sauce and we went into the living room and watched TV. There was a movie on and we watched it until it was over, then we found another one.

"It's going to take him a week to recover from tonight," she said.

"Who?" I asked her.

"My grandfather. He's not supposed to drink anymore. He's an asshole when he drinks. It's why no one ever comes here."

We were silent for a long time.

"Can I ask you a question?"

"Okay," she said.

"Why do you stay here? He seems really mean."

"I don't know where else to go," she said, and then she reached over to the end table and opened a drawer and took a pack of Werther's candy and gave me one. Our legs touched as we sat next to each other on the small couch and it felt good that they were. Then Mike came in and got me and told me we were leaving. I told the woman goodbye and we went outside. Mike started the car and we drove down the side of their property to a hay shelter. He got out and climbed up a huge stack of hay and threw a bale down.

He put it on top of the car and we started driving again.

They were both so drunk they could hardly talk. Dallas had the music loud and we drove out the driveway onto the paved road and went fifteen miles an hour along it. We were halfway to the trailer when Dallas opened the door, leaned out, and puked.

"Don't get any on my car," Mike said and stopped. He laughed and got out of the car. I got out, too.

"You should stop puking and look at these stars," Mike said and lit another cigarette.

"I hate sloppy joes," Dallas said. He sat up, wiped his face with his shirt, and got out of the car. "I've always hated them."

They both sat on the hood and Mike started talking about the army but I couldn't understand what he was saying. After a while we drove back. Mike had to help Dallas out of the car because he was so drunk and he practically carried him into the trailer.

I pushed the bale off the roof and carried it over to Pete. I cut the bale strings and gave him three flakes and filled his water.

"I like you a lot, Pete," I told him. "I'm sorry about what happened today. I'll stand up for you better next time." I pet him, then went inside.

The TV was going but they weren't in the living room. I walked down the hall towards the bedrooms and saw Dallas face down on a twin bed, passed out. He lay there on the bed snoring. I called out to Mike but when I went back to his room he was passed out with headphones on and I could hear music coming from them.

I went into the bathroom and locked the door. I started the shower and took off my clothes and got in. I stayed there for a long time. When I got out I used a towel that was on the floor, then I looked through the medicine cabinet and found a tube of toothpaste and I put some on my finger and tried to brush my teeth.

When I went back out they were both still asleep. I went into the kitchen and looked through the cupboards. I found two cans of stew, a can of soup, and a couple cans of corn and I put them in a plastic sack. There were two empty gallon jugs and I filled both those with water, then I found a piece of paper and I wrote them a note. I thanked them and told them I'd pay them back for the canned food and the hay. I put the note on the counter and left.

Pete was still eating when I went to him and I waited until he finished.

The night was full of stars and it wasn't cold. I sat down in the dirt and leaned against the barn and fell asleep. When I woke it was still dark and Pete was just standing there. I got up and put as much hay as I could in the duffel, then took a rope and tied one end around a jug of water and the other end around the other jug. I put the halter on him and opened the gate. I put my sleeping bag over my shoulder and carried the duffel and the plastic sack of canned food and the water and led Pete out of the pen and onto the road.

19

When it got light we moved off the road and began following it from a distance as we had before. We kept walking
and the landscape stayed the same, just sagebrush and
rock and dirt and desert. We went through gullies and
across long straight stretches of nothing.

We came to a fence. It was barbed wire running north and
south and it blocked us from going east. I took us south, farther away from the highway, and we went for miles until there
was a break and we went across there. I couldn't see the
highway anymore and I couldn't hear it. Pete took shorter
steps and I knew the rocks hurt his feet. At one point I
stopped and looked at his shoes and saw he was missing his
hind right. I didn't know what to do so we just kept going. I
came to a dirt road. We followed it for hours but I never once
heard the sound of cars or trucks and I didn't see any house
or building either. Above us there were no clouds and it was
really hot. There were no trees or shade anywhere.

Late in the afternoon we stopped to rest. I put out a flake
of hay for Pete and while he ate I drank as much water as I
could, then I cut the top off the plastic jug and held it in
front of him. He didn't drink from it for a while, then he
finally did. I sat down on the road and opened a can of stew
and ate.

We started walking again but I was tired and sunburned.
I saw a ranch in the distance, maybe a mile away. It was

dusk by then so I unrolled the sleeping bag and sat down. I took the extra rope and tied it to Pete's lead so he'd have more room to move around, then I tied the end to my ankle and held on to the rope with my hand and night came.

We heard coyotes whine and it seemed like an ocean of them surrounding us. A wind picked up and it got cold. I put on my coat and fell asleep. In the middle of the night Pete pulled away from me and the rope around my ankle tugged and I woke up. I untied the rope and went to him and pet him and we stood in darkness and you could tell he was worried. I told him what a good horse he was, and how fast he was. I told him we'd find a place where both of us could stay for a long time. A place where his feet would get fixed, a place where there was a lot of food.

I kept talking to him. I told him about a time my dad and me and some friends of his spent a weekend at a cabin in the snow, and I told him about school, about teachers I had. About changing schools four times. About girls I saw and sat next to, about friends I had. I liked the school part of school alright, but I barely got good enough grades to play sports. I told him about getting free lunch and being embarrassed by it, and running to the cafeteria so I could eat before anyone I knew saw. Then I told him about my mother. About how I used to have a picture of her but that I threw it away one night when I was mad and how I tried never to think about her.

Her name was Nancy and she was my dad's girlfriend when they worked together at a grocery store. She had black hair and was tall and was ten years older than him. My dad broke up with her but after a while they got back together and he got her pregnant. Then they broke up again. When I was born I stayed with her but when I was a year old she left me with him for a week and never came back. He thought she might have moved to North Dakota because that was where she was from but he didn't know. He always said he wasn't sure why she left, but said he was glad she did. When I was younger I used to ask him about her all the time, but he'd never say anything at all. Then one night when he was drunk he told me she was the moodiest person he'd ever met. He said there were times when she'd walk in the door and you'd swear she was a different person. Even the way she talked was different. He said she could be mean one hour and then nice the next, then mean again. She could spend days on the edge of both at the same time.

"I ain't gonna lie to you," he said. "She ain't called or sent a card but I know deep down she loves you. She really does. She's just fucked-up in the head and likes to party too much. I know it's hard to hear, but its a good thing she's gone. I ain't shit but I like being here with you."

When it was light enough to walk I rolled up my sleeping bag and gave Pete the last of the hay from the duffel. I watched him eat and while he did I drank water and the last can of stew.

When I saw the ranch again in the morning light I could see it was a pretty big operation. Trucks and cars were parked in front of the house and there were two barns to the side of it and a huge hay field behind it. A tractor was heading down a dirt road. There were too many people and it made me nervous so I headed further south, where I could see nothing but more hills and more sagebrush. I figured I'd go around the ranch and then make my way back near the highway.

The day went slow and was hotter than it had been. A couple times I got so tired that I wanted to sit down in the sun but I knew if I did I'd be ruined. We came to a steep gully and it took us a long time to get down it. I moved Pete as slow as I could because there were so many rocks, but he ran into me and I fell and I let go of the lead rope. I wasn't hurt or anything and he just moved ahead of me and made it to the bottom. I thought he might run off but he didn't, he just stopped.

We came to a small muddy creek. The water moved slow and was brown. It was maybe three feet wide and there were a handful of aspen trees that lined it. Pete ate grass from the small patches that lined the banks. I decided we'd rest there. I tied his lead to the base of the largest tree and laid out my sleeping bag in the shade and sat on it. I ate a can of soup, then drank the brown muddy water from the creek and rested. When I woke it was late afternoon. Pete was just standing there. He had sagebrush stuck to his tail and he was dusty. Every once in a while he'd stomp or move his tail to chase away a fly but other than that it looked like he was sleeping. I got up and went to him. I got the brush off his tail and pet him, then took off my shoes and set my feet in the water.

"This ain't so bad," I said to Pete. "If there was enough food we could probably stay here all summer." I lay back and looked up at the sky. There were clouds but none of them blocked out the sun.

"I just have to figure out how to make us money. I'll make sure you're alright so don't worry about that. We're a family now. And if I can't find my aunt I'll get a job at a place where you and me can live until we figure something else out. Last night I started dreaming that I made a ton of money and one day Del came by our place looking for a job. 'Well, Del,' I said to him as I sat behind a huge desk. 'If you weren't such an asshole I might give you a try. If you weren't such a mean pervert cocksucker I'd at least lend you a twenty. But let me talk to my partner, maybe he'll help you out.' Then you'd come in and Del's eyes would get huge with worry and he'd start shaking, he'd be scared out of his skin. He'd be sweating bullets and then you'd push him outside and he'd start screaming and then he'd get hit by a huge Greyhound bus!"

I started laughing at that, but Pete just stood there dozing in the heat. Only his tail moved as it worked against the flies.

When night neared I got hungry again and ate a can of corn, then I got inside my sleeping bag. I lay awake for hours. It was the first night I was really scared. I could hear coyotes yelping and they seemed right next to us and you could tell it was making Pete uneasy, too. Then it got windy and the leaves on the trees shook. It sounded like someone was walking towards us and I couldn't sleep. It was only with daylight finally approaching that I conked out.

I woke hours later from a nightmare. I was in a restaurant and the Samoan was there. My dad had gone to use the restroom and the Samoan came in and sat at a table and stared at me. You could tell he was angry, it was boiling over in him. He began hitting the table, almost breaking it. I thought that at any moment he'd come and attack me but he didn't, he just waited. I couldn't leave, it was like I was glued to my seat. Then my dad came back and I tried to warn him but I couldn't say anything. I tried and tried but no words came out. Then the Samoan jumped up out of his chair and ran as hard as he could and tackled my dad and strangled him to death. He had his big hands around my dad's throat and my dad's face turned red and then purple and he looked at me, he looked at me like it was my fault.

When I opened my eyes I was sweating and the sun was over me. I moved to the shade of the trees and I sat there for a long time and tried to clear my head. Then I rolled the sleeping bag up, filled the jug with water from the creek, ate my last can of corn, and we left. We followed the creek and I hoped we'd find bits of grass he could eat and for a while there was some, then the creek became mud and then it disappeared altogether. We kept walking. It got so hot out that I took off my pants and walked in my underwear and by the late afternoon we'd finished all the water.

We went up one ridge and then down another. We didn't stop for a long time. Then I saw a series of ranches and houses and fences. There was a paved road. I put my pants back on and we waited until past dusk, then walked down the ridge and towards the people.

It was completely dark when we made it to the paved street and we walked on it for a long while. Seven or eight different ranches and houses passed before us but we didn't see anyone and we kept going. We came to a hay field, I could smell it, and we walked along it until we came to a rusted-out old gate. It was tied with wire but I opened it and Pete and I went through it and out onto the field. I took us as far from the road as I could and stopped and Pete ate.

I laid the sleeping bag down and the moon was out and gave off enough light that I could watch Pete eat. I extended the lead rope again and tied it to my ankle and lay down. I was tired and thirsty and I fell asleep. Pete moved throughout the night and the rope pulled on my ankle, but I was so tired I just moved the sleeping bag closer to him and lay back down.

I woke the next morning to a Mexican shaking me with his foot. He was standing over me. He was old, in his fifties or more. He was short and wore a baseball hat and had on a stained long-sleeve dress shirt and jeans.

"*Hola*," the man said.

"Hello," I said and looked up at him.

"*¿Es tuyo ese caballo?*" he said.

"What?"

"You horse?" he said and his accent was really thick.

"No," I said and stood up. I looked around the field but there was no one else there, just a truck parked alongside the road near the gate.

He looked at the rope tied from Pete to my ankle.

"*Eso es muy peligroso*," he said and shook his head. "*No es una buena idea.*"

I bent down and untied the rope. He took it from the ground, looped it, and held it. He ran his hands along Pete's back.

"*¿De quién es el caballo?*"

I shrugged my shoulders.

"Who own him?"

"No one," I said. "He's his own horse."

"His own horse?"

"Yeah," I said.

The man laughed out loud. He kept petting Pete and said things to him in Mexican.

"*¿Eres un fugitivo?*"

"What?"

"Runaway?"

"No," I said.

"Where are you from?"

"Portland."

"Portland?"

"Yes."

The man laughed, then shook his head.

"Far."

I nodded.

"Where going?"

"Wyoming."

"Wyoming?"

I nodded again.

"Walking?"

"I guess," I said. "I don't know."

"Guillermo," he said and put out his hand.

"Charley," I told him.

"*¿Tienes hambre?*"

"What?"

"Hungry?" he said and patted his stomach.

I nodded.

"Come with me," he said and pointed to my sleeping bag. I went over to it, rolled it up, and followed him.

We walked to the side of the road where his pickup sat parked.

He tied Pete to a fence post, then went to his truck and came back with a cup of coffee and a McDonald's bag. He opened the tailgate, sat down on it, and told me to come over. He tried to hand me an Egg McMuffin.

"I don't have any money," I said.

"*¿No tienes dinero?*"

"No," I told him.

He shook his head.

"*Estás loco,*" he said and put the sandwich in my hands.

I took it and ate it while he drank coffee. When I finished he handed me another one.

I shook my head but he put it in front of me again.

"It's your breakfast, isn't it?" I said.

He pointed to his bulging belly and laughed, so I took it. When I was done he stood up. He finished his coffee and threw the empty cup in the bed of the truck and shut the tailgate. He reached into his back pocket and took ten dollars from his wallet and handed it to me.

"No," I said.

"Careful where you sleep. You're have a hard time."

"If you send me your address I'll mail it back to you when I can."

"No," he said and waved me off trying to give it back. I put the money in my pants pocket and we shook hands.

"*Puede que sea su propio caballo, pero éste es un mundo de hombres. Ten cuidado con él.*"

I shrugged my shoulders.

"Wyoming is far," he said, then shook his head and smiled. "Good luck."

"Thank you," I said and smiled back to him.

Then he got into his truck and drove off and I never saw him again.

We walked down the road and there wasn't a cloud anywhere and the heat hadn't set in. Pete and I were both full and for the first time I felt that we weren't cursed.

"Maybe this is the start of a lucky run," I told him. His hooves clanked next to me on the pavement. "When we get a dog, maybe we'll name him Guillermo, alright?"

Pete just kept walking.

"Alright," I said and pet him. "I'm glad you agree."

20

We walked along the paved road for hours and we couldn't get off because every property was lined with barbed-wire fences. Cars slowed when they saw us, but not one stopped or rolled down their window and said anything. The day went along and we kept going, and it was alright except we had no water and my stomach was beginning to hurt because of it. We went up a long hill and came down the other side and saw a house set off the road. It wasn't a ranch or a big property like the others we passed, it was just an old white house with a separate garage and a yard that had a few trees. It was the first place I'd seen where no cars were parked so I walked towards it.

We went up the drive and I tied Pete to the chain-link fence that surrounded the yard and I knocked on the front door. I stood there for a while but no one answered. I walked around the property and found an old plastic bucket behind the garage. I took it to the backyard where there was a hose and washed it out and filled it. I drank as much water as I could, then carried the bucket back to Pete and set it down for him to drink.

I sat down on the ground and looked at the map and my heart sank when I saw how far we still had to walk to get to Wyoming. I knew then that I'd probably have to steal a truck and trailer to get there.

Pete drank until the bucket was empty. I went back and filled it again, then left him and looked for an open window on the house and found one. It had a screen, and I tried not to break it, but I did. I left it on the ground outside, climbed in, and stepped down into the kitchen.

It was an old person's house. There was a quilt hanging on the wall and dozens of pictures of families and kids. The place was clean and there was a TV and a couch, a couple of easy chairs and a fireplace. In the cupboards I found a row of canned food. I took two black beans, one green beans, one vegetable soup, and a can of tuna fish. In a drawer there were dozens of plastic sacks and I took one and put the cans in there. I looked in the fridge and took a couple cans of soda and crawled back outside. I took the broken screen and hopped over the chain-link and walked a long way from the house and put dirt and rocks over it to hide it and walked back to the house.

Pete just stood there half asleep and the bucket was nearly empty. I dumped out the last of the water and set it back where I found it. I drank as much water as I could out of the hose and we left.

We walked by a hay field that was fenced off but there was grass growing under the barbed wire and near the road. I stopped, sat down, and let Pete eat there for a long time.

"Maybe we'll find a place with a pool," I said. "And maybe the guy that owns it is a vet and he's got a nice wife who is a good cook. The vet is so busy he doesn't have time to work on his place so he hires you and me. And then the woman makes me go to school and the vet fixes your feet and they let me live in a trailer near their house. The trailer's really nice and it has its own bathroom and there's cable TV. And they have a fridge that's always full of food."

Pete looked up as a truck drove past us on the road. He startled at the sound, but then he calmed back down and started eating again. His black coat was full of dust and it was fading brown from the sun. It was no longer shiny. Every once in a while he'd snort or look around, but really all he was interested in was the grass. I looked in the plastic sack and took out a can of black beans, opened it, and began eating them.

"And the vet has a huge hay field and he lets you eat on it all the time and their pool has a slide and the bed-in trailer has an electric blanket and the barn you sleep in has a stereo in it and there's always new dogs and horses there trying to heal up. And on Fridays they have movie night. We all sit out there and watch movies in the barn."

We started walking again. As dusk fell we came to more houses and ranches. It felt like we were getting near a town. I knew I should get us off the road, but everywhere was fenced. I could find no open land so we just kept walking and it grew dark. The cars that passed seemed to be going faster and their lights would shine bright on us making Pete uneasy.

Not much later I heard the sound of motorcycle engines. I looked all over but I couldn't see where they were coming from. It was a sea of noise. Pete got worried. He was pacing back and forth and it was hard to hold him. I tried to calm him, but he didn't even notice me. He pulled back and I almost lost the lead rope. The engines grew even louder, but even so I couldn't see anything. Then behind us suddenly was a group of dirt-bike motorcycles.

I held on to Pete the best I could but he reared up and spooked and tried to take off and I fell down. I dropped the cans of food on the pavement. I dropped the duffel bag. He was dragging me and I tried to hang on but in the end I let go and he sprinted off down the road. The people on the dirt bikes passed on the opposite shoulder. I tried to yell at them to stop but they couldn't hear me.

I got up and ran after Pete. The dirt bikes turned off on a side road and Pete was fifty yards away sprinting in a panic down the street. The road went up a hill and he kept going and as he neared the top of it I saw a truck's headlights heading towards him. It was a pickup truck. I screamed out his name, but he didn't hear me, and they crashed into each other.

The truck stopped and Pete was knocked over, and he was trying to get up. His front leg was broken. It hung on by skin and swung in the wrong direction. Pete was frantic. He got up once for a moment, then he fell back onto the pavement.

When I got to him he was still alive and breathing. There was blood all over him and the ground. You could hear him crying out. I got down on my knees and pet his neck. I began crying. The truck headlights reflected off his eye. He tried to raise his head and move his legs but couldn't.

An old lady got out of the pickup truck that hit him. She was saying something but I couldn't hear what. Pete tried to move and you could tell it hurt him to do so, and then all of a sudden he just stopped moving. I put my arms around his neck. There was blood all over me and all over Pete.

"I'm sorry," I told him over and over. "I'm sorry."

I held on to him but he was just heat and blood and sweat.

"Don't hate me," I begged him. "Please don't hate me."

I looked up and the old-woman driver was standing next to me, crying.

21

A police car came. Its lights flashed in the darkness. An officer got out of the car and went to the old woman and asked her questions, then walked over to me.

"Are you alright?" he asked.

He had a flashlight and he was shining it on me and Pete.

"Are you okay?"

I shook my head.

"Are you hurt?"

I shook my head.

"Is this your horse?"

"No," I said barely. "He's his own horse."

The policeman went back to the old woman and talked to her and she went to her truck and started it. It took a while but she got it going. One of her headlights was out, her hood was crushed, and her windshield was cracked all over. The engine didn't sound right, but she moved it to the side of the road. The officer used his radio and called for a tow truck, then told them about Pete and he spoke on the radio asking for a tractor and a flatbed truck. He came over to me.

"Can you stand up?" he asked. "Can you walk over to the car?"

"I can't leave Pete," I said.

"Pete's the horse?"

I nodded.

"Where do you live?"

"I don't know."

"Where's your family?"

"I don't know."

"What's your name?"

"Charley Thompson," I said.

"Where did you used to live?"

"Portland," I told him.

"Okay," he said, "Just stay here, alright?"

I nodded and he went back to his police car and he was there for a long time.

When he came back he shined the flashlight in my face.

"Did you steal a truck and a trailer? Did you steal this horse?"

I just held on to Pete. I didn't say anything.

"Are you that Charley Thompson?"

I nodded.

The flashlight was pointing right at my face and he wouldn't take it away.

"I didn't mean to," I said. "Del was going to send him to Mexico. I know he was."

"Del's the owner of the horse?"

"Yeah."

"Where were you heading?"

"Wyoming."

"What's in Wyoming?"

"My aunt," I said and started crying.

"So you're a runaway?"

"No," I told him.

"Where are your parents?"

"I don't know," I said.

The officer looked at me for a while. He wasn't mad, he had a kind voice. "We'll take you in and get you cleaned up. We'll figure out what's going on. Okay?"

"Okay," I said.

Pete's head was lying on the asphalt. His tongue was hanging out. There was blood everywhere and you could see his broken leg bent up towards his neck.

I looked up at the old lady. She stood there on the side of the road looking at me. She was still crying. I saw the officer go back to his patrol car and open the trunk and when he did I just got up and started running down the road. I could hear the officer yell but I couldn't make out what he said. I saw a field and went through a barbed-wire fence and ran as hard as I could into the darkness.

When that field ended I went through another barbed-wire fence and into sagebrush. The moon was half full and there was enough light for me to keep going. Every once in a while I'd look around, but I didn't see any lights shining towards me; no one was following me.

I walked for hours. I could see house lights in the distance and they kept getting further from me. I walked until I got so tired that I just sat down on the dirt. I could hear coyotes cry and once in a while I'd hear other things, rustling or movement. But I didn't care. I just sat there, then I lay down and closed my eyes.

When I woke the next morning the sun was over me and I was sweating. My clothes were covered in dried blood and dirt. My arms were painted in it and I felt my hair and it was in there too.

In the daylight I could see no buildings or anything,

only sagebrush and hills. I took the Polaroid of my aunt and me from my pocket. It had a new tear in it and was beginning to wear out. I stared at it and my thoughts were black. Because of me, Pete was dead. I took him when I didn't have a plan and I didn't even know where my aunt lived or if she was still alive. And if she was, maybe she wouldn't want me. The images of him wouldn't stop and I hated myself more than I ever had. I looked at the picture and I almost tore it up but I couldn't, I just couldn't. I put it back in my pants pocket and stood up. I picked a direction and began walking.

I walked up and down hills and through miles of brush until I came to a green trailer home. There were no cars parked in front of it, there was nothing else around it except a dried-out lawn, a barbecue, and a metal shed.

I stood by the front door and listened but I couldn't hear anything. I knocked on it but no one answered. It was locked. I checked all the windows and found one open. I moved an old metal burn drum that was in the shed and set it underneath the window sill, then I got up on it and crawled through the window into a bedroom.

There was a double bed and a TV and a dresser. There were clothes all over the floor and there was nothing on the walls. The bed was unmade and near it on a night stand was an ashtray full of cigarette butts. I walked down a hall. I passed a laundry room and another room that was empty. I came to the living room that had a TV sitting on an entertainment center. There was a couch and an easy chair. There were beer cans and another ashtray full of cigarette butts. There were fast-food bags and pizza cartons, but there were no pictures or paintings on the walls.

The kitchen didn't have a table to sit at. In the sink there were dirty knives and forks and spoons. I put my mouth underneath the kitchen faucet and drank as much water as I could. I looked in the cupboards but there was no food. Not even a can of soup. There were dishes and coffee cups and glasses, bowls, and a frying pan, but they all looked new and unused. Inside the refrigerator were three eggs in a carton behind cans of beer, and on another rack there was a half a loaf of white bread, a plastic bottle of pancake syrup, and some margarine.

I went back to the window and looked out, but I saw no one coming and I could barely see the main road it was so far away. I emptied out my pockets. I had the ten dollars from the Mexican, the Polaroid of my aunt and me, the map, a can opener, my pocket knife, and a lighter. I set it all on the kitchen counter. I took off my clothes and walked back to the laundry room and put them in the washer, added the soap, and started it. I moved the La-Z-Boy chair so it blocked the front door. I looked out the window again but it was still clear.

I went into the bathroom and started the shower and got in. I washed myself as fast as I could but it took a while. My hair had blood and dirt in it and my arms were the same but it was worse because they were sunburned and it hurt pretty bad to try and scrub them. It took a long time. I shut the water off every so often because I'd think I'd hear something, but when I shut it off all I could hear was the washing machine running so I'd start the water again. When I got out there was a towel on the floor. It was old and smelled but I dried myself with it and wrapped it around my waist.

There was toothpaste laying on the sink and I brushed my teeth with my finger then walked to the main room and looked out the window but there was nothing out there. I lit a burner on the stove and put the frying pan on it and put some margarine in it. I broke the eggs into a bowl and mixed them and soaked the bread in the eggs to make French toast. I used all the eggs and ate the rest of the bread while the French toast cooked. I ate five pieces covered in syrup while I looked out the window and watched the road. I put my clothes in the dryer and went back to the kitchen and did the dishes and put everything back to where it was.

I went outside and sat behind the metal shed in a lawn chair and watched the road. The sun was beating down but it felt alright because there was a breeze. When I heard the buzzer for the dryer I got up and went inside. My jeans looked alright but my shirt was ruined with bloodstains. I put on my underwear, socks, and pants. I put on my shoes. In the bedroom closet I found a light blue long-sleeve Western shirt, I put it on and it fit alright.

I went back out to the kitchen and grabbed my money and things and drank as much water as I could. I opened the windows to air things out and put the towel in the dryer, then set it back in the same place it was. I left the window in the bathroom open and hoped everything would dry by the time the man who lived there got home. I moved the La-Z-Boy back, shut the rest of the windows, and left.

22

I walked down the drive, then took another dirt road for a while before coming to a paved street. I went along it, trying to hitchhike. Car after car passed but no one stopped. It was hours before a car finally pulled over. It was an old-looking tan station wagon with fake wood panels. I ran up to the passenger side window and leaned down and looked in.

There was an old man inside and he was alone. He rolled down the window. When he spoke it wasn't through his mouth, he spoke through a box on his throat. I could understand him alright but the voice sounded like it was coming out of an old AM radio.

"Are you looking for a ride?" he asked. He had a gray moustache and was wearing a suit and had a gut that sat in his lap like a dog. He was bald on top and the hair on the sides was so black that I knew it was dyed. It was greased back and combed.

"Where are you going?" I asked him.

"Boise," his voice said. The box made me uneasy, but it was better than walking.

"Would it be alright if I rode with you until then?"

The man nodded and unlocked his door and I got in and he started driving. We drove for a while, then he put up the windows and started the A/C.

"What are you doing out here?"

"My car broke down," I said.

"I didn't see a car back there."

"It's farther back off the road."

"What happened?"

"The clutch went out."

"Where are you heading?"

"Wyoming," I told him.

We sat there quiet for a long time after that, then he said, "Do you smoke?"

"No," I told him.

"I smoked three packs a day. That's sixty cigarettes."

I nodded. I looked out the window at the houses and ranches we were passing.

"Did you hear me?"

"Yeah," I said. I looked over at him.

"I'm just telling you not to smoke."

"Okay," I said.

"There's a pack of cigarettes on my dash. Do you see them?"

"Yeah," I said.

"They're there as temptation. Man is ruled by temptation. Do you understand that?"

I nodded. He looked over at me.

"Temptation leads to excess and excess leads to talking through a box. Do you understand that?"

"I think so," I said and then he quit talking again. We drove on and I saw a sign that said we were entering Idaho. We drove for a while longer, then we got on the interstate.

"Do you like the world as it is today?"

"I don't know," I said.

"You don't know if you like the state of the world?" he

said and shook his head. "Do you like AIDS and murder and alcoholism and rape?"

"No."

"They're the standard bearers for the state of the modern world and you say you don't know if you like the state of the world. So tell me the truth, do you like the state of the world?"

"No," I said.

"Did you graduate from school?"

"No."

"Can you read?"

"Sure," I told him.

I tried not to look at the man, but you could smell him. He smelled like he hadn't changed his clothes in a long time.

"Do you believe in lying and cheating and gambling?"

"No," I said.

"Do you get drunk? Are you a druggie?"

"No."

"Wouldn't it be nice if you lived in a world where people didn't shove gallons of ice cream down their throats while other people in the world only have a handful of rice to eat all week?"

"Yeah," I said. "I guess."

"Yeah, I guess," he said and shook his head. "Do you think all these problems are just going to go away?"

"I don't know."

"You don't know?"

"No."

"I bet you watch five hours of TV a day."

"I don't have a TV anymore."

"TV leads to sloth. Laziness leads to temptation and temptation leads to excess."

I nodded and he quit talking again. We drove another hour in silence, and I could feel him want to talk but he didn't. Then he pulled off the interstate and drove us to a truck stop and pulled in front of a gas pump.

"How much money do you have?"

"Me?"

"I need money for gas."

I had ten dollars but I told him I didn't have anything.

"You're flat broke?"

"Yeah," I said.

"You still want a ride to Boise?"

I nodded.

The man reached into the backseat where a row of boxes sat and took out copies of a magazine called *The Watchtower*.

"Go up and give these to the people walking in and out of the restaurant. They're free, so don't charge anybody."

"What kind of magazine is it?"

"A good one," he said. "I got to take a leak, then I'll go around to the other entrance."

"How long are we going to be here?"

"Not long, they don't like us here."

He put them in my hand.

We got out of the car and both walked to the entrance. There was a row of newspapers for sale and he told me to stand near them. When people walked by I put the magazine out towards them, but nobody looked at them or even stopped.

The man went to the toilet, then went back to the car and took a stack of magazines and walked to the other entrance. I stood there for a long time and held them out. I thought about the man and the smell in the car and I set the magazines down on a newspaper box and went inside the truck stop.

There was an Arby's fast-food restaurant and I waited in line and ordered the 5 for 5 to go. Five sandwiches for five dollars. I went to the truck stop mini-mart and bought a gallon of water. I had a little over two dollars left.

I looked out the entrance where I was supposed to be and saw his car still sitting there empty. I walked near the other entrance and saw him standing alone holding a stack of the magazines. I went to the opposite side of the truck stop and left. I found a side road that ran near the freeway and took it.

I started eating the sandwiches while I walked. I kept going for almost an hour. I'd eaten three of the sandwiches when the station wagon pulled up alongside of me and stopped. He rolled down the passenger side window. I stopped and leaned down and looked in at the old man sitting in the driver's seat. He had an Arby's sack next to him and a soda between his legs.

"You do have money," he said in his box voice. You could tell he was mad, but his voice sounded the same, it didn't change. "I knew you did."

I didn't say anything. He took a drink off his soda and it took him a long time to do so.

"Did you find the magazines alright?"

He nodded.

"That was pretty low down of you. Did you give any away?" he asked.

"No," I said.

"How much money do you have left?"

"A little over two dollars."

"Give me the money and I'll drive you to Boise."

It was thirty miles to Boise so I reached in my pocket and gave him the two dollars.

"What about the change?"

I took that out and handed it to him and got back in the car. He rolled up the windows and started the air conditioner. He turned the car around and got us on the road back to the freeway. He didn't say anything for a time. He just ate and drove. Parts of his sandwich began falling down on his legs and stomach and you could tell it made him mad. When he was done he began feeling around his legs and stomach and on the seat for anything that fell. If he found something he'd put it in his mouth.

He turned on the radio and flipped through the stations but he never stayed on one long enough for you to hear it, then he shut it off again.

He took a long drink off his soda, then said, "Do you understand what human kindness is?"

"I'm not sure," I told him.

"Well, you didn't show any of it back there. I wasn't asking much. Just a little payment for the ride. Do you know how much gas costs?"

"Three dollars a gallon."

"That's right. That's a lot of money." He coughed and when he did it seemed like it really hurt him.

"Have you ever heard the story of the stranger?

"No," I said.

"Do you know anything?"

"I don't know."

"I don't know," the man said with his mechanical voice. He was agitated. He couldn't stop moving his hands around, he couldn't sit still. "You're a piece of work. A real piece of work. The stranger comes to a village. His clothes are threadbare, his eyes are sunken and lonely. His skin lays over his bones like a death sheet. He's dying of hunger. Of real hunger. A hunger that you wouldn't know anything about. A hunger that would kill you. The townspeople feed him. They heal his starved body. They clothe him, they put shoes on his feet. They heal his soul through kindness, they introduce him to the Lord. Time passes and the weather changes and it begins to rain. The rain won't stop and the river is about to flood the village. Everyone is in a panic, they are all going to be washed away, but the stranger tells the people not to worry. He cuts tributaries off the river to ease the pressure and the village is saved. They had never heard of such a thing. Without his help the village would have been swallowed in water. Crawdads would be sucking on dead baby's eyeballs. Virgin girls would be rammed into rocks and old men split in two by passing logs. Their guts spewed about like a drunken sailor's dinner on the sidewalk of porno alley. Do you understand what I'm saying?"

I didn't answer.

"Kindness breeds kindness. To get you must give."

He finished his soda, then looked in the rearview and threw it out the window.

197

"Why are you going to Boise?" he said.

"I don't know."

"You don't know?"

"No."

"You don't know much."

"No."

"Do you believe in God?"

"Me?"

"You're the only one here."

"I don't know."

"If you don't watch it all your 'I don't knows' will get you syphilis from one of your girlfriends."

"I don't have a girlfriend."

"You don't have a girlfriend?"

"No."

"What are you, some sort of pervert?"

"No."

"God punishes those who let the devil inside them. You have to fight it. You have to battle it. It's a struggle. But I guess you're not much of a fighter."

As I sat listening to him images of Pete began coming to me and they wouldn't stop. Pete's lying in the middle of the freeway and cars are rushing past him. He's too hurt to stand but he keeps trying and he's crying and scared. He's in horrible pain. He really wants to get somewhere safe but he isn't able to. I can see the fear in his eyes, I can see tears. Blood's everywhere and cars are missing him by inches and they're not even slowing down. I look in the cars and every driver and passenger is mad and yelling and spit's flying out of their mouths.

"I had a co-worker," the man said. "He had all the good accounts, but he was poking our only sales lady. They were both married to other people. They did it on company time. He banged her in motels and in cars and in alleys. They fornicated in the building where we all worked. I know they did. I almost caught them once. So one day I left an anonymous letter on the vice president's desk. I told him how to catch them. I told him how the salesman was using his expense account to pay for their motel rooms. I laid it all out for him. The vice president brought my co-worker in, and he confessed and was fired. The saleswoman was put on probation. When it was clear public knowledge I went to the vice president and told him I would be happy to look after the good accounts, the accounts that my co-worker had, that I was ready for the challenge. That I was the right man for the job. But in the end, when it was all settled, I was overlooked. He didn't give the accounts to me. He transferred Bob Harbuckle out of the Salt Lake City branch. Do you understand what I'm saying to you? Does it make sense?"

I nodded but he didn't see me.

"Do you know how to listen?"

"I heard you." In the distance I could see Boise. I could see high-rise buildings and miles of houses and stores beginning to appear.

"Do you have a learning disability?"

"No," I said.

"I'm talking about justice. Do you know what justice is?"

I nodded my head.

"I sweated and toiled for those dirty uncouth cocksuckers

199

and what do I get? I get transferred to Eastern Washington and three years later the branch is closed. And the bitch who spread her legs from here to Sacramento ends up running the Salt Lake City branch and now drives a brand-new Mercedes. Is that justice?"

I didn't say anything.

"Is it?"

"No, I guess not."

"Have you ever heard the story of the lost dolphin?"

"No," I said.

The man coughed and shook his head. "You're a tribute to our education system. A real champ. The dolphin was lost from his family during a big storm in the Pacific Ocean. He ends up alone two hundred miles away from anything he knows and he's got a broken fin. He keeps trying and going day after day and month after month. He's lonely, he's tired. He's physically tired but, worse than that, he's soul tired. He's tired in a way that would kill you if you felt it for thirty seconds. But he keeps going until he comes to a cave and in the cave is the devil. The devil is part man and part sea beast. He tells the dolphin that if he gives up he'll get to live forever in comfort. He'll be snorting lines of cocaine and frolicking with naked women and eating bonbons for breakfast. But to get all that he has to kill one fellow dolphin. The dolphin could be his family, it could be a stranger, he wouldn't know who it was until he did it. The dolphin is so beat up he can hardly move forward and his broken fin hurts, and the devil calls him and begs him towards the cave, towards the comfort."

The man left the freeway and kept talking about the dolphin. We came to a stoplight and while we waited for it to change I opened the car door and got out. I didn't say anything. I started walking down the shoulder of the road. I kept my head down and didn't look back. He honked his horn over and over. When the light changed he drove slowly past me and I looked at him. He had the passenger side window rolled down and was yelling at me but I couldn't hear him over the sound of the horn. Then he sped off and I made my own way into Boise.

23

I walked into downtown and spent the afternoon looking around. There were big buildings and shops and people all around. I still had two Arby's sandwiches and I ate one and saved the other. I went to the bus station and asked the counter lady how much a one-way ticket to Rock Springs, Wyoming was and she told me a hundred and thirty-eight dollars.

There was a university and a river that ran by it. People were swimming in the water and others were lying in the sun next to it. I walked across a bridge and there was a park on the other side and I went to it and sat down and rested by the river in a place where no one could see me. I sat there for hours and ate my last sandwich and I didn't leave until it was nearly dark.

I headed back downtown and went to a pizza parlor and stood in the video arcade. The whole place was crowded with families, and I saw a birthday party going on and I watched them as they ate. When they left they left half of a pizza. Before the busboy could get to it I went over and sat down. There was a full glass of Coke and I drank that and ate as much pizza as I could. Then I stacked the rest of the slices on a paper plate and left.

I went back to the park and hid by the river in a bunch of bushes. I used my lighter so I could find my way. Inside the bushes I found a small space and I sat there and it wasn't too cold. I ate the rest of the pizza and finally sometime during the night I fell asleep.

I woke up at dawn and it was cold. I sat there for a long time and I couldn't stop thinking about Pete, then I got up and crawled out of the bushes and went across a bridge to the college and went in and out of the buildings. I found a few places where I thought I could hide without getting caught and I found a bathroom that had a separate shower room. I washed my face in the sink and drank water until I couldn't drink any more.

I walked downtown again. There was a skate park and I sat down and watched kids skateboard. A girl was sitting near me doing the same thing. She was alone. She seemed younger than me but when we started talking she told me she was sixteen. Her name was Ruby and she wore all black and had a ring through her bottom lip. She said she was staying at the Cabana Motel with a woman named Sue and a man named Joe. She told me they were heading to Arizona where Joe knew someone who owned a hundred acres out in the desert.

She talked faster than anyone I'd ever met and she played with a rubber band while she talked. She hardly ever looked you in the eye. When the skateboarders left I showed her the river and where I slept. Afterwards we went to the same pizza parlor I went to the day before. She had four dollars so we played video games and then a family left most of a pizza and a pitcher of Coke sitting at their table so we sat down before the busboy came and started eating. It wasn't until we were almost done that the manager came out and gave us a hard time about it. He knew we didn't buy the pizza, because the place was pretty empty and I guess he'd served the family himself. He told us to leave and we got up and started going out when all of a sudden the girl turned around and told the guy off.

"You better watch it, you fat fucking pig," she screamed, "or I'm gonna come back and burn this place down."

He didn't say anything but you could tell he was beginning to get mad.

When we made it outside we ran down the street for awhile, then we stopped and she started laughing uncontrollably.

I wasn't sure what to think about her and I guess she could see that on my face.

"I'm not mean," she said, and suddenly she quit laughing. "I swear I'm not. I was just joking."

After that we went to a CD shop and a clothing store and then we went back to the river. When the sun started going down she said she had to go back to the motel, and said I could go with her.

The Cabana Motel was an old motor lodge set off from the street. The sign was a big hat with lights on it, and the building was white with red doors. Inside the room were two beds, a table with chairs, a dresser, and a television. There was a man sitting on the farthest bed from the door leaning against the headboard watching TV. The bathroom door was shut and you could hear the shower going.

"Where have you been?" the man said. He was older, maybe in his thirties, and he had a beard that came down to his chest and tattoos that ran up and down his arms. His hair was long and brown and he wore black pants and a black T-shirt that read "Biggs Brothers Chicken Wing Shack."

"Walking around," the girl said.

"We're leaving at six tomorrow."

"I know."

"I just don't want to spend half the day trying to get you up."

"I'll get up."

He gave her a half smile.

"Did you fix the truck?"

"I replaced the radiator, both the hoses, and the thermo-stat. We're pulling a lot of weight, though. We'll have to take it easy. So who's he?" the man said and pointed to me.

"His name's Charley."

"Joe," he said and put out his hand. I walked over to him and shook it. "You live around here?"

"He's heading to Wyoming," the girl said.

"What's in Wyoming?"

"I don't know."

"Are you staying at this motel?" he asked.

"He's sleeping by the river," the girl said.

"Boise has a river?"

"It's a big one," she added. "What are we doing for din-ner?"

"Sue wants Chinese," Joe said.

We sat down on the bed and watched TV. Then a naked woman came out of the bathroom. She was drying her hair with a towel when she looked over and saw me.

"Who's he?" she said. She didn't act embarrassed even

though she was completely naked. She was a large woman with black hair. She had big breasts and down between her legs she didn't have any hair. She had tattoos that covered her back and most of her stomach. She had them on her legs, too.

"His name's Charley," the girl said.

The woman said hello and turned around. There was a sink and a mirror set next to the bathroom and she stood there and looked at herself in the mirror, then went into a bag and took out a blow dryer and began drying her hair. The tattoo on her back was all black ink and there was a dragon and a skeleton that was swinging a sword and there was a naked woman looking at her reflection in a pool of water. After a while she turned off the hair dryer and put on black underwear and sat next to Joe on the bed. We all watched TV and then the woman got dressed.

"Let's go eat," she said.

"Can Charley come?" the girl asked.

"I'm not that hungry," I told her.

"Please," the girl said.

"He can come if he wants," Joe said to the girl and then he got up and put on his shoes and we all left and walked towards downtown. It was dusk and nice out and Ruby and I fell a half of a block behind them.

"I don't have any money," I told her.

"You already told me that," Ruby said and smiled. "But you don't need any money when Joe's around. Joe pays for everything."

We kept walking until we found a rundown-looking Chinese restaurant. We went inside and sat at a table and

Joe ordered food for everyone. Ruby and I each got a Coke and we sat there and no one said hardly anything at all. Once in a while Ruby would ask Joe questions about the truck or about how long it would take, or what it was like in Arizona or what he thought about Boise. The whole time she played with the same rubber band. Sue just sat there and smoked cigarettes, and it was like she was somewhere else. Then the food came and we all ate. When we were done Sue went to the bathroom and we all just sat there and the bill came and Joe asked me for ten dollars.

I looked at Ruby and she looked back at me.

Then he got up and went to the bathroom.

"I don't have any money," I said.

"Nothing?"

"No," I said. "I told you I didn't."

Then Sue came back and then Joe did.

"Joe," I told him. "I'm sorry, I don't have any money."

"You don't have any money?" he said and shook his head. "What did you think was going to happen?"

"I don't know," I said.

"You just thought I was going to pay?"

"I guess I just didn't think about it."

Sue laughed at that, then lit another cigarette.

"I could pay you back," I said.

"I bet," Sue said.

Joe shook his head. You could tell he was annoyed but he paid the bill. We left after that. Joe and Sue were in front and Ruby and I trailed behind them.

"I'm sorry," she said. "He usually always pays. I've never seen him do that."

"Is he your dad?"

"No," she said and shook her head. "I just met them a while ago."

"Where?"

"In Medford. That's where I'm from."

"That's in Oregon, right?"

"Yeah," the girl said.

"Are you going to get in trouble?"

"No," the girl said. "Joe loves me."

"Maybe I should go."

"Don't leave," she said, and then suddenly she stopped and looked at me. "Don't go, okay? Maybe you can come with us to Arizona."

"I don't know," I said, and then we began walking again. The sun had set and it was warm and the sky was clear and it was fading dark. When we got to the motel we all went inside and Joe turned on the TV and sat back just as he was before. Sue went into the bathroom again, then came out and sat next to him. We were all there for a while, then Ruby told them we were going to go to the pool and she went into the bathroom with her bag of clothes and came out wearing a black one-piece swimsuit and we left. We walked down to the pool and no one else was there so I stripped down to my underwear and got in with her. The water was warm and we swam around for a long time. When we got out we sat on the side with our feet in the water.

"Where's your family?" she said.

I told her about my dad and my mom and not being able to find my aunt.

"Maybe you should hire a private investigator," she said. She sounded excited.

"If I had the money, I would."

"Maybe Joe would pay for it," she said and then we became silent.

"So Sue's not your mom?"

"No," the girl said. "My mom lives in the same apartment complex as they did. Then she got a boyfriend and I hated being around him so I used to go over there all the time."

Then suddenly Ruby began crying.

"I'd visit Sue and Joe and they let me stay over. Pretty soon it was like they adopted me."

"My dad had a lot of girlfriends," I said.

"I bet they didn't steal your underwear."

"No."

"My mom's a retard and I don't care if she gets all her skin cut off and gets tortured for the rest of her life."

I started laughing at that, and then so did she.

"Anything's better than that place. Will you come with me?" She took my hand in hers.

"I don't think they like me," I said.

"Joe and Sue love me. They'll do anything I say." Then all of a sudden she jumped into the water and I followed her in. We goofed around for a long time, then we lay by the side of the pool until the manager came out and told us the pool was closed.

When we got back to the room Sue and Joe were in bed sleeping. The TV and the A/C were on and I sat in a chair near the door and watched TV while Ruby went into the bathroom and took a shower. She came out in pajamas and got into the empty bed.

I stood up and went over to her and told her goodbye, but when I did she grabbed my hand and whispered, "You can sleep here, okay?"

"I don't think they'd like it."

"Joe doesn't care. Just sleep on the floor next to me, then he won't even know." She took the bedspread off the bed and handed me a pillow. I knew I should have left but I liked her and I was tired and the room was cool and nice. I lay down and put the bedspread over me and tried to tell myself I'd wake up before Joe and Sue did.

Ruby turned off the TV and moved to the edge of the bed, right above me.

"Are you hungry?" she asked.

"I'm always hungry," I said and smiled to her in the darkness.

"I'd love pancakes and syrup and bacon and a chocolate milkshake."

She let her hand fall near mine and I took it and we held hands.

"Do you have a picture of yourself?"

"I have a picture of my aunt and me," I said.

"Can I see it?"

I took the picture out of my back pocket. I gave it to her along with my lighter.

She looked at the worn-out photo by the light of the flame. She set it on the table next to her.

"Will you come with us to Arizona?"

"I don't know," I whispered. "I don't think they'd want me to."

"I know they would," she said and we kept holding hands. She'd squeeze mine and then I'd squeeze back. She'd squeeze twice and so I'd squeeze twice. A couple times it made her giggle. Then she leaned over with half her body hanging off the bed and she kissed me. I'd never kissed a girl. We kissed for a long time and every once in a while she'd giggle or laugh.

She pulled up her top and took my hand and put it on her breast.

"I love you, Charley. Don't leave, okay?"

"I've never been to Arizona," I said.

"Me neither," she whispered back.

"Does your mom know you're going down there?"

"I left her a note saying I was running away."

Then Sue coughed and rustled around in the bed so Ruby moved back and lay still. When the room fell silent again Ruby leaned over the bed and took my hand in hers.

"Goodnight, Charley."

I told her goodnight and we kept holding hands.

When I woke it was just getting light out. Ruby was knocking on the bathroom door.

"Sue, I gotta pee. Is it alright if I come in?"

Sue said it was and Ruby went in there. The shower was going and after a while you could hear Ruby in the shower with her. They were talking.

The alarm went off and Joe coughed and got up and went in there as well.

You could hear Ruby giggle and then you could hear Joe

saying things and I put the pillow over my ear and pressed down but still I could hear them. I got up and put on my shoes and went to Ruby's bedside table to get my photo but it wasn't there. I turned on the lights and I looked everywhere I could think of but I couldn't find it. Then I heard the shower stop. I saw her rubber band sitting on the TV so I took that, put it in my pocket, and left.

24

Outside, the motel sign was still lit and there was no one around. I walked through the parking lot and saw a camper hooked to an older Chevy truck. It had Oregon plates so I figured it was Joe's. I thought of Ruby in the truck with them and her sleeping in the back with them in Arizona.

I went to the river and hid in the bushes where I had slept before. I sat there and it was cold and I couldn't sleep. I kept thinking of Ruby and then I started thinking about Pete and my thoughts grew dark. I lay down on the dirt and curled in a ball and fell asleep.

When I woke up I could hear kids laughing and I looked out to see a group of people having a picnic. There were kids playing football and kids kicking a soccer ball and two older men were barbecuing. I snuck out and no one noticed.

I went into a 7-Eleven. There was an old lady working behind the counter and there was a line of construction workers in there getting hot dogs. I went up and down the aisles. I took two cans of SpaghettiOs and a loaf of white bread and walked out. I waited until I was out of the parking lot, then I started jogging and took an alley and ran down it until I found a place in between two buildings and sat down.

I grabbed the can opener from my pocket and opened one of the cans. I poured some of it out onto the bread and ate it like that. I finished a whole can and half the loaf of bread.

After that I walked back to the Cabana Motel. I decided I'd go with Ruby to Arizona if they'd let me. Maybe Sue and Joe weren't bad, and if they were then Ruby and I could go off on our own. I started feeling alright about it, even excited, but when I got to the motel the truck and camper were gone. I beat on their room door but no one answered and when I asked the front desk lady if they'd checked out she said they had.

"Did they leave a note?"

"No," she said.

"Did they leave a photo?"

"A photo?"

"An old Polaroid."

"Nothing," she said. "I cleaned the room myself and they didn't leave anything."

"Are you sure?"

"Yes."

"It's a picture of my aunt and me."

"I'm sorry."

"Could we check the room?"

The woman shook her head, then called to a man who was in the back of the office and then she grabbed a set of keys and I followed her out to the room. The inside was cleaned and the beds were made. It didn't seem like the same room even though it was. I looked under the bed, I looked in the drawers, but there was nothing.

I sat out on the sidewalk and waited but they didn't come back. When night came I went to the university and went inside one of the buildings and hid underneath a stairwell and ate the last of my food. It was pretty boring in there but it felt safe. When I woke up it was the next morning and I went to the bathroom that had the shower and I sat under the hot water for a long time.

That day I went to the library and looked around. I read magazines and newspapers and talked for a long time with an old man who only had one arm and lived in an abandoned railcar with his brother. When the library closed I went back to the Cabana Motel but the truck was still gone so I went back to the river and slept in the bushes.

The next day I went to a thrift store and took a pair of underwear, a couple shirts, and a blanket and ran out the door with them. No one followed me but I jogged for almost a mile before I stopped. I made my way back to the park and spread out the blanket and lay down and fell asleep. When I woke it was late afternoon. I hid the blanket and my extra clothes in the bushes and followed the river maybe two miles past the city until I came to another park. There was no one there, nothing except an old Cadillac sitting on the far side of a gravel lot in the shade. Huge trees lined the park and there was green grass and picnic tables and a nice area to get into the river. I sat down there. It got hot out and after a while I went swimming. I hid my clothes near the bank and swam in my underwear.

That afternoon I fell asleep on the grass. I was woken up sometime later by the sound of the Cadillac honking its horn. I sat up and looked over but I couldn't see it very well. The honking wouldn't stop so I went over to it.

The car was a two door and it was green and dusty and had a dent on the right side that ran from the front tire all the way to the trunk. The dent was rusted out and one of the headlights was busted. The car sat underneath an old cottonwood tree.

The horn stopped as I got near it.

"Are you okay?" I yelled.

"No," a man's voice said.

I walked to the driver's side and the window rolled down. Inside was a man who had long greasy brown hair and wore a jacket and had a blue tarp wrapped around himself. He was older, middle-aged. His neck had bruises on it and his hands were pale and there were scabs along them. The car was full of trash and clothes and newspapers. There was no place to sit.

"I'm stuck," he said. He was missing some teeth and there was dried snot around his nose.

"The door won't open?" I asked.

"The door opens but I'm stuck between the steering wheel and the seat."

"Do you want me to call the police?"

"No," he said.

"What if we took some of the stuff out so you could move the seat back. Would that work?"

The man looked at me. You could tell he was worried.

"The seat moves back and forward by a switch. That's what got me stuck. I tried to move it back but it wouldn't go so I moved it forward hoping it would break something free. It went forward alright but now it won't even go back even a little. I'm stuck and it hurts."

"The seat's probably just caught on something," I said. "We could try moving a few things out."

"Okay," he said.

He unlocked the passenger side door but it made him nervous to do so. When I opened it I could barely see him there was so much stuff in there. It was stacked up past the dash and left him barely enough room to sit.

I moved piles of clothes and records and trash off the front seat and it all smelled horrible. I took it all outside and set it on the hood. It took me a while but I got the front seat cleared so it would fold forward. I could finally see him sitting there, the steering wheel pressed into his legs and stomach. I looked down and saw he'd peed himself. He had on tan pants and they were wet and stained.

There was an empty grocery sack and I filled it with fast-food bags and newspapers and empty soda cans. When it was full I walked over to a park trash can and emptied it. When I got back the man was shaking.

"What are you doing?" he said in a broken sort of way.

"I'm getting rid of the trash. Some of it really smells, some of the stuff in here is rotten."

"Don't," he begged.

"I won't throw anything good out," I said. He just sat there upset. He began rocking his head back and forth, but I kept moving things. I cleared the backseat and then the floor behind the front seat. I found two dead mice and a stack of moldy baby clothes and a broken wooden hanger jammed in the seat track, blocking it from moving. I put it all in the paper sack and dumped it in the trash.

He started the car and moved the seat back. It hurt him a bit, but he was finally free. He opened the door and got out.

He was short and the parka he wore was a heavy winter coat that came down to his knees. The blue tarp wrapped around him was old and worn. He went to the hood and found a pair of pants and underwear and hurried towards the park outhouse.

When he came back he began frantically putting his things back in the car, then got in the driver's side and locked the doors.

"Thank you," he said and then he rolled up the windows. He gave me the thumbs up sign. His face relaxed and you could tell he felt better.

I stood there for a bit, but he didn't say anything more so I walked back to the river. It was late afternoon by then but it was still warm out so I went swimming again. Sometime after that the man drove up near where I was and asked me if I was hungry and I told him I was and he drove off. He came back after a while and began honking his horn. I walked up to him and he handed me a bag of food from Wendy's. I thanked him and then after that he just rolled the window back up and drove away and I never saw him again.

Inside the bag were two cheeseburgers, a large fry, a salad, and a Coke. I ate the salad, fries, and one of the burgers and saved the other. No one else showed up there that day so I decided I'd spend the night there. I went to the trash can and got part of a newspaper and gathered wood and started a fire in the barbecue pit.

When it got dark I let the fire die so no one would see it and tried to sleep. I was tired but I just lay there most of the night awake.

The next morning I walked back to the city. There were a few restaurants downtown that had outside seating near the sidewalk. I picked one and stood next to a parked car and when a table got up I'd walk over and see if they had left anything and if they did I'd grab it. I ate alright that way for a couple days until a waiter yelled at me and I started running and I wasn't looking and I knocked into an old man who was holding hands with a kid. I knocked him over and he fell to the ground. I stopped and looked at his old body lying there, and you could tell he was hurt. He was dressed up and the kid with him was dressed up too, and I knew I'd ruined whatever they were doing. I started running again and went back to the river and hid in the bushes for the rest of that day. I felt horrible about myself and decided then that I'd get out of Boise and try to hitchhike to Wyoming that night.

I began walking towards the highway, but I was already hungry and knew I'd need food and water while I waited out a ride. Near the outside of town I found a mini-mart on the corner of a pretty quiet street and went in. There were two customers. One was a middle-aged man looking at the beer cooler and the other was a woman buying cigarettes. It took me until the woman was gone to find the canned foods. I grabbed a can of soup and a can of chili and a gallon of water. The clerk was an Asian man. When he rang up for the man buying beer I went for the door, but when I did another man came from behind the counter and grabbed me by the shirt. I hadn't seen him and he was strong and he didn't let go. He took the water and the two cans from my hand.

"I already paid," I said.

"You didn't pay," he said with a thick foreign accent. "We have tape. You gonna pay now?"

"I don't have any money," I said.

"You don't have any money?"

I shook my head and I knew just looking at him that I was going to get it.

He kept hold of me until the man who was buying beer left, then he said something to the cashier in a language I didn't understand. The man behind the register got up and went to the front door, locked it and turned around the sign to read closed. Another man came from a back room carrying a baseball bat, and they took me to their office.

I sat in a chair. The guy behind the register went back out front but the other two stayed and watched me. Maybe an hour passed when two police officers came and the store owners told them what had happened. The whole time they were all looking at me.

"What's your name?" a woman officer finally said to me. She had short blonde hair that was cut like a man's and it looked like she lifted weights.

"Del," I said.

"Del what?" she asked.

"Del Montgomery."

She wrote it down in her book.

"Do you have any ID, Del?"

"No," I said.

"How old are you?"

"Fifteen."

"Where do you live?" the other officer said. He was bald

and short and heavy. He had a big moustache and his face was tan except around his eyes, where they were white.

"I've been sleeping by the river."

"By the river?" the woman officer said.

"Yeah," I said.

"Where did you live before that?" the other officer asked.

"All around."

"You don't have any family."

"No," I said.

"Where do you go to school?" the woman officer said.

"I don't go to school."

"At some point you must have."

"Not really," I said.

The man officer asked the store owner what I tried to steal and he showed them.

"Why were you stealing the cans?"

"I haven't eaten since yesterday," I said.

He nodded, then told me to stand up.

I did and he handcuffed me. We went through the store and to their police car and they put me in the backseat and drove to the main city jail. It was a big old place and I got so nervous I thought I'd start bawling but I didn't. They got me out of the car and took me in and sat me down in a chair in a room by myself. I was there for a long while, then the woman cop came back and sat down in a chair across from me.

"Del, we're going to take you to Ada County Juvenile Detention Center. If you give us more information we can help you, but until then, and since you say you're only fifteen, that's where you're going."

She told me to stand up, then took me back to the police car and they drove me to the juvenile center. It was the middle of the night when we got there so I couldn't see much except that it was a big tan concrete building.

The woman cop led me into a room and took my handcuffs off. I sat on a bench seat and she left and I never saw her again. After a while another officer came and took me to a room where they took my picture and fingerprinted me. The officer asked me my name and where I was from. I said I was from Los Angeles, California and that my name was Del Montgomery. He took me into another room and told me to get completely undressed. So I did and I stood there like that and he looked through my clothes and put them in a sack. He gave me a towel and a set of issued clothes and pointed to a room where I was supposed to take a shower. I put the towel around me and went in there and cleaned up. I dressed in the underwear, socks, blue pants, and green T-shirt. He gave me tennis shoes, then led me to a cell that had a green mattress, a pillow, a blanket, and sheets. On a small table there was a paper cup, a cup of toothpaste, a comb, a small bar of soap, and a handbook with the rules of the place. I went in there and sat on the mattress and the officer left.

I made the bed and lay down. As uneasy as it was, it was nice to sleep in a place where I knew it was alright to sleep. It was sometime later when another man woke me up and led me to an office where a big man with gray hair and a gray beard sat behind a desk.

"My name is Harvey," he said and put out his hand and I shook it.

"You were caught shoplifting, is that correct?"

"Yes," I said.

"Why were you shoplifting?"

"I was hungry."

"It says you stole two cans of soup."

"A can of soup, a can of chili, and a gallon of water."

"Where were you going to cook them?"

"I wasn't. I eat them cold."

"It says you don't have any family?"

"No," I said.

"Everybody's got somebody."

"I'm not sure I do," I said.

"Have you ever been in lockup before?"

"No."

"Where did you go to school."

"A lot of places."

"Name one."

"I went to elementary school in Los Angeles but I can't remember what it was called."

The man sighed.

I tried not to look at him but I knew he was staring at me.

"What's your mother's name."

"I don't know."

"Do you have a mother?"

"Sort of," I said.

"If you aren't honest I can't do a thing to help you," the man said and leaned back in his chair. He was frustrated with me. He asked me a few more questions, then ended the meeting and I was put back in my room. I was let out again for dinner. I stood in line with other kids, but I didn't say anything to any of them and they didn't say anything to me. I got a tray of food, went back to a table, and ate. It was meatloaf and mashed potatoes and cooked carrots and a roll. I ate the whole thing and then went back to my cell.

The next morning I ate breakfast and was told to take another shower. I did and then I was taken to a juvenile magistrate. She was a fat old lady who wore glasses and had a big mole on her chin and she asked me the same questions the other guy did. If I did drugs, where I slept, what I ate. She asked me if I liked sleeping by the river, and if I had any friends that slept there too. What states I'd lived in, how I got from one place to the next. She asked me what my favorite subject was in school, and if I was abused by my parents. She asked the same questions over and over. She'd change them around a little to confuse me, and it went on but I liked her alright. When it was over I was sent back to my room.

I ate lunch and nothing happened but at dinner a kid started saying things to me while we ate. I didn't say anything back, I just looked at him. He was part Indian and he was a lot bigger than me and he had tattoos on his hands. I thought he was going to want to fight but nothing happened and I went back to my cell. The next morning came and I was told to get back in my own clothes and they drove me to a group home where I was to live with six other kids.

The place was in a suburban neighborhood. The house was white and two stories high. I went inside and was introduced to an old man named Skip. He had a gut that was so big it hung over his pants, nearly reaching his crotch. The driver handed him my file and left. Skip took me to a room that had two sets of bunk beds in it and I was shown a bottom bunk and was told it was mine. He showed me a dresser that was assigned to that bed and he gave me a toothbrush, toothpaste, and a towel. He took me to the basement where they had boxes of clothes. He found me a pair of jeans, a few shirts, and five pairs of underwear and socks. Then I was led outside where three other kids were mowing the lawn and weeding and I was told to help them.

For dinner we all sat at a long table with Skip and his wife Charlene who was overweight as well. She had long gray hair pulled back in a bun, and wore an old-lady sort of dress and made us hold hands while she said grace. After that we got to eat. There were six kids in all. A couple were younger but most seemed around my age. We ate macaroni and cheese mixed with hot dogs and there was a big bowl of mixed vegetables that Charlene told us we had to eat. There was a pitcher of red Kool-Aid and a loaf of white bread and I ate until I couldn't eat any more. Afterwards I helped clear the table and do the dishes. There was a big living room with four separate couches and we all sat around and watched TV until it was nine, then we were told to go to bed.

As I lay there that night I could hear the other kids talking. Some of it was about their various jobs or about girls and then they started talking about a kid named Weston who had my bunk before me. He was released and sent back to his foster parents. It seemed like everyone there hated him and they went on and on about it. They didn't talk to me so I didn't say anything and I felt alright. I didn't care. I just wasn't hungry and the bed was soft and the sheets smelled good. I lay there and listened until Skip came by and banged on the door and told them to cut it out.

That night I dreamt about Pete. He and I were walking by a swimming pool and we stopped and he drank from the water but the water was so full of chlorine and chemicals that it was smoking. I tried to make him stop. I yelled at him.

"Pete, don't," I screamed. "For Christ's sake, Pete, please."

I pulled on the lead rope and when I did he spooked and reared and fell into the pool. But the pool had no bottom and he couldn't get out and he couldn't stand or rest. He just trod water and tried to hang on. I ran around looking for a way to get him out, but every time I tried to think my mind would freeze. It seemed like it all went on for hours and days, through sunlight and darkness. He was sinking into the water. He was getting tired. I tried my best to hold him up but I wasn't strong enough and then he just disappeared. He was gone.

At seven o'clock Skip came in and told us to get up and by seven thirty we all went down to breakfast where we ate cornflakes and orange juice and toast. Skip told four of the kids to hurry or they'd be late for work and he told me and one other kid to be back by five o'clock or he'd call the police. Charlene gave us each a sack lunch and we left.

Me and the other kid walked down the street together. His name was Kevin Sheraton and he was younger than me. His face was covered in acne and he was the skinniest kid I'd ever seen. He had black hair and it was shaved down like he was in the army and one of his ears was smaller and deformed, like it never grew from when he was small. He told me his mom married a born-again Christian and they kicked him out of the house for smoking cigarettes. After two months they let him move back in, but then they said he'd tried to finger his little sister.

"But it ain't true, man. I'd never do that. My sister's seven. My mom's husband hates me, that's all. He's the fucking pervert. He's the one."

We walked around downtown and both ate our lunches and then we went into a hardware store and looked around. When we came out we went down near this canal where there were shops and restaurants and people walking by. I followed him until he sat down right near the water. He took a tube of glue out of his pants pocket.

"You didn't even see me do it, did you?"

"You mean the glue?"

"Yeah," he said.

"You took it when we were in the hardware store?"

He nodded. He opened the glue and put it up his nose and inhaled as hard as he could. He did that a few times, then he handed it to me, but I told him I didn't want to do it so he put the tube back in his pocket. We sat there for a long time, then we got up and I showed him where I slept by the river.

"That's rough, man," he said. My blanket was still there along with the shirts I had. He pulled out the glue and stuck it up his nose again. "At least the house is better than this. Skip's alright but it's Charlene who's the real bitch. I've lived there two months now. You'll see. She's the worst. She's got a real temper and she's mad at me right now. But it wasn't my fault. Skip, all he gives a fuck about is watching TV. That guy can sit in front of the TV all day. The problem is he always picks what we watch and all he likes are hunting and fishing shows."

"How come they just let us out all day?"

"What else are they gonna do? We ain't fucked-up enough for juvie. We can't get jobs 'cause we're too young, and they don't want us wasting their lives back at the house. You just can't be late, man. If you are they get seriously pissed and then you're fucked."

We sat down in the bushes and talked for a while, but it was hot out so we both stripped down to our underwear and went swimming in the river and the day passed. When it got near five we got dressed and made our way back to the house.

Skip was washing his car when we got there so Kevin and I helped him. We dried it and waxed it and then we helped him rearrange the garage and sweep the driveway. That night for dinner we had Hamburger Helper and a bowl of mixed vegetables and a loaf of white bread. There were two pitchers of red Kool-Aid and we all held hands and said grace again, then we sat in silence and ate. Since Kevin and I were the only ones without jobs, Charlene had us clear the table and do the dishes. A couple of the other guys went upstairs and the rest followed Skip into the living room to watch TV.

The next morning it was the same thing, toast and cornflakes and juice. We left with the same sort of sack lunch we had the day before and Kevin and I went downtown and walked in and out of stores. Then we went to the river and ate our lunches and went swimming.

When we got back that evening at five Skip had Kevin and I vacuum the carpets and mop the kitchen and bathroom floors and then Charlene came home. She put two pounds of ground meat in a pan and had me stir it around, then she threw in a bunch of onions and added a gallon can of spaghetti sauce. She boiled two big pots of water and threw in the spaghetti. The whole time she didn't talk or say much of anything.

We all ate together and afterwards Kevin and I did the dishes again. When we'd finished, Charlene told me to stay behind. She took me into a back room that had a desk and a couple chairs and a computer. We went inside and she shut the door and told me to sit down.

"I've done this for over ten years," she said. She was sweating and you could see it leaking through her dress. She moved her big body behind the desk and sat. On the walls in the small room were two religious posters. One had a picture of a bird flying through the sky. It said "Jesus loves you" and the other was a picture of a green meadow and it read "With *His* gift you will be set free. With *His* gift you will finally be."

"I have certain rules and if those rules are broken, then you're gone. It's the way I've run my home since the beginning, and it works. There's no discussions or second chances here and I told you that when you arrived. Del, you'll be leaving us."

"Me?"

"We found a tube of glue, a baggy with what looks like marijuana, and four cigarettes in the back of your dresser."

"In my dresser?"

She nodded.

"I don't even have anything to put in the dresser but the things you've given me."

She just sat there sweating, looking at me.

"I don't smoke anything and I don't stick glue up my nose," I told her.

"We've never found anything like this before with any of the other residents. That's the truth. You arrive and suddenly there's marijuana, a tube of glue, and cigarettes in your dresser. I called your assigned juvenile magistrate and she remembered you. She looked in your file and made a call and tomorrow you're being sent to the Idaho Youth Ranch in south-west Idaho. It's a year-long residency."

"A year?"

"A year," she said. "It's on a five hundred and fifty-acre ranch and is a more intensively structured living situation than this."

"But none of that stuff is mine."

"Then whose is it?"

"I don't know," I told her. "I don't know anyone here."

Her face didn't change or make any sort of expression.

"Someone will be here by nine tomorrow morning to take you. I'm sorry it didn't work out for you. You can watch TV with the rest of the boys or you can go to your room and get your things ready for tomorrow. Okay?"

"I swear it wasn't my stuff."

"You have two options tonight, Del. You can go watch TV or you can go to your room and get your things ready for tomorrow."

"I don't have any things to get ready."

"Then you can watch TV. Okay?" She turned on the computer. "You can leave now."

I shut the door to her office and went up to my room, lay on my bunk, and tried to think. I couldn't sleep. Kevin and two other kids came in at nine and they talked for a long time and I just lay there with my eyes closed. I waited until they were sleeping, then I got up and found my clothes and dressed as quietly as I could. I took the sheet and blanket and rolled them up like a sleeping bag, then lay back down and listened as hard as I could. I didn't hear anything so I got up again and walked over to Kevin. He was in the lower bunk across from me and was sleeping on his back. Looking at him in the dim light made me see red. I don't know why he'd do that to me. I'd gone over and over the two days we spent together and it didn't make sense.

I put my hand over his mouth until he woke up. His eyes got wide when he saw me and I hit him as hard as I could in the stomach. Then I took my hand off his mouth and grabbed his throat to hold him down and hit him two more times in the guts. He hit me back once in the eye but it didn't hurt. I hit him again. He cried out that time, but I knocked the wind out of him so he just lay there out of breath looking at me. I made my way downstairs, went to the front door. The alarm went off when I opened it, but I just ran down the street, turned a corner, and kept running.

25

I made it to the freeway and walked alongside it for a couple miles until I was outside of town. It was still dark out. Cars and trucks rushed by and none stopped and I didn't see any police. I kept walking until I saw a truck stop in the distance. I got off the interstate and went towards it. There were tractor trailers going in and out and there were dozens of them parked in the lot.

I sat in the dirt across from the main building and waited out the rest of the night. Just past dawn a pickup stopped for gas. A man got out and filled the tank, then drove over to near where I was and stopped. He got out, opened the hood of the truck, and leaned over and began working on the engine.

I could hear him talking to himself and then he stopped, took a pack of cigarettes from his shirt pocket, and lit one. He looked out and saw me sitting there staring at him.

"You much of a mechanic?" he yelled out to me.

"No," I said and got up and walked over to him.

"It would be alright if you were," he said and smiled, and when he did you could see he was missing his front top four teeth. He was young, maybe twenty or so, and he wore a white T-shirt and jeans and boots. His hair was brown and short and it looked like he hadn't taken a shower in a while.

"What are you doing here, sitting in the dirt?"

"I'm hoping to catch a ride," I told him.

"Where you going?"

"Wyoming. Where you going?" I asked him.

"Grand Junction, Colorado."

"Can I get a ride with you?"

"Grand Junction ain't on the way to Wyoming, man," he said.

"That's okay. Anywhere is better than here."

He looked at me.

"Alright, but don't give me a hard time if we break down going over the mountains."

"I won't," I said and got up.

"I got to haul ass too."

"Alright," I said.

I walked over to him and introduced myself, and he told me his name was Lonnie Dixon.

"What's wrong with your truck?"

"It's just old, and I shouldn't be making this sort of trip in it. The top radiator hose is bulging so I duct taped the shit out of it. I got an extra but I'd have to wait until it cooled down to change it and I don't have the time so I'm gonna chance it. The alternator belt's loose too. Its been howling for a while so I went in there and bought a spare and tightened the old one. It'll be alright, I hope. I go through about a quart of oil an hour and it'll be a miracle if the tranny holds. I've been running this fucker all the way from Tonopah, Nevada."

I looked at the engine. The battery was sitting on a makeshift wooden platform and circled with wire to hold it in place. I could see where the hose was duct taped. There were other hoses that had duct tape on them, too, and the

233

whole engine looked rusty and where it wasn't rusty it was covered thick in dirt and oil. He started the engine and came back with a screwdriver and began adjusting the carburetor. He did it for a long time.

"It's a moody old fucking truck," he said when he was done. "And she's pissed at me 'cause I've been going fourteen hours straight. You ready?"

I nodded and he shut the hood and we both got in the cab and he drove onto the highway. There was a case of Coke sitting between us and a half dozen empties on the floor in front of my seat. On the dash sat a dental bridge with four front teeth. The windows were rolled down and the truck shook and rattled as we went down the road. The sun came up and it got warmer and the farther we got from Boise the more I relaxed. We were an hour out of Boise when I fell asleep.

Lean on Pete came to me when I did. He was in a city. He was lost and the buildings went straight up into the sky, and he couldn't tell which way to go. He couldn't find a way out. He had to dodge cars and trucks and people, but the farther he ran the more cars and people there were. He went up one street and down another and ran block after block, but nothing ever changed. His black coat grew shiny with sweat. He became frantic. His hooves cracked and began to fall apart. Then blood began leaking out of his nose and legs. He was in horrible pain. Finally, in exhaustion, he fell. He forced himself to get up again, but then he fell a second time and couldn't get up. Speeding cars missed him by inches. He began moaning in pain, crying so loud that it was deafening, crying so loud I woke up.

When I opened my eyes I knew I was crying. My heart pounded, it was really hot out and I was sweating. Even the wind blowing through the truck was hot. Lonnie was driving and smoking a cigarette.

"You have a bad dream?"

I wiped my face. "Yeah."

"I could hear you whimpering. You sounded like my dog when he gets a nightmare."

"It's really hot now," I said.

"That's what probably did it. You're getting hit by the sun. You're on the wrong side of the truck. I always get nightmares when you fall asleep in the heat. Take a Coke. Sorry they ain't cold, but I forgot to bring my cooler. Coffee never keeps me awake. I can drink a pot of coffee and go right to sleep, but Coke keeps me up if I keep drinking it."

I took a can and opened it.

"How long was I asleep?"

"Three or four hours," he said. "That must have been a shit-ass nightmare."

"It was," I said.

"What are you doing out on the road by yourself?"

"I'm trying to find my aunt."

"In Wyoming?"

"Yeah."

"Why don't you just take a bus?"

"I don't have any money," I said.

"I know how that is. I had to borrow five hundred bucks just to make this trip."

"Why are you going to Grand Junction?"

"My brother works out there on a construction crew and

yesterday he fell off a scaffold and broke his neck."

"I'm sorry," I said.

"Fuck, me too," he said. "He's a good guy and he's got a kid and a wife."

"Where do you live?"

"I work on a ranch way out in bumfuck Nevada. Before that I worked on a ranch in Montana."

"Is it hard working on a ranch?"

"Sometimes," he said. "It just depends. You don't get paid shit."

"But you don't have to have finished high school?"

"Fuck no. I mean, I graduated from high school but it hasn't helped. As long as you can read and count."

He took another cigarette, lit it, then grabbed a can of Coke and opened it. He ran his fingers through his hair and kept driving.

We stopped at a truck stop outside of Salt Lake City, Utah. Lonnie put in his front teeth and we both went inside and used the toilet. Afterwards he gave me five dollars and we went to Taco Bell, ordered food to go, and then we gassed up the truck and left.

He drank nearly a whole twelve pack of soda through the day and into the night. He told me about a girl named Linda who broke up with him and about him riding in a rodeo and getting his teeth knocked out. He said the owner of the ranch was losing his mind and that once he went to a whorehouse and saw the boss walking around in women's clothes.

He talked all night long and I tried to stay awake. He told

me about his brother and how they were raised Mormon, and how they both got excommunicated and now they couldn't even go home because both of their parents disowned them, and how the only contact they have with their family is a sister in Kansas City.

He told me about his brother and him living in Mexico for a couple months and them working on a ranch in Utah for a summer. He talked about his brother meeting a girl and getting her pregnant. He told me how he once worked for a guy who couldn't pay him so he gave him a beat-up Pontiac Lemans instead of a paycheck and how he and his brother fixed it up and sold it to a drug dealer. He told me about a time when he saw a guy hang-gliding and the glider caught an updraft and flipped over and crashed into the side of a mountain and another time when he was at a bar and saw a guy hit a good-looking girl right in the face. Her jaw broke and she fell unconscious. He said it was the weirdest thing he'd ever seen. Her disconnected jaw just hung off to the side of her face.

Once I had to ask him to stop so I could take a leak and when I did he admitted he had to go so bad he didn't think he could stand but that he was scared to slow the truck, thinking it might finally give up and quit.

We went over a bunch of mountains and you could tell the old truck had a hard time. I fell asleep sometime in the night and when I woke the next morning Lonnie was still smoking and drinking Cokes. When we finally got outside Grand Junction he pulled off at a truck stop and gassed up.

"I guess this is it. Probably have an easier time catching a ride out here than in town. If you ever need a job, I could

237

probably get you one."

"Really?" I said.

"He's so weird he has a hard time keeping people," Lonnie said.

"Thanks for the ride. I wish I had money I could give you."

"It doesn't matter."

"I hope your brother's alright," I said.

"Me too," he said.

"I guess I'll see you, then."

"Maybe," he said and put in his teeth.

He gave me five more dollars and wrote his number on a scrap of paper and I put it in my pocket. I shook his hand, grabbed my blanket, and got out.

26

I went into the truck stop and got a pre-made sandwich and a gallon of water and waited out on the sidewalk. Every once in a while I'd ask someone who looked alright for a ride, but I didn't have any luck. It wasn't until around three o'clock in the afternoon that I saw four long-haired guys pull up in a small red compact car. They were all dressed in black pants and black T-shirts. They told me they were going to Denver. I asked them if I could get a ride there and they told me I could. They went into the store and I waited by their car.

When they came out they were each carrying a bottle of Mountain Dew. I got in the backseat and we left. They were in high school and were going to see a concert. They smoked clove cigarettes and drank soda and ate candy bars and beef jerky and played the stereo so loud that they blew one of the speakers and then two of the guys almost got in a fight about it.

They didn't talk to me so I didn't talk to them and mostly I just looked out the window. My thoughts raced and for a while I couldn't stop thinking about Pete. Then I began falling asleep, but I was so scared I would dream about him that I stayed awake.

We drove into Denver and they parked their car across the street from a place called the Bluebird Theater on Colfax Avenue. I told them thanks and started walking down the street. It was night and I came to a closed store and hid my blanket behind a dumpster in their back lot and went looking for food. But every mini-mart I came to looked like the one where I got caught and my nerves wouldn't let me go in.

It wasn't a good part of town. There were liquor stores and bars and dirty magazine places. I saw a drunk black man pushing an empty baby stroller and I saw a guy whose face was deformed and a woman who yelled at a man and said horrible things to him and chased him around a Walgreens parking lot.

I came to a Carrow's Restaurant and went in. There was a lady who sat people and she came up to me and I told her I was waiting for my parents and she told me I could sit on the couch by the entrance. I stayed there until a group of people got up from a booth near where the restrooms were. One of them left most of a hamburger and fries. They went to the counter to pay and I got up and went to the table and took the burger and as many fries as I could. I went into the bathroom, found a stall and sat down on the seat. There was a guy next to me using the toilet and it smelled horrible and he kept coughing and grunting. The walls had things written on them. There were drawings of naked women, there was a swastika and phone numbers, and dirty things written. I ate the food, but it was hard.

When I made it back out onto the street and really saw where I was I got really down. I didn't mind Skip and Charlene's. They would have let me go to school, they probably would have let me play football. I didn't mind being called Del Montgomery and I liked the bed and the sheets and the food and I liked having people around.

As I walked down Colfax Avenue I got more and more worried. What if my aunt lived in Florida or in Maine? What if she had died? What if she wouldn't want me? What if she had never really liked me in the first place? I was only eleven years old the last time I saw her. I didn't know anything back then. I got my blanket from behind the dumpster and kept walking until I saw an office building that had a bunch of bushes alongside it. I crawled inside them until I found an alright place to lie down. I put the blanket over me and waited until morning.

The next day I met a man who called himself Silver and he lived in the back of his camper. He was tall and heavy-set with a thick beard that was gray and black. His truck had broken down and he was parked on a side street in front of an apartment building. He told me he had to move it at least once a week but that his battery was dead and if I helped him steal one he'd let me spend the night in there with him.

I told him I'd think about it, then he asked me if I was hungry and I told him I was and we walked to the Denver Rescue Mission and ate lunch there. They served a bowl of split-pea soup, a cheese sandwich, a carton of milk, and a couple cookies. Silver hardly ate anything and he gave me what he didn't eat. After that we separated and I spent the day in the park watching people play soccer and another bunch of people play touch football. When night came I went back to the mission and had dinner there. They had stew and bread and salad and milk and pound cake for dessert.

When I left I went up and down Colfax again. I saw two

men get in a fight and I saw a girl that had a tattoo on her face and a man and a woman having sex in a car. Then I ran into Silver as he was walking with a skinny blonde woman who, I found out, was called Martha. They said I could come with them to Silver's camper. We walked for a long time until we reached a neighborhood where it was parked. The camper was big and white and had a huge dent on the side of it. It sat on a pickup truck. Inside there was a table, a bed, a booth to sit at, a stove, and an ice box. The windows were taped over with black garbage bags so you couldn't see in or out. It wasn't in as bad a shape as you'd think. He kept it alright. Both he and Martha drank off a bottle of vodka and we all watched a small battery-powered TV.

There was a big bag of potato chips on the table and they said I could have some and so I just sat there and ate them and watched a police detective show on TV. They smoked cigarettes and drank the whole bottle. Later on they moved up to the bed. I asked Silver if I could stay the night and he said it was okay so I slept on the bench seat.

A couple hours later I woke to him standing above me. The TV was still on but there wasn't any program playing. It was just static. I could see that he was naked. He began punching me in the stomach and in the face.

"You nigger faggot," he yelled. "You cock-sucking faggot."

Martha woke up and shined a flashlight down and yelled at him. I tried to sit up but couldn't. He was too strong.

I begged him not to hit me, but he wouldn't stop. I tried to cover my face but there wasn't enough room to move.

"Goddamnit, Silver, stop!" Martha screamed at him. "He

ain't who you think he is."

She got down out of the bunk and pushed him and he fell into the back of the camper against the door. He didn't get up and she turned on the light. She stood there naked. Her body was old. It was like the skin on her was falling towards the ground. Silver was on the floor mumbling and Martha turned to me.

"You better get out of here," she said.

I sat up and could feel blood leaking down from my nose. I was having a hard time breathing.

"He's blocking the door," I told her.

"Stand on the bench seat and stay in the corner. I'll get him up on to the bed and then you leave, alright?"

I nodded and she went to Silver and talked to him for a bit, then helped him up. His leg was bleeding. He'd cut it when he fell. He leaned on her and was talking but I couldn't understand anything he said. As she tried to get him up onto the bed I got down off the bench seat, unlocked the camper door, and jumped out.

27

I walked down the road but it hurt every time I breathed. I kept looking back even though I knew he wasn't going to follow me. It was late and everything was shut down. I went to the bushes by the office building. When I got there I lay down and wrapped the blanket around me and fell asleep.

When I woke the next morning my head was pounding and my ribs hurt so bad I could barely sit up. I just lay there most of the day and tried to sleep. By late afternoon I got up and walked to the parking lot and looked at my reflection in a car mirror. There was dried blood everywhere and my nose was swollen and hurt pretty bad. I knew I had to find a place and clean up. I passed a bar called the Lion's Lair. The door was open and I looked inside and there were nothing but a few old people sitting around the bar drinking. I couldn't see the bartender so I walked in and found the men's room and shut the door and locked it. I spent a long time washing my face and cleaning myself up. I washed my hair in the sink using a bar of soap. I took off my shirt and looked at my chest but I couldn't see anything wrong except bruises. I put my shirt back on and combed my hair with my hands. I looked alright. My nose didn't look too bad. My coat was covered in dried blood though. I tried to wash it in the sink but I couldn't get any of it out so I left it in the trash can. My shirt looked fine though and I tucked it into my pants and left.

I spent the rest of the day walking around and that evening I went to the mission for dinner and sat next to three men. They all wore the same shirts that read "Green Grass We Cut It Fast." They were talking in Mexican but one of them spoke English alright.

"You guys mow lawns?" I asked him.

Two of the men just looked at me.

The other one nodded.

"You think they're hiring?"

"He always hires," the one man said and grinned. "But you won't like him."

I asked him where the place was and he told me the address. I got a pen from another guy and wrote it on a napkin. When I finished eating I thanked them and left. I went back to the office building and got my blanket and started walking.

There was a lady who worked at a donut shop and she was standing outside it smoking a cigarette. I showed her the address and she told me where to go. It was five miles away and it took me most of the evening to find it because I kept having to stop and rest due to the pain in my ribs.

The lawn-mowing company was a warehouse door among a sea of others. I waited there for a while, then walked around to the end of the complex where hundreds of wood pallets were stacked in tall rows. There was a space between them and a chain-link fence and I sat down there and fell asleep.

When I woke it was cold and still dark, but dawn was coming. My ribs hurt worse and I was pretty sure they were broken. I hid my blanket, then got up and left and walked until I came to a row of houses. I snuck up on the front lawn of one of them and found an outdoor faucet. I turned it on and drank as much water as I could, then kept walking until the sun was up. I went back and waited outside the warehouse door and a bald-headed man dressed in shorts and a "Green Grass We Cut It Fast" T-shirt got out of a car.

"What do you want?" he said. He was smoking a cigarette and drinking from a liter bottle of Dr. Pepper. He was tall and lanky and had the skinniest legs I'd ever seen on a man.

"Are you hiring?"

"Have you ever done lawn maintenance?" he said.

"Yeah," I said.

"What have you done?"

"I know how to mow lawns. My dad's friend let me borrow his mower and I'd walk around the neighborhood and get jobs."

"How old are you?"

"Sixteen," I told him.

"Are you a drug addict?"

"No."

"You ever been in jail?"

"No," I told him.

"Well I'm three guys short. I'll try you," he said. "When can you start?"

"Right now."

"Alright," he said.

"My name is Sid," he said and we shook hands.

He led me inside and I filled out an application. I lied about everything. I told him my name was Del Montgomery.

I gave him a false phone number, address, and social security number. He gave me a company T-shirt and told me to change, but my ribs hurt so bad that I couldn't lift my arms and I asked him if he had a bathroom and I went in there and locked the door. I took my other shirt off alright because it had snap buttons, but it took me a long while to put the new T-shirt on. I broke out in sweat and I almost cried out a couple times but I got it on and walked back out to the room.

He told me I'd make seven dollars and twenty-eight cents an hour, then he had me sit down and wait in a chair by his desk. Twenty minutes later men started arriving and Sid got up from his desk and opened two warehouse doors. Inside were three pickup trucks and three trailers full of lawn mowers, trimmers, blowers, rakes, and shovels. Sid introduced me to a Mexican named Santiago and told me I was in his crew and I got in the truck with him and another man named Bob and we left.

Santiago drove and I sat in the middle. Bob sat in the passenger seat and ate two Milky Way candy bars and drank coffee while we drove to the first job. No one talked at all.

We mowed lawns until noon. Santiago showed me what to do and it didn't hurt too bad because I didn't have to lift my arms over my head very often. On lunch break we stopped at Burger King. Bob went inside but Santiago took a cooler from the bed of the truck and carried it underneath a tree in the parking lot and ate by himself. I went inside to the bathroom and drank as much water as I could from the sink and went back out and waited by the truck.

That afternoon we mowed and weeded a huge fancy house and then we mowed five businesses and drove back to the warehouse at three. Sid was there at his desk smoking a cigarette and doing paperwork. He looked up at me and said, "Tomorrow at seven," then he went back to his papers and I left.

I walked to the mission but it was too early and they were closed. I sat there for a while, then walked to a park down the road. There was a girl playing Frisbee with her boyfriend. They were around my age. They played for a long time, then they sat next to each other on the grass and started kissing. I couldn't stop staring at them. It made me think of Ruby, and I sat there for a long time and wondered about her in Arizona.

When I went back to the mission it was open for dinner. There were guys sitting all around me who wouldn't eat this or that and I'd ask them for it and most of the time they'd give it to me. I asked one of the ladies working there if I could get lunch for tomorrow, but she said I couldn't.

I didn't go down Colfax that night because I was worried I'd run into Silver. I took side streets and walked the five miles back to the warehouse and sat behind the pallets, found my blanket, wrapped it around me, and waited.

That night I had a dream where my dad and I were in a laundromat. He was sitting next to me reading a magazine and then he looked over and told me a story about a coyote that wandered into the warehouse where he was loading freight. It was small, it was a female, and she was really scared and no one knew what to do.

"Did someone catch her?" I asked.

"Hold your horses, I'm getting to that."

"Maybe we could keep her if she needs a home."

"Keep the coyote?"

"Yeah," I said.

"You can't have a coyote as a pet. They're wild."

"Maybe we could."

"It doesn't work like that," my dad said. "Anyway, so what happened was a guy threw a roll of paper towels at it. You would think the coyote would run off after that, but she didn't. She just moved towards me, looking at me in a strange way. She was a tiny thing. She wasn't mad – I don't know what she was – and then she ran off."

"Where did she go?"

"I don't know," he said, and then he went back to reading his magazine. When the washer ended I put our things in the dryer and when I did the Samoan walked into the laundromat carrying a basket of clothes. I tried to warn my dad but my voice didn't work and I was suddenly stuck. No matter what I did I couldn't move. Then my dad got up to go outside and smoke a cigarette and when he did the Samoan saw him and began yelling at him. He tackled my dad into a dryer that had a glass door and the door broke and my dad fell inside and the Samoan wouldn't stop hitting him. There was blood everywhere and the Samoan kept hitting him harder and harder and it was so awful it woke me up and after that I couldn't sleep at all.

I rode again with Santiago and Bob that next day. We mowed a lawn in front of a huge office building, then we drove to a different job and while we were in the truck Bob told me he'd just been let out of jail for beating up his brother in-law. He said he hit him so hard that he shattered the man's eye socket. He and his wife were living in an apartment out in the suburbs. He was older and had tattoos running up and down his arms. He talked about the fight for a bit, then about a TV show he'd seen the night before, then about a jet ski his neighbor was going to sell him. He didn't talk to Santiago at all and I could tell he didn't like him. We mowed two more lawns that morning and at lunch we stopped at a Burger King and I did the same thing I did the day before. After that we mowed more office buildings and then went back to the warehouse.

That evening I went to the mission for dinner, then I walked back to the warehouse and hid behind the pallets and waited. I did that for the rest of the week and then on Friday Sid gave us our checks and told me to be there on Monday. I put the check in my pocket and ran down to where Santiago was getting into a pickup truck and I asked him how to cash it. I told him the truth, that I didn't have any ID. He just shook his head but let me get in his truck and we drove to a bank that would cash the boss's checks. I waited in line with him and when it was our turn he waited until there was a clerk he knew. They spoke in Mexican and she cashed his and then mine.

"I can give you some money for gas," I told him when we were in the parking lot.

"Don't worry, I was coming here anyway."

"This is the most money I've had in a long time," I said and smiled. "Thank you."

"It's okay," he said. "I'll see you on Monday." He got into

his truck and drove off. The bank was even farther out, but it didn't matter because I had a hundred and three dollars.

I walked back into town and ate at a place called Pete's Kitchen. They had a fried chicken special with mashed potatoes and collard greens and I ate the whole thing and drank two Cokes. I decided I'd find a movie theater and spend the rest of the night there. I stopped at a donut shop and got two glazed and I ate them while I walked down the street.

I passed a bar called the Satire Lounge, and when I did I saw Silver and another man walking towards me. I tried to keep my head down but I couldn't help it: I looked up at him and he looked at me, but it was like he didn't even recognize me.

After that I didn't go to the movies, I just went to the bushes by the office building and hid. But I didn't have my blanket so I froze most of the night and didn't sleep much. That morning I went to the mission for breakfast and after I went to a thrift store and bought a coat, a couple pairs of underwear, a pair of shorts, a T-shirt, three pairs of socks, and a pair of swimming trunks. There was a public swimming pool named La Alma and I went there. It only cost two dollars to get in and I showered and cleaned up in the men's locker room.

There were a group of kids with a dad and they got in the shower room to wash off before they went to the pool and they all saw the bruises around my ribs and chest, but none of them said anything. When I got out I changed into my new clothes and left. I walked around for a while, then went to a laundromat and washed my work shirt and the rest of the clothes I had.

* * *

On Sunday evening I bought a loaf of bread, a package of cheese slices, and a six pack of soda and went to the warehouse and slept behind the pallets. Just after sunrise I put on my work shirt and made three sandwiches out of the bread and cheese. I put them and two sodas in a plastic sack and sat by the warehouse door until Sid showed up.

The week went along alright. One day at Burger King Santiago asked me to sit with him in the shade of some trees that ran alongside the edge of the parking lot.

"How come your mother makes you eat cheese and white bread every day?" he asked while we ate.

"I make my own lunch."

"You're not very good at it," he said and smiled.

"I'm trying to save money," I said.

"Why?"

"I have to go to Wyoming."

"Wyoming?"

"Yeah," I said.

He nodded and we kept eating for a while.

"What's wrong with your arms?" he asked.

"What do you mean?"

"Every time you lift the grass bag I can see your face in pain."

"I got beat up."

"Why?"

"I don't know," I said.

"Who did it?"

"Just some guy," I said.

Santiago just nodded and we finished eating.

* * *

On Thursday night when I was sleeping behind the pallets a car pulled up. Four guys got out. I could see them by the street light. They left the radio playing and drank beer and stayed there for a long time. Once in a while they'd throw a beer bottle against a concrete wall and it would break. A couple times they wandered over near where I was, and when they did I could see they were young, maybe a little older than me. I began to get nervous that they'd find me, and I was ready to run but in the end they just got back in their car and drove away.

On Friday morning Bob didn't show up and we worked with an old man named Cliff. He was retired but his daughter and grandkid had just moved back in with him so he didn't have enough money. He had to go back to work. He seemed like an alright guy. When he was young he was in the military and lived in Guam and at lunch he told us about it there. When the day was done Santiago let me ride with him to the bank and again he helped me cash my check. I had almost three hundred dollars in my pocket. We said goodbye and I began walking down the street when he pulled up beside me and stopped. He got out of his truck.

"Do you need a ride home?" he asked.

"I don't live far from here. I'm pretty close," I told him.

"Close to what?" he said. "There's nothing out here. Where do you live?"

"Not far."

"What's your address?"

I just stood there. "My address?"

"Yeah."

"I don't know."

"You don't know?"

He shook his head, then asked if I wanted to have dinner at his house. I nodded and he wrote down his address and the directions on the back of an envelope, gave it to me, and drove off.

I walked back to the pallets and put all the money I had except for twenty in my left shoe and changed into my jeans and my clean blue shirt. I walked down to a grocery store and washed my face and hands in their bathroom and bought a carton of cake donuts and left.

It took me nearly an hour to walk to Santiago's house. It was a small brick home set off from the sidewalk. It had a front yard with grass. There were two kids playing on it and there was an old man sitting in a chair watching them. I went to him and asked him if Santiago lived there but I don't think he understood what I was saying. Then one of the kids ran into the house and came out with Santiago. He was dressed in tan pants and a white buttondown short-sleeved shirt. He wore a baseball hat and flip-flops.

"I didn't think you would come," he said.

I walked up to him and handed him the donuts.

"What are these for?"

"For your family," I said.

He laughed at that and we went inside. I met his wife Nuria and her brother Carlos. Their house was nice, it had pictures of their family on the walls and it smelled good and they had music playing on a stereo. We sat around for a while, then we all went into the backyard where there was a picnic table that had a white cloth over it. We sat there and ate carnitas with homemade tortillas. They spoke in Mexican and the kids laughed and Santiago smiled and said things that made them laugh harder. His wife sat across from him and she was young and good-looking.

When dinner was over I helped clear the plates and his wife did the dishes. Everyone else stayed outside except Santiago, who I saw in the living room lighting a candle in front of a picture on the mantle.

"It's my mother," he told me. "She left us five years ago. Every Friday I light a candle for her to let her know that I miss her and that I have work and that I'm okay."

The picture was old and in black and white and the woman in it was young and wearing a dress and a hat. She was leaning against a car.

"Was she nice?"

"She was my mother. Of course she was nice."

I didn't say anything. I just stood there with him, then one of the kids came and asked him to come back outside and so we did.

The box of donuts were sitting on a plate in the center of the table.

"You don't have to eat those if you don't want," I told them and I was embarrassed.

He laughed. "I like donuts. My kids like donuts."

"I'm gonna go now," I said.

"You're not going to have one?"

"I eat them every day," I said and put out my hand. He shook it and I said goodbye to his family and he walked me out. When I left there I was pretty down. I never understand why seeing something nice can get you so down but it can.

I went to Colfax Avenue and stopped and bought an ice cream sandwich from a mini-mart and ate it while I was walking. It was Friday night and there were a lot of people out and I wasn't paying attention and suddenly someone grabbed me from behind. I looked up to see it was Silver. He was with a skinny man who had a shaved head and tattoos on his neck. I'd never seen him before. They smelled. Even from where I was I could smell them. It was part smoke and alcohol and part sweat and wearing the same clothes for too long.

"Where's my TV?" His eyes were red, he was upset.

"Your TV?" I asked.

"I remember you. You're the little fucker that ran down my battery and ate all my food and skipped out."

"You said I could have the chips," I said.

"I let you stay in my place and now my TV and radio are missing."

"I didn't take them," I said.

"Where do you live?"

"I don't live anywhere."

"He probably pawned them," the other man said and coughed.

Silver grabbed me by the shirt and led me to a side street and then down to an empty parking lot. There was no one around. He made me empty my pockets. He took the fifteen dollars and the pocket knife I had in them.

"Where do you live?" the tattooed man said.

"I don't live anywhere. I've been sleeping behind a stack of pallets where I work."

"You have a job?" the tattooed man said.

"I mow lawns."

"Where do you keep your money?"

"I don't have any more money."

"That's bullshit," Silver said. "If you got a job, you got more money than this."

"He probably has it hidden somewhere," the tattooed man said.

"Let's go to where you're sleeping," Silver said.

"But I don't keep anything there," I said.

"Then take your shirt off," Silver yelled and grabbed me by my hair.

I took it off.

"Take off your shoes and pants," the tattooed man said.

I began to unlace my shoes and then I tried to get away but he kept pulling hard on my hair and then the tattooed man hit me in the stomach. Silver put his other hand around my neck.

The tattooed man took off my shoes and then my pants. He looked through the pants, then he felt in my shoes and found the money.

"I knew he'd have money," he said and grinned. "I just knew it."

"It's all I have," I said and started crying.

28

Silver threw me down on the ground, then the tattooed man kicked me in the guts and they left. I just lay there. When I got up it was minutes later and I found my clothes and shoes and dressed. I made my way to Colfax Avenue but I didn't see them anywhere. I began to panic. I was tired of being broke and I was tired of sleeping outside. I walked up and down long stretches of the avenue looking for them but they were nowhere. I didn't know what to do so I began looking in bars and restaurants and stores.

Maybe two hours passed and I looked in a place called the Monroe Tavern and saw them sitting in a corner drinking. I went back outside, walked across the street, sat down on the curb, and waited.

They didn't come out for hours. When they did you could tell they were drunk because the man with the tattooed neck kept dropping a cigarette he was trying to light. They talked for a couple minutes, then separated, and I followed Silver.

He walked slowly down Colfax, then took a turn and walked down an alley and I saw his truck and camper parked there. He got to it, stood outside and took a leak, then unlocked the door, and went inside.

I waited to make sure he was going to stay in there, then I walked to Walgreens. I took five packages of thumb tacks and a roll of masking tape and ran out the door. No one followed me but I kept running for a couple blocks, then I went behind a restaurant and looked through their dumpster and found a cardboard box. I ripped it down so there was a piece that would cover my chest and stomach, then I took off my shirt and taped it on my body the best I could. I stretched out a line of tape and stuck the end to my knee and began sticking thumb tacks all the way through it so the tape would hold them but nearly all the tack was facing out. I did four rows of this, then I taped those to the cardboard on my chest. In the end I had almost a hundred tacks facing out on my chest and stomach.

I put my shirt back on and began walking down the alley looking for an unlocked car. I found an old Toyota pickup that had a busted-out window and I opened the door and looked behind the seat and found a tire iron.

I walked back to the camper. I wasn't even that nervous or scared, I was just mad and tired. I beat on the door and called out Silver's name but there was no answer. I walked around to the side and knocked on the camper's aluminum walls, then finally I just swung the tire iron into one of the windows and broke it.

It wasn't much after that that Silver opened the door. He was drunk and naked.

"What the fuck?" he yelled.

I swung the tire iron at him but missed.

He jumped down from the camper and grabbed me and hit me in the face but it didn't hurt that bad. Then he grabbed me by the hair and hit me in the stomach but when he did he also hit the tacks. He yelled out and looked at his hand and when he did I hit him in the knee with the tire iron and he fell to the ground. Then I swung it as hard as I could and hit him on the side of the head and he collapsed. His naked body lay on the pavement, and there was blood coming out of his head and he was slobbering, trying to move his lips to speak.

I went into the camper and found the flashlight sitting on the table and I shined it around until I found his pants and his wallet. There was only a hundred and nine dollars left. I took it and jumped down to the street. I shined the light on Silver. He was still lying there. His hair was dark with blood but he was still breathing when I threw the flashlight back in the camper and left.

29

I walked a half a mile before I put the tire iron in a trash can. I took off my shirt and pulled the tacks and the cardboard off me. I hid in some bushes alongside a bank and waited for morning. I didn't sleep at all. At sunrise I started walking again. I ate breakfast at a diner that was open and ordered two turkey sandwiches to go and left. I walked to the Greyhound bus station and bought a one way ticket to Rock Springs, Wyoming for sixty-eight dollars.

The bus wasn't scheduled to depart until the afternoon but I didn't leave the station. I sat in a chair next to where a security guard stood and kept a lookout for Silver. When the bus came I sat in the front near the driver and once we got out of the station I felt better and by the time we got out of Denver I couldn't keep my eyes open.

It was three in the morning when we pulled into Rock Springs and it was cold. There were three other people that got off and then the bus moved on. There was a Denny's sign in the far distance and I walked towards it.

Inside I sat at a booth and ordered a chocolate milkshake and fries and when the waitress wasn't looking I took out my last turkey sandwich and ate it. I bought a paper and sat there and tried to read it to kill time but I started falling asleep so I left.

I walked around the rest of the night just going up and

down the main streets and neighborhoods. I couldn't recall much of it, but in every house and apartment and car that I passed I looked for my aunt.

When the sun came up I walked down a street and saw the auto parts store where my aunt had once worked. The front sign had an angry-looking man in a kilt holding a wrench. It was called Scottish Sam's Auto Parts. I waited outside until they opened, then I asked a woman behind a counter if she knew Margy Thompson and she began laughing.

"You're the guy that keeps calling here," she said.

"Yeah," I said.

"Like I've said, there ain't a Margy that works here, and I've worked here the longest except for the boss. But the good news is that he's started to come back to work. I could ask him." She was chewing gum and drinking a bottle of diet Coke. She was pregnant.

"Is he here today?"

"No," she said. "He only comes in on Mondays to do the books. So he'll be here tomorrow."

"What time?"

"I'm not sure," she said. "But he'll be here by lunch I bet." Then another customer came and she began helping him.

I sat outside the building for a long time. I counted my money but I only had nineteen dollars. I began walking around town but I saw two police cars go by and they made me nervous so I found a movie theater and went to the first show at noon and then I jumped from movie to movie until the last one was over sometime past eleven o'clock. When I got out I was starving. I went to a mini-mart, bought a couple cans of SpaghettiOs and hid behind a dumpster at a grocery store, ate, and spent the night there.

When I got to Scottish Sam's the next morning the same girl was there behind the register eating a Pop Tart and drinking a diet Coke.

"You're back?" she said.

I nodded. "Is the owner here yet?"

"He's in the office."

"Can I talk to him?"

"Sure," she said and went into the back and came out with a fat old man in a wheelchair. He only had one leg.

"You're looking for who?"

"Margy Thompson?"

"Why do you want to know?"

"She's my aunt and I'm trying to find her."

"Well," he said, "she used to work in the office here years ago. She did the accounts payable and receivable."

"Do you know where she is now?" I asked.

"I know she left here to go work at the library."

"The library?"

He nodded.

"Do you know where she lives?"

"Like I said, I haven't seen her in years. But the library is just up the road, maybe they know." I asked him for directions, he gave them to me, and I left.

It was Monday and the library was closed until Tuesday. I had to wait out another night. I sat down on their front steps and worried. I was almost out of money and what if I couldn't find her? And if I did, what if she had a new family and didn't want me around? Then I started thinking about Pete and then about Silver and things started spiraling. I made myself get up and start walking. I ate my last can of SpaghettiOs and counted my money. In my pants pocket I found Lonnie Dixon's phone number and that afternoon I got quarters from a grocery store and called his ranch in Nevada.

An old woman's voice answered.

"Is Lonnie there?" I asked her.

"No," the woman said. "He's in Colorado. His brother just died."

"Oh," I said. "Is he gonna be back?"

"He said he would be, sooner or later."

"He told me you guys might be hiring."

"You'll have to talk to Ralph about that and he ain't here right now."

"Will he be back today?"

"He'll be back tonight. The best thing would be to call him tomorrow."

"Did Lonnie leave a number?"

"No," the woman said.

"Alright," I told her, and then I left my name and we hung up.

I spent the rest of the day in a park, then I went back to the movies and watched all the same ones I had the day before. After that I hid behind the grocery store dumpster, but I couldn't sleep.

In the morning I cleaned up in the grocery store bathroom. I was down to three dollars. I bought a couple donuts and sat by the library and waited for it to open. When it did I went to the front desk where a middle-aged woman stood and I asked her if she knew Margy Thompson.

"Of course I know Margy," the lady said and smiled.

"She's my aunt."

"Really?"

"Does she live here?" I asked.

"She moved to Laramie maybe three years ago. She got married and last I knew she worked at the university library."

"She got married?"

"She did. I was at her wedding."

"Who did she marry?"

"A guy named Jerry."

"Jerry?"

"He was a chemical salesman when I met him. I don't know if he still does that. I didn't really know him."

"But she got married?"

"Yeah."

"What's his last name?"

"Piotrowski, I think. It's a hard one."

"Could you spell it out?"

She wrote it on a slip of paper and handed it to me. "I think that's right," she said.

"In Laramie?" I asked.

"That's where they moved."

"When was the last time you talked to her?"

"A year or a year and half ago," she said and smiled.

"Okay," I said and then I left.

I walked towards the freeway and it took me a while but I made it to the on ramp heading east towards Laramie. I waited most of the day trying to hitchhike but no one ever stopped. Near dusk a man pulled over in a dented old Datsun truck. I ran up to him and asked him if was going to Laramie and he said he was going right past it and that he'd give me a ride.

His truck was as beat up on the inside as the outside. Everything had duct tape on it and there was no stereo or anything on the dash except the speedometer. The man had long sandy blond hair and wore a stained white T-shirt and cut-offs. He was smoking cigarettes that he rolled himself while he drove. He said his name was Dan.

The truck could only go fifty miles an hour. We had the windows rolled down so it was hard to hear, but he started talking about cameras and how he'd just bought a bunch of them and thousands of dollars' worth of film from a guy in North Dakota for five hundred dollars.

He kept talking but with the wind and the heat I fell asleep. When I woke up he was shaking me. We were parked at a truck stop called Little America. We both went inside and used the toilet, and afterwards I waited by the truck and he came out with two ice-cream cones and handed me one.

"Thanks," I said.

He nodded. "They have great toilets here, don't you think?"

"Yeah," I said.

"The cans have their own little rooms. You could live in there if you had to. Plus the ice cream. Guess how much it costs?"

"I don't know."

"Thirty-five cents."

"Really?"

"And its good," he said.

I looked in the back of his truck and it was filled with old coolers. "Why do you have the coolers?"

"The film I bought is expired. They don't make the film I like anymore but the guy said he kept it in a huge fridge. That's why I have all the coolers in the back of the truck. If you keep the film cold it lasts a lot longer."

"But what if the ice melts on it?" I asked him.

"Dry ice," he said and smiled. "That shit's the best. You ever used it?"

"No," I said.

"You should," he said.

We finished the cones, then got back in the truck, but it wouldn't start. We both got out, pushed it down the parking lot, then he jumped in and compression started it. He let it idle for a bit, then we got on the freeway and he talked about how he could control his dreams. He said he was trying to bring his camera into his dreams so he could take pictures of the things he saw. He said a whole bunch more things like that but I couldn't really hear him because of the wind. I fell asleep sometime later and when I woke he was shaking me again. We were on the side of the highway.

"There's Laramie," he said and pointed to lights in the distance. We were maybe a mile away from town.

"You ever been there?" I asked him.

"No, man. What are you doing there?"

"I think my aunt lives there."

"You don't know for sure?"

267

"No," I said.

"You know anyone else in town?"

"No."

"Damn, that's rough," he said and put out his hand. We shook. "Good luck."

"I hope your film still works, even though it's expired."

"Me too," he said.

"I like your truck."

"It's called a Little Hustler. It's a piece of shit but it runs."

"Well thanks," I said and got out. He put the truck in gear and drove off down the side of the freeway trying to pick up speed. The little truck coughed and sputtered its way down the road until its tail lights just disappeared in the night.

I don't know what time it was as I made my way into town. I walked down a main road where there were businesses and shops but everything was closed. Cars and trucks passed me and I saw a police car go by so I got off that road and took side streets until I came to a bridge. Below it was a dried-out irrigation ditch and I jumped down there and hid underneath the overpass. Once in a while I thought I saw police lights but I couldn't tell for sure and I knew I was just nervous. I stayed in the ditch and waited out the rest of the night.

30

When it was light out I walked downtown. I found a pay-phone with a phone book. I took out the piece of paper the librarian had given me and looked in the Ps and saw a listing for M. Piotrowski. It gave an address which I memorized. Then I went to a sporting goods store across the street and asked them where it was.

They gave me directions and as I followed them I tried not to think about anything, but in my heart I knew she wouldn't be there. I went through a neighborhood and at the end of the street I came to a rundown mustard-yellow apartment building. I climbed up the stairs and knocked on the door of apartment number seventeen, but no one answered. I sat there for an hour or so, then left. I walked back downtown and counted my money, but I only had two dollars in change. I went to a payphone and called Lonnie's ranch in Nevada but no one answered. I walked in and out of stores to kill time, then called there again but no one ever picked up.

It was past six when I went back to the yellow apartment building. I knocked on the door and within thirty seconds a woman answered. She stood there and it took me a while to realize who it was. She was much heavier than when I knew her and she hadn't aged well. Her hair was gray and cut very short and her face was bloated. There were dark circles under her eyes.

"You're so tall," was the first thing she said when she saw me. "Oh, Charley, it's you, isn't it?" Her voice broke when she said it. She opened her arms and hugged me. She invited me inside her apartment. It was small with a couch and a table and plants and paintings on the walls. It was a really nice place. We sat in the kitchen across from each other and tears fell down her face. We sat there staring at each other, and then finally I told her about the Samoan and my dad and Del and Lean on Pete and some of the things I'd seen to get to her.

"I can't believe Ray's dead," she said barely. "You must miss him bad?"

"I don't know," I said.

She tried to say something else but she began sobbing so hard she couldn't. "I prayed you would come to me," she said and wiped her eyes on her shirt. "I tried to get ahold of your dad, but you guys kept moving and it was impossible to find you because he hated phones. He never wanted to be found by me."

"You tried?" I said and tears filled my eyes.

She nodded. "He didn't want me to be in your life."

"I did," I said.

She nodded again, then got up and went to the counter and took a paper towel and blew her nose into it. She sat back down and told me that she was married but that her husband and her were in the process of getting a divorce and he was living with a woman somewhere in New Mexico.

"Can I ask you a question?" I said.

"Of course."

"You don't hate me?"

"Why would I hate you?" she said.

"I don't know. He said a couple things."

"Don't believe anything like that. He was just mad at me. I love you, Charley."

"Can I ask you another question?"

She nodded.

"You're really my aunt?"

"Yes, you know I am."

"Then can I stay here with you for a while?"

She wiped her eyes and smiled. "Of course you can." She leaned back in her chair, set her hands on the table, and looked at me and smiled. "I wouldn't have it any other way."

I smiled at her.

"Are you hungry?" she asked.

"I'm always hungry," I told her.

She got up from her chair and went into the kitchen and put two Weight Watcher meals in the microwave and we ate them at the table. Afterwards she made me a bed on the couch in her living room. She put a sheet down and laid a blanket over that and left me one of her pillows. She gave me a towel and a toothbrush, and told me she would take the next day off work and we'd spend the day together and buy me new clothes.

That night I lay there in bed for a long time but I couldn't sleep. I got up and walked back to her room and knocked on the door. A few seconds later she turned on a bedside lamp and told me to come in.

Her room was small but it was nice. There was a double bed and a dresser and a couple paintings on the walls. Next to her was a bedside table that held the lamp, a radio, and an older phone that was off the hook.

"Do you leave your phone off the hook every night?"

"Yeah," she said.

"Why?"

"My ex calls sometimes in the middle of the night."

"Oh," I said.

"What do you need?"

"I just wanted to let you know something."

"What?"

"If in a week or so you don't like me, you can kick me out."

"I'm not going to kick you out."

"But if you do, you don't have to feel bad about it."

"Fair enough," she said.

"I'll get a job, too. I'm not going to cost you much."

"I'm not worried about that."

"I had one other thing."

"Yeah?"

"Do you think it would be alright if I went to school here?"

"You can live here as long as you want, and you have to go to school, it's the law."

"Do you think it would be alright if I played football when I go back to school?"

She nodded. "We just have to call Del and figure out what we're going to do about his horse and his truck and trailer."

"If I have to go to jail can I still live here when I get out?"

"You won't have to go to jail."

"Maybe I will."

"You can stay here when you get out," she said and smiled. "Now go get some sleep."

"You're sure?"

"Of course I'm sure," she said and yawned. "Now go back to bed."

"Alright, good night," I told her and walked back to the living room and lay down on the couch. But still I couldn't sleep and I didn't feel any better. I hadn't told her about hitting Silver or all the shoplifting or the group home. I didn't tell her anything that might make her hate me.

When I woke up the next morning she was in the kitchen cooking breakfast. I lay there for a while and listened. The couch was nice and the sun was coming through the window and the room smelled like coffee and bacon. The radio was playing quietly.

"I went to the store," she said when she saw me. "We can't have you eating Weight Watchers if you're going to play football."

She smiled at me, then went back to cooking. I sat at the table and drank orange juice and watched her. We ate together at the table and listened to the radio.

"Can I ask you a question?"

"Sure," she said.

"What if your husband comes back? Do you think he'll want me to leave?"

"He's not going to come back. It's the last thing I want."

"But if he does, what then?"

"I know what you're doing. You can't worry so much, okay? And we don't need to talk about my husband anymore.

I don't like him, and I'll never live with him again. So that's the end of the discussion on him. Okay?"

"Okay."

"The real question is, what if I'm too boring? I don't have a TV and I never go anywhere. I spend my weekends in bed reading. You won't leave me, will you?"

"I don't mind not having a TV," I told her.

"I'll get you some good books. You're stuck with a librarian, you know."

"I like reading alright," I said.

"We'll have a nice time together," she said. "I know we will."

After breakfast we left to go shopping, and as we went out to her car I noticed she walked with a slight shuffle. She wasn't the same lady I once knew, but then I guess I wasn't the same boy either. We drove to a thrift store and she bought me three pairs of pants and a half-dozen shirts. Then we drove to JC Penny's and she got me socks and underwear, a winter coat, sweats and shorts, and a pair of running shoes.

When we were done we ate lunch at a Mexican restaurant and after I finished my plate she shook her head and laughed.

"You eat faster than anyone I've ever seen. I don't remember that."

"I'm sorry," I said. "I can't help it."

"Don't be sorry. You're just hungry."

"Del used to say my manners were so bad it made him hate eating."

"He was just being mean," my aunt said. "Look at my

274

plate. It's almost empty too."

"I don't disgust you?"

"No," she said, "of course not. But you might enjoy it more if you slow down."

"I'll be better," I told her.

"You don't have to be," she said.

"I will though, you'll see. I'll work on my manners."

"Maybe we should both work on our manners," she said.

When we left the restaurant she drove me around town. We stopped at the high school and walked around. We even went to the football field. We drove past the library where she worked and the old house she'd lived in with her husband.

It was late afternoon when we got back to the apartment. I put my clothes in the wash and she made soup. When the clothes were done I changed into my sweats, put on my new shoes, and went running. I took a road up to the university and ran through the campus and I felt okay.

When I got back to the apartment I took a shower and dressed in my new clothes. My aunt had set three novels on the couch. Two Westerns and a James Bond novel, and I sat down and opened a Western and tried to read it.

That night we had soup, cornbread, and salad. I wanted to ask her about Del, about what she was thinking, or if she'd called him, but I was too nervous to bring it up and I hoped that maybe the whole thing would just disappear.

Later that night I lay down on the couch but I couldn't sleep for a long time. When I finally conked out I dreamt that I was in a rowboat and I was in the middle of the ocean.

Pete was next to me in the water. I was trying to get him in the boat but I didn't know how. I kept trying to lift him by his halter but I wasn't strong enough. Pete didn't seem that worried at first because he knew I'd figure it out. He trusted me. But time went on and nothing I did worked. I think after a while he knew I wasn't going to be able to save him. Then morning came and Pete went into a panic. He splashed and screamed and waved his head around. He became exhausted. His head began slipping down into the ocean. I'd try to hold him up but I couldn't. Then finally his head went under and he didn't come back up, he disappeared. I dove in after him but I couldn't find him anywhere. The water was cold. I dove deeper and deeper but I could never see him. I swam to the surface and I was tired and by then the boat had begun to drift. It was maybe thirty yards away and I swam as hard as I could towards it but I could never get closer.

When I woke I was crying and I could hardly breathe. I lay there too scared to go back to sleep. I got up and went to my aunt's room. Her door was half open and her bedside light was on. She was asleep with a book on her chest and her clock radio was playing. I sat down across from her and leaned against the wall. The night passed and I sat there and waited.

In the morning I woke to her shaking me.

"Charley," she said, "are you okay?"

"I'm alright," I said and opened my eyes.

She was dressed in her bathrobe. She had slippers on her feet.

"I get nightmares," I said.

"They'll get easier the more good times we have together."

"You think so?"

"I'm pretty sure," she said.

"I ain't gonna be a pain in the ass," I told her.

"Good," she said.

"Are you going to work today?"

"I have to," she said.

"But you'll come back?"

"Of course I will," she said and put out her hand. "Now come on, get up."

PACIFIC OCEAN

Match Spokane
Races

Portland

R.I.P.
Pete
†

Pinto's
Trailer

Boise

Burns

Rock
Springs

Laramie

Cheyenne

Grand
Junction

Denver

N
W   E
S

by Charley Thompson
for his friend Lean on Pete

COLUMBIA RIVER

My Dad's Work

Movie Theater

Taqueria

N. Lombard

St. John's

WILLAMETTE RIVER

Delta Park

Our House

Lean on Pete

Portland Meadows

I-5

Jefferson Highschool

PORTLAND, OREGON

A Motorcycle for a Horse

A spoken word short story featuring Charley Thompson, Lean on Pete and Lonnie Dixon.

Read by Willy with music by members of Richmond Fontaine.

DOWNLOAD
Willy Vlautin's exclusive audio story at
FABER.CO.UK/LEANONPETE